D0170651

BOOKS-BY-MAIL
MAINE STATE LIBRARY
LMA BLDG. STATION #64
AUGUSTA, ME 04333

WITHDRAWN

L481be

A Bed of Earth

THE SECRET BOOKS OF VENUS
BOOK III

A BED OF EARTH

(The Gravedigger's Tale)

TANITH LEE

THE OVERLOOK PRESS
WOODSTOCK & NEW YORK

SEP 1 7 2002

First published in the United States in 2002 by
The Overlook Press, Peter Mayer Publishers, Inc.
Woodstock & New York

WOODSTOCK:
One Overlook Drive
Woodstock, NY 12498
www.overlookpress.com
[for individual orders, bulk and special sales, contact our Woodstock office]

NEW YORK:
141 Wooster Street
New York, NY 10012

Copyright © 2002 Tanith Lee

All Rights Reserved. No part of this publication may be
reproduced or transmitted in any form or by any means, electronic
or mechanical, including photocopy, recording, or any information
storage and retrieval system now known or to be invented without
permission in writing from the publisher, except by a reviewer who
wishes to quote brief passages in connection with a review written
for inclusion in a magazine, newspaper, or broadcast.

∞ The paper used in this book meets the requirements for paper
permanence as described in the ANSI Z39.48-1992 standard.

Library of Congress Cataloging-in-Publication Data

Lee, Tanith.
A bed of earth (the gravedigger's tale) / Tanith Lee.— 1st ed.
p. cm. — (The secret books of Venus ; bk. 3)
1. Venice (Italy)—Fiction. 2. Gravediggers—Fiction. 3. Cemeteries—
Fiction. 4. Nobility—Fiction. 5. Vendetta—Fiction. I. Title
PR6062.E4163 B43 2002   823'.914—dc21   2002070368

Book design and type formatting by Bernard Schleifer
Manufactured in the United States of America
FIRST EDITION
ISBN 1-58567-261-0
1 3 5 7 9 8 6 4 2

In memoriam Dennis Barrett—
a powerful healer and kind friend.

Contents

Contents

AUTHOR'S NOTE

In the known world (i.e., our own), Cesare Borgia lost his power in 1503, with the death of his father, Pope Alexander VI, and was dead himself within four more years. However, the City-State of Venus is located in an Italy where history follows a different path.

Since this *is* a parallel Italy, some names are spelled phonetically. But an *e* at the end of a name is always sounded, (as *ay* to rhyme with *day*).

Meanwhile, it should be pointed out that the Latin used in this book is sometimes also that of a parallel Italy. In some cases nevertheless, it will be recognized as correct, too, for this world. For most of these recognizable and correct passages, the author extends her grateful thanks to Barbara Levick, of St. Hilda's College, Oxford.

The fragment of song sung by Dionyssa in Part Three is based (in free translation), on an anonymous French song, approximate to the early 1500s.

Finally, one moment of this story has already appeared, over thirty years ago, in largely different form, and in a private publication—under my name, and the title *The Betrothed*.

PART ONE

Death

My trade is to flatter the dead, not the
living—I am a tomb-maker.

JOHN WEBSTER
The Duchess of Malfi

BARTOLOME

I, BARTOLOME DA LOURA DI AN'SANTA, being in sound health, and sane, in this the forty-first year of my life on God's earth, and a Settera Master of the Guild of Gravemakers, declare hereby this account is rendered by my own hand. And that it is, so far as eye or mind can evidence, true. There are to be no witnesses.

You may wonder perhaps that I can write. But it is no wonder at all, for the guild, to which I was apprenticed when very young, saw to it that I learned the knack, and similar abilities, along with my trade.

My purpose is not to speak of my trade especially. My work is secret, as with the fashioners of stone for mausoleums and markers, and the custodians of the Cremarias. The making of a proper grave, and altogether the care of the dead (aside from their spiritual needs, for which the priests cater): that is my province, and it is not fitting to say much of it, here. But even so, it is a skill, as with all right work. Though some may be wary of the gravemaker, since few of us avoid him at the last, I account myself no less a man than the next.

As a boy, I lived in my father's house on the Canal of Scarlets, in the Butchers' Quarter of the City. My father was a butcher, but also a drunkard, and when drunk he would grow angry and beat me. When he was sober, he would beat me, too, being in a foul mood from wanting drink. My mother had nothing to say on this. She liked the cup as well. When I was six, my Uncle Thimeo came and found me bruised like a kicked fruit and lying in filth. I do not remember the scene, nor anything much, before I found myself in his own house, which was farther along the canal, against the Laguna Silvia. The lagoon had entirely filled up only in the last three decades; it had been mostly tidal marshland before. There were many wonders drowned in it, ancient statues and monuments, treasure-troves of coins and gems, it was said, and an antique Roman Circus. There, gladiators had fought in the time of the Caesars, and later sinners and heretics had been burned alive there by the will of the terrible Council of the Lamb. This dire religious authority, though by then gone for most of a century, was yet still spoken of in hushed tones, or with curses.

My uncle's house, after my father's, was like Heaven.

It was kept clean and comfortable, warm in winter and cool in summer, and food came to the table regularly. Thimeo had a housekeeper, Rossa, a big, red woman, who made me sugar pancakes and other sweet things as a treat, and told me stories of heroes and kings while she kneaded dough or plucked a chicken. Only when I was twelve did I learn she was also my uncle's mistress, and then only because they let me notice, judging me by that time to be old enough to be as discreet as they were themselves.

They were a curious couple: he, very thin and sallow; she, large and glowing as the tasty dishes she cooked. But they were happy enough, and indeed she was clever in more than cookery—he had taught her to read and write. In the evenings, I have seen the works of Petronius and Pliny, to name only two, under her hands, and sometimes she read pieces of them aloud to me, translating their Latin as she went.

Meanwhile, I was getting my own schooling from the guild and, by the age of eight, I would read aloud to her, translation now superfluous.

The other things I learned I did not speak of nor, as I have said, shall I do so very much here. All guilds bind their men by powerful oaths, as you will understand.

However, there is one episode I will put down, for it bears on what comes presently.

Two weeks after I turned thirteen, there was a burial on the Isle of the Dead—which place, in common talk, is coming to be called more often, *Saint Smoke*.

Indeed, there is a good reason for the popular name. The fires of the Cremarias, going on day and night, and sending up their smoulder, are what have earned it.

The City of Venus is built on water, either upon her seven major islands, or on stages and stilts driven down into the oceanic clay floor, in the shallower parts of the lagoons. Here she had balanced some centuries, to the astonishment of the outer world.

Evidently then, despite her many gardens, Venus has little space for burials. Therefore she sends them out to the Isle, which lies near the far edge of the Laguna Silvia where, even in the days of the marsh, the sea had always been deep. Nevertheless, not every person can be buried on one island. And most of the dead, it is a fact, are burned—under the unique dispensation of a past pope, which assures us that, even in ashes, they will be reassembled on the Last Day. (For myself, I think it does not matter much in any case, whether the dead are burned or buried, providing it is well and honorably done. But I, of course, have reasons for such a thought, as you will see.)

Until now, as a young apprentice of the guild, I had done my share of grave-digging, but all these graves had been small ones, meant to receive the little casks and pots of ashes brought from the Cremarias.

Now, however, there was to be a burial in earth, on the Isle. And my uncle took me aside and said that I should go over to attend it, providing I was circumspect and did all as he told me beforehand. This was of course not in any way meant as a show to disturb or thrill me. Rather, it was considered a necessary portion of my education. One learns both by deed and by example.

I do not recall if I was at all nervous. Perhaps I was, I think so, for the burial was to be of a nobleman of the della Scorpia family, who can trace their roots in the City back five hundred years.

Though I had by then seen the funeral boats Venus knows as "Charons," I had never ridden on one, let alone one so grand.

It was some fifty to sixty feet in length, lacquered black with golden trim, and its cabin, where the corpse was to lie, draped in black velvet with a nap of two heights. At prow and stern stood a carved angel with gilded black wings, stretching out its arms in prayer, its head bowed. The oarsmen were dressed also in black, as were the musicians, who were seated forward, to provide stately sad music. But my uncle, a Guild Master, his six assistants, and I were clad in grey, with the badge of the guild in silver to the left over the heart.

Our badge is curious, to those who do not know

what it represents. It is a circle sliced by a single horizontal straight line, and it is significant, coming from ancient Rome herself, where it was the symbol of Mors Plutonius: Death.

I have described the funeral boat, but in all there were three vessels, for it was an occasion. On the others stood members of the della Scorpias themselves, clothed in mourning. One woman, who was old, was weeping pitifully, pale as a pearl. But her black was thickly embroidered with gold and her veil was of samite from the Indus. They were very rich, I saw. But riches, of course, still cannot usually keep death away. There were besides several other boats, painted and draped with black, and these, too, set out with us.

The thing was this: The body of the old nobleman was taken first across the Laguna Aquila, then through the wider canals to the basilica of the Primo, which stands on the lagoon of Fulvia. Here a Mass was to be sung for the dead man, and the guild was needed to carry him with dignity first to the boat, then to the basilica, then to the boat again for his final journey. Which meant that my Uncle Thimeo and his assistants, who were to bear the open coffin, went first of all into the palace of the della Scorpia family. Naturally, I, the apprentice, only waited outside, as I had been told to do. Even so, standing by the mooring place, I had space to view the palazzo of the della Scorpias, which I had never seen before.

It was an afternoon of early winter, the sky curded and dim, and little light fell on the palazzo's front. The building stood back from the water's edge, across an open square, and some people idled here respectfully, or merely vulgarly, to watch.

The house plaster was yellowish, and the great

timbered door stayed so far shut, behind its colonnade of marble, just as the long, carved tracery windows looked blind, above. And yet it seemed to me there was a marble stair behind the door; and on the wall, a painting of something like dark shapes running, and a chariot, and a wreath of gold, and a man's head half turned with a speck of light fixed in his eye.

Then next the door was undone, to let the coffin and the household out, and I glimpsed inside. I saw the stair, and a mural of a robed man my uncle later told me was a Caesar in his victory chariot, with the wreath of an emperor being offered him.

After we had crossed through to Fulvia and the Mass had been sung, the body was rowed out to the Isle.

By then there were dark rain clouds, and tears fell also from the sky. As we reached the island I could see, away beyond the bar and the sea-walls, the great, slow, silken tumble of the outer ocean.

Then we came to shore, and the guild took up the coffin again, and we passed in through the high gates in the wall. Everywhere ahead lay slopes where graves and the houses of death were planted, and white stone angels. And through this landscape we walked, even the lords and ladies, along a paved road railed by great cypresses, while the rain fell thick as syrup.

So we reached, in about one third of an hour, the della Scorpia burial garden. Which is itself the reason for this tale I would tell.

Those of our trade are called, commonly, gravediggers. Certainly most of us, even the stonemasons of our guild, have taken their turn at the digging of graves, so that everything of our work should be known to us and understood. However, as I said, I had not yet come to the digging of the larger graves, only the little ones for ashes, and so I had not seen many of such burial spots, let alone a burial garden such as belonged to the della Scorpias.

There was a big outer wall, taller than three tall men and very thick. Carved over the gate, and over the chapel portico beyond, was the armorial symbol of the della Scorpias, which is, not surprisingly, the Scorpion who is also a guardian of the City. The della Scorpia Scorpion, though, carries in his foreclaws a flowering branch. I had seen something similar in their banners on the palazzo, and the larger boats, those done in yellow and gold on a chestnut ground.

Attendants of the family had already undone the gate. The procession went inside.

The garden, even under a heavy sky, was beautiful, and lush, and immaculately kept. The somber box hedges were, in spots, trained and cut to the shape of ancient stelae, such as are found about the tombs of the Greeks and Romans. The pillared cypresses had a similar form. At the end of an avenue stood the mausoleum, also marked with the della Scorpia escutcheon. But the mausoleum was, it seemed, full, and the dead lord was to have his bed in the earth. So we went on, the priest who had come from the chapel leading us, and a boy in white ringing the little bell.

Beyond the cultivated hedges lay a wood of beech, one of thousands that scatter the isle. But between the trees, the pallid shoulders of the graves were many. Once, the old lady stumbled, and her servant and a young man of the family steadied her. But the guild, bowed with the weight of the coffin, never missed their step.

The wood ended suddenly, where the trees had been cut down. Here there was a strange, low wall, not three feet high, and very broken in places, although nowhere was it completely fallen. Over this wall, the beech trees began again about ten paces off, and then continued thickly, but there were no graves or markers to be seen among them.

When we reached the area of felled trees, the procession halted. And then immediately the old woman in black and gold began to shout in a thin, frightened, raging voice: "Must it be here? Why must it be so close? . . . It's too close! . . . No, this must not be! . . . No, I won't permit this . . . Gido, tell them this mustn't be done."

The men of the family gathered about the old woman, who afterwards I learned was a Donna Julia, and was the dead lord's sister. They spoke to her quietly, trying to calm her, indicating the grave which had been, of course, ready-prepared, its edges laid with velvets, garlands of laurel, and the paper flowers made for death. Then another woman moved forward, large-boned and ugly but with a marvelous, complex crown of coal-black hair. And she said sternly, "Mother, you mustn't protest like this. They wouldn't dare to insult him here. They have never dared it. See how the other tombs are. Not one of them is defaced."

And then the old woman began to weep again, but she had stopped shouting, and the funeral proceeded.

Obviously, I kept my attention on the business in hand, as I knew I was expected to. However, I could hardly help my curiosity: What had the old lady meant by her cries, or the younger one with her declaration that nothing had been vandalized? So rough and sacrilegious an act was surely rare. What might, then, have caused the chance of such an incident here, in the della Scorpia burial garden?

The last rites took a while. The priest spoke darkly of resurrection. Then the box went down and for a second I saw the old man's powdered face. He looked grim enough, as sometimes corpses do, though others seem to smile. The garlands were thrown in, and the concluding words spoken. It was very quiet, no bell to sound, and no bird inclined to sing in the island trees.

The grave would be filled in presently, and this time I was to stay to observe it. So we remained behind after the della Scorpias and their people had gone away. But I knew better than to question my uncle about them before his duties were completed.

That evening, we took our supper at midnight, my Uncle Thimeo and I. But Rossa had provided a good hot meal: a platter of sausages, a noodle soup, and semolina tortelli with pine nuts.

"Uncle," I said at last, "what was the meaning of that scene by the grave? What did the old lady fear would happen to her dead?"

Rossa had gone out, as she usually did after she served, and left us to eat and discuss what we would. Yet still Thimeo paused, looking into the fire. Then he said, "I will tell you what I know, for you'll come to things of this sort, now and then. But, you grasp, these matters aren't to be talked of outside the guild, even where other men know all about them."

"But if it's common knowledge—"

"Even so, Bartolo."

"Then of course not, sir."

"Well, then. The house of Scorpia has, for a century, more or less, been the second party in a feud with another great house here. The name of which house, I will also tell you, since that too is well enough known. They are the Barbarons."

"I've seen their palazzo from the Triumph Canal. A huge palace. They call it Castello Barbaron."

"Just so. And they possess a fortress-castle too, at Veronavera, and a great deal of land there. Their wealth is mostly from commerce."

"And the feud? Is it about trade? Land?"

"In a way, about land," he said. "I've heard myself that it began with some dispute between them during a siege of the City long ago, when the Eastern Infidel of Jurneia sailed into the very lagoons and were only driven off when courageous men got aboard their vessels, under cover of night, and set them afire."

I stared, always amazed by this heroic story, which Rossa had already recounted when I was younger—save, in her version, it had had a slightly different plot.

"As I was told," my uncle said, "there was fighting between the two families when the Barbarons were trying to keep ahold of what they had in Venus, and the della Scorpias were trying to escape before Jurneian ships arrived. I don't know the facts well. Suffice it to say, the families took a dislike to each other. And it happens that the burial ground of each, meanwhile, abuts that of the other."

"Then," I said, breathless with surprise, "that place beyond the little broken wall—"

"Is disputed earth."

"So the trees were cut and the wall built to keep out the Barbarons—or show them they can't come in—"

"Supposedly. And you will find something like that too, when and if you must serve the Barbaron burial garden. Of course, neither would truly encroach inside the other's wall. It is the stretch of ground between, that they haggle over. So neither may use *that*."

"Why do they dispute it? Has one family tried to steal part of it—or done so?"

"They have tried. Each house says it belongs only to them. And you know, don't you, Bartolo, how ground for full burial, not for the ashes only, is valued on the Isle."

I stared now at the fire. I was perturbed, but not enough, I admit, to prevent my taking another sausage. It had been a prolonged wait for me, cold and wet, on the Isle of the Dead. Although, naturally, the dead wait there longer.

Finally I said, "What about the Barbaron lands at Veronavera? Can't they bury their dead there?"

"They do sometimes. But think—a journey of two or three days—in summer, it's not always possible, or in winter, if the road is bad. Besides, it's to do with the honor of their houses."

"Have they never gone to the courts—or to the Ducem—to settle it?"

"It seems so, but nothing *was* settled, and that was five or six decades back, when the legal rights to the burial ground must have been better remembered."

"Do they fight openly?" I said, abruptly intrigued at the idea of wild swordplay in the alleys.

"Sometimes. More to the point, they keep a distance from each other, and hate each other. It's ingrained with them. If the Ducem holds a feast and asks Andrea Barbaron, he does not also ask Como della Scorpia. And conversely."

I had heard of such things with several of the high families of Venus. Perhaps I was losing interest, turning to the sweet gelatina and the grapes Rossa had left on the old black sideboard.

"There was one terrible thing," said my uncle. His voice was now so soft it thoroughly caught my attention, and for some reason the hairs stood up along my neck and scalp. "I don't know if I would be right to tell you. But I will, I think, since you'll hear of it one day I expect, though it occurred some fourteen years ago. Again, I impress upon you, Bartolome, chat about this with no other. It's a horrible tale, and even though all the City probably has some version of it, we who see to the result of such things, the Grave Guild, must always know more—and say less."

MERALDA

AT FIRST ALL SHE COULD RECALL of him were his eyes. She had been told that they were fine, just as she had been told he was rich and of a noble house—Ciara. She kept the image of him, standing at the end of the long table, in the smoke of the candles, which much activity to and fro had disturbed.

Her father led her forward and put her hand into the pale, narrow, ringed hand of this lord of Ciara. Everyone clapped approvingly. And when she looked up, afraid, into his face, perhaps he was smiling, or not, but she saw nothing save the eyes. And they were an awful molten yellow—like the yolk of eggs.

Meralda was fourteen, the perfect age for betrothal.

They seemed to think, or pretended to think, she should be pleased and excited by it all, as if this were a new toy for her. But at the same time, they lectured her on how she must now put aside childish things and practice the duties of a woman. For, in a year, she would be wed.

At night, after her aunt's women had chattered to her of the splendors of the Palazzo Ciara, which stood somewhere across the City, and other houses and lodges belonging to the Ciara family, Meralda lay on her back, her own eyes tightly shut. And there inside her lids she saw the eyes of her intended husband, floating like candle flames. The reason for her utter revulsion, her panic, she could not have explained.

Meralda was a typical young woman of her class. She had been kept immature, and spoiled—that is, had been given things. But also she had been chastised for every transgression. She knew now she could not approach her confessor, or any of her remaining female kindred. Her mother was long dead. She knew that she could *never* speak to her father on this or any other matter, save to thank him and meekly concur with his wishes.

Justore della Scorpia's position was that of uncle to the young head of the della Scorpia clan, Como. Lord Como, at that time, enjoyed loose living, gave feasts, and had three or four mistress about the City (and two others at Veronavera). Besides, he often drank heavily, gamed, went off hunting for days, and even dabbled in the painting of canvasses of the goddess Venus, under the tutelage of an artist of whom he was the patron. Justore, though still quite young himself, did almost none of those things, though he was said to keep a mistress, an educated courtesan, near the Setapassa market. Of course, he had had to consult Como, as the head of house of Scorpia, on Meralda's betrothal. But Como, having idly agreed, took slight notice. The Ciara family name was good, and the groom was still only thirty, youthful enough to give the girl years of marriage and several sons. And he was wealthy. The della Scorpias, like most of the noble rich, now found themselves not quite as rich as they had been, and would make only profitable alliances among the nobility.

Every bit of this, Meralda also knew. But she knew

it as every child knew the world was flat. What use was it to her? What did it mean? Only that she was a slave to the rules of her household.

So sometimes she lay long awake, or had incoherent nightmares, for the next three or four months of that year. Then, just as they were finishing the golden pomegranates on her bridal gown, she saw Lorenzo Vai.

This took place in the walled garden of the Palazzo Scorpia, one early morning in summer.

Meralda had come out with her younger sister, to sit with straw brims around their heads to shield their white faces and throats, while they left their hair uncovered to bleach in the sunlight. Certainly Meralda's skin was very white and pure, and her hair already a lucent saffron color. In her blanched gown, her hair streaming undressed down her to her waist, the straw brim in her hand, she was undoubtedly very lovely. But Lorenzo was like a lightning flash to her.

He had been kicking his heels in the courtyard for some while, grown bored, and gone through a long passage, uninvited, to the garden.

There he stood under a sculptured tree, among the pots of basil. His hair was also long—brown, thick, and curling—and his skin flawlessly bronzed. His eyes, as she was later to think, were the blue of a star-filled twilight. He was tall and strongly built, and vividly dressed, his sleeves slashed over silk, and pinned to his doublet by golden arrows.

As it happened, he was none other than the nephew of Como's pet painter. He had been brought to the palace in the hope—the painter's—that Lorenzo might gain some lucrative job through the assistance of the della Scorpias. But so far, Como had not given the painter a chance to call his relative in.

There they stood then, the charming girl and the handsome young man of seventeen. The arrows were not only on Lorenzo's sleeves, but in the air. After a second, Meralda charmed Lorenzo further by blushing deeply. But then she hurried away, the sister giggling beside her.

Lorenzo, for all his beauty, was not especially clever. Nor did he think of anything much beyond the gratification of the moment—he was like Como, then, in this; they might have got on.

Soon Lorenzo, having followed the two girls along a path laid with small stones, found Meralda lingering, as if perplexed, by the fountain. Nor did she know what she was doing, but she had sent her sister on an errand.

Reared so elaborately and exclusively, Meralda had learned all the wrong things. Paramount among these was the thought that, in order to experience anything truly desired, it must be thieved, by means of subterfuge and slyness. But as she knew no more what she was at than did Lorenzo, her start at seeing him again was quite real.

"M'donna," he said, "pardon me. I didn't mean to alarm you. But oh, you're like the goddess of day surprised!"

Then, when she neither answered nor took flight, Lorenzo began to make courtly love to her. He did not think he was doing anything more than enjoying himself. Perhaps he would get some privileges from the girl—kisses, leave to caress her breasts—such had gone on elsewhere with other girls, and, never having been discovered, had apparently done no harm.

For her part, Meralda had never been spoken to like this before. (His rather conceited view of his verbal skill was nothing to her appreciation.) Or, if she ever had, never by a man so near her own age and so good-looking. She guessed it would be forbidden, this fruit. So, not even really knowing what she did, she led him into an arbor overgrown with vines, which would conceal them from anyone in the house, or on the path.

How did the conversation go?

The way such conversations go.

"I never saw a girl like you." "Never?" "My brother sets me to study hands for the studio. I should like to draw yours. What a soft pretty hand." "No, you mustn't take my hand." "Don't you like me to?" . . . "Yes."

Once, he kissed her, but only at the corner of her lips. He had found out who she was by then—the daughter of Sre'donno Justore. A mad idea that he might make a high marriage had come over the painter's nephew—crazy indeed. But worse than that, much worse. Her innocence and vulnerable loveliness had abruptly touched him, deeper than the flesh.

As for Meralda, she had fallen in love on sight. It felt to her like recognition. And thus it seemed to her that he was her destined love. How stupid and how strong she was, Meralda della Scorpia, to have thrown off, with one thrust, all they had forced upon her, all those weighty chains of obedience, honor, and female uselessness. Despite every one of them, she had chosen for herself, whether she knew it or not.

A bell roused them from their dream. It was the noon Solus faintly ringing from the Primo, and tolls began everywhere else from the numberless churches of Christian Venus.

The bell, reminding the City of God of the time, reminded Meralda, too, of her plight.

She raised to Lorenzo a face whiter than before, and whispered, "But—I am so afraid."

"Of what?" he cried. He would kill for her. Such a distance, in that short time, they had gone.

Then she told him of her betrothal to a lord of the house of Ciara. She said, meekly, confiding at last to this one being who would understand and assist, "His eyes—they frighten me. They're yellow—yellow as my *hair*—"

"Your hair is like the wheat—like a topaz—" insisted Lorenzo. But he was floundering a little. He said, "I've heard of this man. Why do they give you to him? I've heard bad things of him—"

"Is he diseased?" cried the girl in fresh horror. Her elder sister had been given to such a man. And although Meralda had not quite comprehended the nature of his ailment, she had seen her sister's anguish and, later, the decline in her health.

"The Frankish disease? No—he hasn't that, or I don't believe so. But he has done things, to his enemies, things unproven, but muttered about."

Belatedly he saw her trembling and was sorry, genuinely sorry, and cursed his mouth that should have kissed her, not made her afraid with gossip.

But then, the younger sister came along the path with Meralda's maid, a tall, harsh creature of nineteen.

"Melda! Melda!" cried the sister, looking about the garden.

"M'donna!" called the harsh maid, frowning.

Meralda clung to Lorenzo.

He thought, *She loves me!* He thought, *She longs for me to save her.*

Both of these thoughts were true enough.

When the searchers had passed by without seeing them, Meralda became adult and serious. She sent Lorenzo away for his own sake. But she had heard enough romances to know what to do. Before he left, they had arranged their next secret meeting.

Where they met was a church, the Little Church of Maria Maesta behind the Aquila Lagoon, and not a great way from the Palazzo della Scorpia.

This was the sanctum to which the women of the house generally went. It was therefore simple enough to obtain permission—a girl wanting to visit a church was thought both prudent and seemly, particularly if she were a girl betrothed.

Lorenzo, of course, being male, might move about as he chose.

For some while after, quite regularly, they found each other in a pillared side-chapel where the shadows were deep even at midday. On the wall, a painting of the Virgin, robed and crowned as a queen, watched benignly enough: When she arrived, Meralda would always placate her with a gift of flowers.

The maid, Euniche, was more difficult.

Euniche was an exact product of the codes and practice of the great families of Venus. She thought herself high above the common run, but bound, by holy will, to her superiors. Among these, however, despite her correct politeness toward the girl, she did not yet count her mistress, Meralda.

To herself, Euniche put this down to Meralda's youth, and foolishness. She had not as yet *earned* a loyal servant's approval. Actually, Euniche had that infallible eye which rests always and solely on the main possibility. She was subservient and perfect with the men, even the boys, of the house, never faulting them even in her thoughts. With the ladies of the house, though mentally much more critical, she was also outwardly fawning. With the unmarried girls, Euniche took her time, waiting to see what they were; which was, if they were dangerous or not. Meralda, with her softness, her night fears, her toys and fancies, was not dangerous at all.

At first, Meralda had managed to elude Euniche on her visits to the chapel. She had taken the tone that Euniche needed to be busy with all the preparation for the wedding—the sewing of gowns and sorting of linen and so on. Instead, Meralda was accompanied by another maid, a girl younger than herself, whom it was easy to send off to buy sweetmeats or something of the sort, once they reached the church door.

At Meralda's fifth excursion to the church, Euniche had raised her head from her sparkling needle, like a tiger scenting deer.

"Who is to attend you, M'donna?"

"Oh, the girl."

"That simpleton. It's not fitting. Until last month you had old Cloudia to be your chaperone, which was only proper. A pity she died." (This dismissively, for old Cloudia had been in her sixtieth year, a great age, when death must be hourly expected.) "No, I must go with you. It's entrusted to me, lady."

"Oh no . . . no . . . you mustn't leave my dresses . . . the other women stitch them crooked—"

"What nonsense, lady. I shall be ready in a moment."

And she was—but by then Meralda had escaped her, and was gone.

Of course, Euniche was suspicious. But what did she suspect? The very facts, it seemed. Why else would a fool like Meralda be running off, save to a clandestine lovers' meeting? Enough idiots used the churches in this manner. Euniche even deduced whom the young man might be, for she had glimpsed him that day at the palazzo.

She thought him callow and unruly. In other words, she knew inwardly he would never have turned his head to glance after *her*.

"I believe my servant mistrusts me," Meralda said that day to Lorenzo, standing in the cool indigo shadow of a pillar, her hand fast in his, while the Madonna looked a them kindly under her diadem.

It was then that Lorenzo declared, with near violence, "Let me take you from them. Let me have you. You'd do better with me than in that cruel house. Or do you think otherwise?"

Perhaps he assumed she would refuse, and he was therefore at liberty to make this extraordinary offer. Or again, simply he did not think. At any rate, refuse she did.

"I can't. It would be wicked."

"Why wicked?"

She blushed.

He said, "But I would marry you, Meralda. We could go to one of the churches at Silvia. The priests there will take a present of money and perform the ceremony—"

"No . . . *no*."

"Then you don't love me as you swear to me you do."

"It would ruin us," she murmured.

Her voice was filled by a mixture of terror—and wistfulness.

But then Lorenzo, stirred, began to kiss and feel her all over like his priceless possession, and she succumbed to the singing delight which always took her at such times. Her blood was hot, if anything, hotter than his. She flung her arms about him, clutched the stone-work, shivering in ecstasy as his fingers and tongue found out everything reachable through the gathers of her gown.

That night, however, the Gorgon came to her room. The Gorgon was her own name for Euniche.

"M'donna, I'm very concerned."

"Why?" said Meralda, trying to effect the chill off-putting notes of her della Scorpia aunts. Failing.

The Gorgon told Meralda she was very much afraid Meralda had gone out to meet a young man of the lower orders, a mere artisan, a nephew of the one who came to the palace to give Lord Como painting lessons.

"I'm afraid for you, M'donna. If it were to be found out . . . what would become of you?"

Meralda stood against the wall of her bedchamber, like a rabbit hypnotized before a snake. She tried yet to brazen out her propriety, but she shook, and she was nearly as pale as on the day after she had met her betrothed.

Infallibly the Gorgon now alluded to this very person.

"More dreadful than anything, lady, if news reached Signore-donno Ciara. What might then not happen?"

"How dare you—" croaked the rabbit, petrified, hopeless.

"I dare, M'donna, because I wouldn't see you so disgraced. Cast out to be a harlot in the sinks of the City. Or yet more awful—some stern punishment devised by your father, Lord Justore."

Meralda, despite her attempts not to, began to sob.

Euniche did not smile at this, and did not know she smiled in her heart. Or, in the spot where a heart would normally have been; instead she kept a flint there, off which she sometimes struck silver sparks.

"Please believe, lady, it isn't my intention to bring you down. I only seek to warn you."

"What do you want?" choked Meralda.

What indeed did Euniche want?

Like a sleepwalker, Meralda slid towards her jewel-casket, thinking to take out her necklace of blue pearls (which would naturally have been missed) and offer them to the serpent.

Euniche forestalled her, having quickly reasoned that she was about to be offered a bribe. She did not want that.

"Put your trust in me, lady. I shall say nothing."

"Nothing?" quavered Meralda. She was fourteen, and in the house of enemies that she must treat as her family.

"Be guided by me. Then you can continue a little with your holiday pleasures. I know you'd not do any-thing . . . base—that you would protect your virginity for your lawful husband—" (Euniche knew nothing of the sort) "—it's only your good nature and your guile-lessness that have brought you to this. He's a fine young man—" (she hated Lorenzo) "—and you're tempted. No, you'll do nothing sinful. Of that I'm sure. But in future, let me accompany you to the church. I'll stand guard for you, lady. And later, if needful, be a witness for your protection."

Meralda was astonished.

Well she might be.

She thought, or prayed, she had misjudged the Gorgon, who it seemed wanted to protect her.

In any event, what else was she to do?

"Very well," she said. And softly, unwilling, "Thank you, Euniche."

On the flint heart, such great showerings of lights! Euniche did not even really understand herself. Only that, to get sheer power over her fool of a mistress was worth far more than to get her liking, or her jewels.

The arrows that pinned Lorenzo Vai's sleeves to his doublet were not gold, only painted to resemble it. But the arrow that had pierced his emotions, as he had begun to tell himself, the dart of love, was genuine.

With this in mind, almost confusedly, he began to gather money. Some he stole from his uncle, the painter, out of the chest in the room behind the studio. No one would suspect Lorenzo, the outer chamber was always full of students, everyone went in and out, and thefts had happened before. (This act had seemed wrong to Lorenzo, but that did not prevent him. One day, he thought, when the della Scorpias came round to him, he would pay the cash back.) After this, he got coins from various people who owed them to the Vai studio for commissions. Of these he made an equal split, half to his uncle, for whom they had been intended, and half to himself. The painter was unworldly and never checked anything or pursued debts, his head full only of angels, naked Venuses, and clouds. Privately Lorenzo had long thought the colored pigments had fouled his uncle's brain, and took care himself to handle them as rarely as possible.

Then Lorenzo added the step of borrowing money openly, from his mother. This had taken place many times, and though so far he had never returned any of it to her, she had never pressed him in any way, except fondly in her arms.

Meanwhile, the secret meetings continued.

As for the harsh-faced della Scorpia maid who now accompanied Meralda into the church, Lorenzo did not care for her. When he questioned Meralda on the matter she was evasive, saying only she could no longer avoid Euniche's presence. (Euniche had stressed to Meralda that she must on no account tell Lorenzo that the liaison had been discussed between the two women. It would make the poor young man nervous.)

Euniche would sit down on a bench to one side of the church, while the lovers clung and mumbled their fears and unformed plans in the chapel.

"Come away with me, Meralda. Come tomorrow. I've a bag full of duccas now—"

"I mustn't think of it. You must never speak of it—"

"You don't love me. You play with me—and I'm as easy to wind round your finger as a strand of your hair—"

"I worship you, Lorenzo—you re my god—"

"Then come with me to Silvia and let's be wed."

"I'm afraid."

"Of what, when I'm with you to protect you?"

"Of . . . of my betrothed lord—"

"That one? He's a wretch, but we'll outwit him. He is nothing. And we could go far away from the City. Venus isn't unfriendly to the Franchians, and they are mastering Milano and long for Italian troops. There's brave work for a man in those armies—on either side— and high pay." Seeing her bemused—what did she know of such warlike things—he added, "If you love me, you will let me decide what's to be done, as a woman must."

But still she would not give in. Though this process was like milk resisting a club—so fluid and unhard was she, his assaults passed straight through her and did nothing but make a splash.

Lorenzo next became aware, so he thought, that the

only way to bend her to his wish was to hoist her. Once he had deflowered Meralda, she could not risk the evil Ciara discovering her lapse, and to save her very soul she would have to marry Lorenzo.

It was a vast stride to take. He had enjoyed many girls, but they were not of Meralda's sort, not the daughters of nobility. With the anticipated sexual reward would also come the achievement of plucking such a choice bloom, and the dismay of the deed's enormity.

But it was not to be managed in the church.

The informative romances had seen to it that Meralda outfitted herself with a dark, plain cloak over her most ordinary garments, when she went to meet Lorenzo. Her hair, though, was always marvelously done, the long strands crimped from plaiting, sometimes ribbons threaded through. Only a thin veil ever concealed it. Now that Euniche was party to the deception, she had insisted on a thicker covering. One morning, this proved sensible.

They had entered Maria Maesta as usual—the Mass of Prima Pegno was over and the church empty— Euniche prepared to take her station on the bench, while Meralda hastened to the chapel. Suddenly a boy of about nine appeared breathlessly before them.

"Madonna Melda—here, for you." He thrust a grimy paper into Meralda's hand.

"M'donna is not addressed in that way," said the Gorgon, tartly, but the boy took no notice. He was from the slums, ragged and not clean, his face browned with summer and dirt.

Meralda was no scholar, but she had learned to read well enough to apprehend the message on the paper.

Come at once, Lorenzo had written, in his unwieldy script. *I am sick and alone and cannot move from the house.*

Meralda did not ask herself how, if he were alone and unable to move, he had managed to fetch the boy to bring the paper.

The boy now said, "He told me you would be generous."

This was a lie.

Meralda was at a loss—she had little money of her own and had brought none with her. The journey to the church was short, that was why she had been allowed to make it with only her maid. (It lay through a short alley, over the bridge of a narrow canal, and into a small square, where Maria Maesta stood, crowded to one side.)

At that moment the Gorgon moved into the breach.

"Here," thrusting a penny into the boy's disappointed grip. "What's the matter?" she added kindly to her mistress.

Meralda had never heard a tone of *kindness* from her before.

The boy too was taken in—Lorenzo had not thought to advise him.

"He's ill on his bed and no one to tend him."

"Messer Lorenzo?"

"Lorenzo, yes."

Euniche glanced at her mistress. "Where does the poor young man live?"

"He's written it there," said the boy.

Indeed Lorenzo had. And Euniche could not read. But, after all, this was not a fundamental stumbling block.

She gave the boy another penny with every appearance of ease (false ease, she had none to spare) and waved him off. To Meralda, Euniche said, now nearly tenderly, "Oh, lady. You must go to him."

At which Meralda stared at her, as anyone might have done.

What was the Gorgon up to?

Yes, she might wish for Meralda's downfall, and definitely Euniche must have realized such an adventure might—must—spell her downfall. But the house of Scorpia knew Euniche was her lady's chaperone. If some crisis was the result of this, would they not upbraid Euniche for her carelessness? It would not be enough for her to plead she was only the attendant of her mistress. Euniche had been chosen for the task because of her age and adamantine jailorishness.

As before, Euniche did not know quite what her true motives were. She thought that she would just let the fool make more of a fool of herself, and that afterwards she, Euniche, would find some means to save the situation. And that through all that, she would gain yet more power over Meralda della Scorpia. But somewhere beneath even these layers of guile, the inner Euniche hankered, nebulously, for something else.

Meralda said, "I cannot. How could I go?"

"I'll assist you, M'donna. How can you *leave* him there? He might die.'"

Meralda gave a cry.

It was settled.

Euniche managed everything. She went to the canal and there hailed one of the meandering boats which, for some while now, had been named, in Venus, *Wanderers*. To the wanderlier, a grizzled man in striped hose, she promised a silver venus if he would take herself and her lady by the Wide Canal into the Artisans' Quarter, behind the Temple of Art on Fulvia.

Soon enough, Meralda, her servant, and the wanderlier were through the waterways of Aquila. They emerged on the vast, sun-smashed apron of the Fulvia Lagoon, whose depths were murky, with dragons stirring there.

The alabaster dome of the Primo shone like polished mirror. While around the spire of the basilica, the seven brass mechanical horses (one for each of the City's islands, and not ten years old) trotted, shaking their heads at the stroke of eleven.

At these sights Meralda gazed. She had not seen them very often. Such was the cloistered life of a maiden of a great house. But also she was uneasy, more so at what she had done than the plight of her sick lover.

The minarets of the Temples of Art and Justice (copied from fanes of the East) dazzled above as they went by below, turning from the lagoon into the canal called Wide. This, like the apron of water outside, was packed with craft of every sort. Boats loaded with goods roped beneath canvas, plowed heavily past. A ship with rose-colored sails shot down the channel like one of the Ducem's greyhounds. The wanderlier guided their vessel between, while crystal spray burst from the glaucous water.

Then, following the curve of the canal, they came slowly out of the glory of tall buildings and flame-flagged merchant shipping, into a hot and gloomy tunnel. Here the Wide Canal shrank, and tenements, nearly closing off the sky, overhung the banks, ochre and peeling like vegetables that had been mummified or gone rotten.

"Where is this?" asked the ignorant girl.

"The Artisans' Quarter," said Euniche, who was far from ignorant of the City.

"Does he live *here*?"

"Turn to the left bank," said Euniche arrogantly to the wanderlier, "where the church of San Raphaelo is."

Once they were ashore, Euniche gave the boatman what she had offered, the silver venus, which represented very much to her. Then she led Meralda around San Raphaelo and into the clutch of alleys beyond.

Lorenzo had been pacing about in the upper room. It belonged, this dwelling, to his mother, but she was out at Isole until the evening, with an aunt.

His mother's house, which had been also his when he was a child, and which he still sometimes visited when the studio grew too crowded for his liking, was poor, but well-kept. The lower area was domestic with its broom, lemon-bleached table, pans and crocks neatly stacked by the hearth, water pitchers stored for coldness in their alcove. Up here, the bed (his dead father's) had a frame, and was laid with the cleanest, though coarse, sheets. Upon these, seeing Meralda and Euniche appear abruptly in the alleyway, Lorenzo flung himself.

He could not quite believe his scheme had worked, despite the pains he had taken with it. He himself had paid for his mother's jaunt—from the money she had already loaned him. Now, shocked by his success, his heart pounded. He now easily looked sufficiently feverish to confirm his feigned illness.

The latch of the street door shifted. Lorenzo listened through the roar in his ears. He hoped the girl's servant-woman would stay below, and his luck held. For only Meralda, wide-eyed and lucent as a painted angel, came into the upper room.

Seeing her lover supine, she broke instantly into luminous tears. Lorenzo could not bear this and leapt up at once to take her in his arms.

"Are you so sick, Lorenzo?"

"No longer. Your beauty has cured me."

"But have you seen a doctor—"

"Who would come here but some charlatan? No."

"Oh, what shall I do?"

"Kiss me." Then, after a while, "Where is that girl you call the Gorgon?"

"Shall I send her for medicine?"

"Send her to Hell."

"She brought me here. She's gone to pray at the church for you. I think after all—she is my friend."

"Don't trust her," he said, not seeing he had today put both of them into the palm of Euniche's hand.

"Whom should I trust then?"

"Me. Only me."

Worried by his high color, she urged him to lie down. He agreed, but said she must lie down next to him, to console him. By the bed he had put wine, and a dish of some sweets he knew that she liked. He let her feed him one or two of these, and fed her several, and then he said these sweet meats were not as delicious as her lips, and they drank the wine.

They were young, and passionate, and now they lay together on a great bed, in the sultry hour of noon, their flesh longing only to be one, regardless of whatever morality or strictures had been plastered over their minds.

At first it was as it had been, the kissing and caressing, but then—oh, he had found a way in through Meralda's bodice, swiftly unlacing it, and his warm hands were on her breasts with only the thin linen of her curtella between them.

Outside, at the entry to this particular alley, Meralda had seen a little pagan shrine. It was to Neptune, one of hundreds that had sprung up in Venus after the overthrow of the Council of the Lamb. The half-naked deity, rusty trident in hand, his beard of blue wool twined with tiny shells from the lagoons, had seemed improper to the girl. So she had been brought up. This activity on Lorenzo's bed though, she did not seem to see was the herald of the ultimate impropriety: the taking of her virginity.

Of course, though in some fashion her elders had tried to keep her in complete ignorance, she did suppose that this was sinful. She had felt pangs within her own body even when alone, especially after her meetings with Lorenzo began. But still, she believed she should not let Lorenzo continue because it felt so wonderfully *enjoyable*. The enjoyment's function, she had not identified.

Presently, when Lorenzo had pushed aside her heavy skirts, and started, with an impossibly limpid gentleness, to stroke her core—that he tongued her, she did not even realize—Meralda's will left her entirely. She had no scope for shame. She lay spread for him, her eyes fast shut, abandoned as a maenad from the groves of the wine-god. And he, undoing his own clothing only where it was necessary, in another moment drove home inside her.

He hurt her, for, in his haste he had torn her, but before she could do more than gasp, another sensation took hold of her, and flung her against Lorenzo in a clamor not of pain but delirium. Never had she felt such pleasure. She thought she would burst apart from it. She screamed shrilly and heard Lorenzo's own savage howls.

Uneducated in everything, she was aware that his outcry was no more to do with unhappiness than hers. That it was the prelude to a hideous lament, how could either of them really have been expected to guess?

"What have we done?"

"What do you think? I've made you my wife."

"Your wife—"

"I've broken your seals, beloved."

Then she did not weep, only sat up slowly, stunned, seeing the abyss gape all around them.

"Sweetness," said Lorenzo, "God won't mind— haven't I told you, we'll be wed."

Of all the things her family had hammered into her, this the most insistent: her chastity, she must retain until the selected marriage bed.

"Is there a way—I can hide it?"

Lorenzo laughed. He was pleased, the victor.

"Outwardly. But not from any man that lies with you."

Still no weeping. She wilted from the lack of water.

"I shall die."

"No. You'll live and be mine."

"Ciara will kill me. Or . . . my father will do it."

Lorenzo poured more wine and held it to her lips, which were parched from his eager mouth. He spoke to her carefully, explaining that he, like his uncle, had talent as an artist and would soon get a rich patron. That much was feasible, anywhere in the civilized world. Or he would make a good soldier, and there were the armies of the Franchians. Whatever else, Lorenzo would keep her safe. They could go off together this very night—and then no one should ever harm her. She was his. Finally, he knelt by the bed, handsome and unflawed and, cupping her delicate face in his strong hands, asked her to become his wife, no longer bombastically but with a quiet theatrical eloquence. And Meralda, everything else lost, sitting in the burning shade of his beauty, strength, and fearlessness, felt her love take all doubt from her at last, because he asked so humbly what he knew she must give.

So, it was to be that very night, their escape. Meralda had no loyalty to her house or family—why should she? Only to Lorenzo, whom she loved. But Euniche, as always, was another matter.

If Meralda had been able to buy Euniche off, or to *lose* Euniche somewhere, then there would have been no need to confide in her. But the apparently unbribable Euniche now seemed unlikely ever to leave Meralda alone. Naturally, Euniche sensed developments. As for the act on the bed, how could Euniche have any doubts? She herself had facilitated it.

"M'donna—you seem in such a flurry. Why have you taken these things from your chest? Shall I put them back?"

"No—I—need them."

"How, lady?"

"There's something I must do."

"But your cloak, lady—are you going out again?"

And so on.

Eventually the girl had to confess. If only to prevent Euniche from neatly putting away every item Meralda took up for her journey. Of course, another eloper might have managed things differently. But Meralda was herself, fourteen and at her wit's end.

"Lorenzo and I are to leave the City—" she whispered, at long last.

Euniche pretended amazement and alarm.

Then Meralda also confessed that she had given up her chastity to Lorenzo.

At that Euniche crossed herself, gathered Meralda into her arms, and vowed that it was no one's fault, and that God was forgiving to true lovers, and that she, Euniche, would assist her mistress, regardless of any risk to herself.

Then everything was told; Lorenzo's plan, the boat that would wait by the church of Maria Maesta, its route, the money and papers Lorenzo had garnered. They would be married, but not at Silvia; rather in some rural town farther off, wherever a priest could be made willing.

After this, Euniche helped Meralda to pack up the necessaries for her flight. Then she said that she too had something to do, in order to make everything easier for the fleeing pair. She did not say what this was.

"Rest now, lady. Have a little sleep while you are able. I'll tell them in the house you have a headache from the sun."

This at least Euniche did.

It was now well into the afternoon. The maid left the palazzo by a side door, and walked by a long alley under arches to the market behind Aquila.

Mature sunlight lay across the booths, and piled in ruby sheets against the ribs of carcasses newly butchered. If this omen meant anything to Euniche, she gave no sign.

Straight to the paper shops she went, where sheets of Arabian paper, waxes, goose feathers for pens, and metal styluses from the East were sold. Here, too, you could always find someone to scribe a letter for you.

Because of what her letter needed to say, it had to be organized with care. But the old man, who had once or twice written on her behalf in the past, was also in thrall to Euniche. She had long ago, by lucky accident, learned something about him.

"Ah, my girl," said he, affecting nonchalance and looking at her warily, "how may I help you?"

"I must send a letter on good paper," said Euniche, loftily. "You must see to it. In the back room."

So he took her through into the dark chamber, where parchments, ledgers, and wooden boxes stood in columns, and the sunlight only came in chinks through the shutters.

"Light your lamp," said Euniche.

He obeyed. "To which must I address the letter?" Euniche nodded. "To his lordship, Signore-donno Andrea Barbaron, at the Castello."

The old man's mouth fell open. "You are writing to the *Barbarons*—to the Barbaron eldest son—the *heir*—"

"Are you to question me, or to write, Jacobe?"

"Excuse me, Euniche, but—this is a great house, and besides, you serve the della Scorpias, who are the sworn enemies—"

"Thank you so kindly for telling me this, which I have never known." The old man now cowered, but Euniche added, for good measure, "It is to be our secret, Jacobe, this letter. Like the other secret we have."

"Yes, yes then, Euniche."

"You recall the *other* secret, Jacobe?"

"To my regret—"

"The tally of what you have regularly stolen from your employer, and sold on your own account?"

"Yes—hush, please, please say no more, Euniche—you know I did it to send my grandson to the University. It wasn't for myself."

"Yes. That's the only reason I have never told." Jacobe bowed to the creamy paper.

"Only say what's to put down, Euniche. You know I'm your friend, as you are mine."

They left in darkness, under a sky smooth as velvet, where a quarter moon shone like a silver venus.

Their exit required walking silently, through the garden, then through a snarl of store rooms on the palace's ground floor. Euniche had devised it. But at the outer door, a small one, normally locked (Euniche had gotten the key) and unguarded, the assistant gave her mistress over to the night.

Alone then, Meralda traversed the shorter alley—it seemed long—and came to the bridged canal, where Lorenzo waited for her in a wanderer.

Once in the boat, she lay in his arms, shuddering at the enormity of what she had done. Yet his arms were warm and very strong, as she had remembered. He would keep her safe from all the nightmares of the world.

Euniche meanwhile had gone to the kitchen, where sometimes even the higher maids of the house gathered. Here she sighed and said her mistress had sent her off again, and she feared Meralda was unwell, she had been behaving strangely and secretively for some while.

"I have left her to sleep as she wanted. She was almost hysterical when I remonstrated—what can one do? If things don't improve, I must ask Donna Caterina what to do." (This was one of Meralda's aunts.) "She is very gracious, Donna Caterina."

The people in the kitchen nodded, afraid to disagree, though Caterina della Scorpia was a cold, too-pious woman. Over the hearth the great pots boiled, and tawny feathers fluttered about from a plucking of guinea fowl. Euniche saw no omens in any of that.

Best she liked power over others. With Meralda, she had found the nicest power was that of life and death.

During that hot evening, as the sky had burnt to crimson behind the City, Andrea Barbaron paced about the upper floors of the Castello. Thinking that he was in a bad mood, his siblings and cronies gave him a wide berth. Andrea was seldom to be trifled with.

He was young, the heir, thick-set and heavy in appearance, his fleshy face handsome, his hair a rich russet-brown, cared for like a woman's and hanging down his back. He wore, that day, the colors of Barbaron, deep red and sapphire. The design of the Tower, which was the sigil of Barbaron, had been worked for him into a golden collar.

In his thick, ringed fingers he occasionally turned a piece of paper. Much handling had made it limp and smeared its ink, but he could still make out what it said. There was no seal, no name attached. He would not have expected there to be. Plainly enough some underling had written it—or had it written. Not for gain, it seemed, since the author was anonymous, but out of malice.

One phrase came over and again to Andrea's sharp blue eyes.

"Your lordship may find amusement in promoting the disgrace of one already far-fallen. And in so doing, make of your closest foes a general laughing-stock."

The words were self-consciously chosen, Andrea thought, and one or two were misspelled. It was a man's hand—but that denoted only the writer, who might not be the instigator.

Otherwise, everything was clear enough, providing it were true. A daughter of the della Scorpias had taken up with an artisan, some painter's student, and having already bedded with the fellow, would tonight make off with him. Venus was a City of flights and burrowings, and doubtless they anticipated getting clean away.

There were, however, two complications. For one thing, the girl was already betrothed to one of the noble Ciaras, the one about whom certain sinister stories had recently wafted. Secondly, the handy mischief-maker had outlined both the hour and the escapees' route.

Another man than Andrea might have gone to his father, the old Lord Barbaron, with this news. But Andrea did not even consider it.

The note had been brought by an unseen urchin, for Andrea's eyes. Should he involve his father then, it might add further awkwardness. Besides, and this was more to the point, Andrea did not know that his father would be willing to do anything. Andrea respected and disliked his sire in equal measure. In all forms he was outwardly correct, but he waited impatiently for the old man to die and give up the domain, of Barbaron. And that the old man delayed to do. Andrea felt himself to have been consciously standing on tiptoe, breath held for the event, for well over five years (he was now nineteen, but looked older).

This was typical of how they were. The father chilly, persistent, and slow. Andrea heated and quick, of wit and deed.

Therefore, what use to make of the titbit, how to indulge in retribution, while keeping unsullied the name of Barbaron? Andrea did not intend to pass up an opportunity to harm the della Scorpias. Along with his duty to his house, and a sharp attention to all its interests, both political and mercantile, Andrea kept the score of every tussel with Barbaron's enemies. . . . on which list the della Scorpias traditionally ranked the highest.

To Andrea, revenge was neither mean nor unlawful. It was, at its most simple, a facet of his duty to his class and family. But, it pleased him, too. He liked it, as he liked to fight with swords, eat a good meal, outthink others in business, or rig a vigorous woman. Besides, Andrea also knew his duty to God. Part of which was, for himself and his, to appear at the Last Trumpet fully clad in flesh, stepping out of a grave and not a jar of dust. The contention over the burial ground on the Isle was important to him.

As the sky shed its flames, Andrea made his decision.

Inside the half of an hour, he had summoned three of his younger brothers, his nearest companion, Gualdo, and some of their men. The problem had been presented, and Andrea's solution given. After this, some preparation took place. A gathering of boats came to the canalside doors of Barbaron. And, in its turn, there was the sending of another letter, the content of which was brief.

All this caused very slight comment, for Andrea often went about with his pack. And at night they were seldom at home.

After the furnace of the day, the night had dropped cool. Under that velvet sky with its venus of moon, the channels ran sinuous as snakes of black glass.

They went by the backways of the City, Meralda and Lorenzo, avoiding those spots where torches blazed on the front of buildings, seemingly setting the water itself on fire. The light that was in these narrow fretted windows was soft, and undemanding. Often there was no light, the houses they passed like walls of shadow, glimmering ghostly from the reflections of the moon and the canals.

She did not know the path the boat was taking. Lorenzo knew, that was enough. (It had been enough, too, for others, since Meralda had named the way, even *without* knowing it.)

In Meralda's mind, a timid fantasy was getting hold, of how they would live together, he and she. Unpractical, she did not think of all she would have to learn. That she could neither cook nor darn nor wash clothes—which would doubtless be required of her—that she knew nothing at all, even how to care for a child should one arrive. There had, in the house of non-friends, been always others to look after her. Somehow it seemed this would still continue, even when she was Lorenzo's wife, in some tenement or army camp of the future.

She was drowsy, too. She had not slept, not for a great while, it seemed. It would be wonderful to sleep now, inside the fortress of love.

Meralda drifted, her lullaby the *glok-glok* of the oar in the water, the candle of the moon to keep night-haunts away. Secure forever in Lorenzo's arms.

"Messer—" the boatman's voice, far off, "Messer—who are these?"

And his arms let her go.

"God knows who they are, not I—"

"They're blocking the channel, Messer."

"I can see that. Go to one side."

"It will be impossible."

Meralda opened her eyes and saw, too.

There were four boats, half veiled in darkness, yet

each with a lantern hanging at the prow. Men stood up on the boats, cloaked also in black. But there, and there again, a curious glint of gold, or steel.

And now they were very near.

"Turn back," said Lorenzo. "They're robbers." His tones were uneven with nervousness.

But just then a man called along the few feet of separating canal. "Hail to you, Lorenzo Vai. The greetings of this night."

The salute was given in a voice of stone.

"He knows you, Messer."

"Christ's heart."

One of the boats detached itself and eased gracefully forward. It was not a wanderer, but well-handled and agile. As it came, the lantern seemed to catch, as if by magic, a shining golden tower *within* a cloak. Lorenzo finally noticed who they really were.

"They're Barbarons," said Lorenzo. "Oh, God . . . your worst adversaries . . . Meralda, don't say a word—"

But this was of no use, for now the approaching boat ground lightly against their own. There, standing up in its prow, the man who had shown his colors, was Andrea Barbaron. He said, "Well met, Messer Vai. And M'donna Meralda. I think you are attempting to desert our glorious City of Venus. I think you must not. No, I think, M'donna, for the sake of your own fairest name, you'd better accept my protection. We shan't hurt you. We only want to take you to your rightful lord."

Meralda sat transfixed. A lance might have gone through her and pinned her to the boat, which all the while seemed to be withdrawing from around her (as had Lorenzo s arms) so that she hung there suspended, between night and water, weightless, in the still air.

Lorenzo said, his voice shaking, "To her father? No, her father is cruel to her. Why would *you* help the della Scorpias—let them sink to Hell. Only let us by, Signore, only let us go on—"

"No," said Andrea. That was all. It cut the night in two, that one word. Then, after a pause he added, urbanely, "But don't fear it's her father we'll take you both to. I meant her intended husband, Ciara."

This was the same darkness, through which she and Lorenzo had drifted. How changed.

They had come on to a lagoon. Meralda did not know which one. It might have been anywhere. It might have been in Hell.

Far off, too far and all indifferent, were the lamps and tapers of the City, the walls that held the water from the sky. And then an islet appeared, a little black hump. There was the winey smell of overripen pomegranates. The boat bumped against stone.

She had been put into this boat with Andrea Barbaron and some others. Another boat held Lorenzo, but he had struggled, there in the dark on the canal, and been felled by Andrea's cousin, the useful Gualdo. Since then, Lorenzo made no protests.

Most devastating of all perhaps, was Meralda's sense of utter aloneness. It was as if her lover were not even there with her. As if he had abandoned her—not for involuntary unconciousness, but by running miles away.

This fate was hers, and no one could save her from it. If she had stupidly believed Lorenzo Vai could do so, now she was enlightened.

Andrea helped Meralda ashore quite courteously.

Steps led up towards a low, brick house. It was old, had been erected some two centuries before, and the endless encroachment of the lagoon had marked it, inwardly and out. But in the dark, that same darkness, it was only the most terrible spot in the world.

"A house of secrets," remarked Andrea, as Gualdo and another of the Barbaron men dumped Lorenzo's inert body on the landing-place. "The story is, some priest of the Primo kept his mistress here, and his boys. They say you can catch huge eels here as easy as blinking."

She did not say to him, *Why am I here?*

He told her, anyway.

"This is his solitary-house now. I mean, your betrothed. Sometimes he likes to come here, quietly, for a private festivity of his own."

He was not sadistic. He was only telling her, grimly enough, what lay in wait for her. Andrea, with his codes of honor, had no time for women who transgressed the only duty required of them, faithfulness.

Then other men came down the steps. They were all one with the darkness, and they gathered up Lorenzo and carried him away. At this Meralda would have shrieked, but since they were also hustling her in the same direction, the shriek died within her.

By then Andrea, his part in the drama played (and hungry too, for he had missed his dinner through this), had gotten back into the boat with Gualdo.

As the night-house received her, Meralda heard male laughter rowed off over the lagoon.

And now there was only this dark room. And through the dark came two points of light, lit by a third point, all floating. Three candles: one flame, two eyes.

Ciara.

He held the candlestick in his thin and too-white hand. Every second she saw more of him, as the chamber bloomed up into light. It was full of candles now, and he had set his down. The servants—or had they been unseen things, minions of the dark—had withdrawn.

He nodded.

"I am honored, madonna, to entertain you as my guest. A joy I hadn't anticipated so soon."

There were tapestries on the walls, to hide the damp perhaps, in dull ancient colors picked out with brackish silver thread. And there was a table with a damask cloth, figured with flowers. On this, were dishes of silver, and goblets of the finest Venus glass, pale red and sulfur, and, in their oval wombs, tiny curled embryos of candlelight.

Courteous as a gallant, he had seated her at the table.

"You must pardon me, madam. My poor house is hardly properly supplied for your visit. Your visit being so unexpected. But try a little of this cheese and fruit. The bread. The wine is good, and will refresh you." Perhaps he smiled, or not. There were only his eyes, his hands—his hands also watched her with their optical rings. "Tomorrow I must summon a feast for you, something to charm a dainty maiden."

Even his clothing was invisible to Meralda.

But—now he had a voice. This awful voice, so soft and mannered, so unlike the rough enamored tones of her lover.

"Where—" she started. Her throat clenched.

"Where, madonna?"

"Where is Lorenzo?"

"Ah," said the Lord Ciara. "Where I have him."

"You must let him go," she said. She did not know how, or why. It was no good.

"But, madam, I can't. How can I?"

"Don't . . . don't—"

"Yes, madam?"

"Don't harm him—"

"Why should I harm him?" Ciara asked, reasonably. "Why should I want to? Is there any cause? What crime has he committed against me? Or what crime have you committed, for the matter of that?"

Meralda shriveled. She closed and curled together like a scorched leaf, not only her spirit, but her body, too, and put her face into her hands. No tears came from her.

"Come now, Meralda," the first use of her name, "why this display? Rest assured, your father would entrust you to me, under such circumstances, since you've left his own defending walls."

To placate him, did she sip the wine, taste the peach or the candied nuts? Did she speak any more? Did he? Did someone come and conduct her from the room? They must have done, for here she lay now, in another room, very bare, yet with a bed. There was no light now, while beyond the narrow window, latticed over by iron, she heard the slipping of the Laguna Aquila, on which, though she did not know, lay the Isle of Eels. This island, currently the retreat of her betrothed.

She cried eventually against the pillow, which was of the finest linen and smelled musty, unlike the coarse herb-scented pillows of Lorenzo's bed.

Then Meralda prayed. To God. Who else was left?

Did she believe in God? Yes, but only as one more father, one more lord, the God of Laws and Thunders and Jealous Rage—and Christ, who suffered so and therefore did not grasp that others did not have His endurance and could not bear what He had borne.

Yet, her need was limitless. It seemed to become a creature in the room, calling out to a Heaven that did not hear. But the night heard, and the night answered. It answered with the voice of a man. A voice that screamed once, and then was silent.

Meralda turned to ice. Frozen, she lay, her dead prayers cold-burnt to her lips. And then a void like death came upwards from beneath the house, the ground, the water, the earth, and smothered her in a kind of sleep.

The morning brought a woman, with a dish of bread sopped in milk, as if for a child. Meralda ate some of this, and then the woman indicated she would dress her, and arrange her hair.

Meralda was accustomed to that, of course, but not here, and not to the woman, who had a leaning, warped shape. The room was hot already with sun, and the lagoon blistered outside. Through this window she could make out nothing but the water.

Was it possible to escape? To what? Lorenzo was here. She must find Lorenzo.

"The young man who was with me—"her new attendant glanced into Meralda's face "—do you know where he is kept? He's of good family and they may become angry—" Meralda stopped. Her own threats frightened her with their weakness and unsuitability. But the woman only grunted. Meralda tried again. "I heard a man . . . I heard a man . . . in the night . . . he cried out. . ."

The woman's hands were in Meralda's hair, combing, braiding, looping and coiling, fastening strands with clasps set by beryls and two or three strings of pearls. Why was this done? Did Ciara want to see her so, as if for a festival?

"Is . . . your master kind to you?"

The woman looked full at her then and laughed, with a peculiar noise. As she did it, Meralda saw that she had no tongue, only a blackened stump.

Oh God . . . please . . . sweet God—The prescribed words: *Merciful Father, help me in my hour of night, when all men turn from me their faces. I shall not be afraid for the arrow of the sun, nor the pestilence that comes down from the moon. For You are with me, Lord, You are my guide and my only hope*—

She did not see Ciara again until sunset.

Movement in the house, which was not large, alerted her to activity among the servants. Then a heavy smell of food and roses began to wash through the rooms. Apparently they were to have the feast he had promised.

She had heard romances about feasts. Would he poison her?

But when she went perforce (*driven* there almost, by the tongueless woman) to the dark-lit table, where the fragile goblets flamed softly and roses spilled about, only two meticulous servants waited on her. Ciara did not appear.

"Where is . . . where is my lord, Signore-donno Ciara?"

"At his studies, madonna. He has already dined."

She was young, her body hungry and thirsty despite her fear, the desert of her bewilderment. She drank wine, and when they served her things from the several dishes, she ate some, every mouthful perfumed from the flowers. She looked for Lorenzo in the room, in their faces, in vain.

Nevertheless, the dinner revived her. Her revival was very sudden—perhaps due to spices in the meat, or some drug? Anything, anything.

Meralda got to her feet and said, "Take me at once to my lord."

They hesitated. Then one said, "As you wish, M'donna."

She walked behind the man with the candle, up a narrow stair through night (*in my hour of night, be with me, God . . .*)

Long ago, almost a century, this house was a place of secrets, true, but also one of delights and kindnesses, of love.

Did the young girl feel them brushing at her as she went, those others who once had sported and been happy here? Their hands, no longer substantial, reaching out to soothe and anchor her?

No, not that. It was only she had come to a conclusion, and thought it might save her, save Lorenzo even, thought it might bring him back from the dead somehow (for a part of her knew, she had heard his cries before—agony or orgasm—they could have a similar sound). She was mad, in this. She was a fool, naturally. But she was young, she was alone. Hope, which is both friend and foe, had not yet let her fall.

There was a large chamber, curtained off by thick velvet. The servant went in, then returned and let her enter. Inside sat the lord they had betrothed her to, at a long table spread with huge, heavy books, some of them open, with pages illustrated in jewelry tints.

The servant went out.

Meralda stood and clasped her hands.

"My lord . . ."

"A moment, madam. If you'd be so good."

He was reading. Those yellow yolks of eyes fixed still on the page.

Then, one of the hands picked itself up and beckoned to her. "Come here, and see."

She did what he said. That was her ploy, now. To do what he said, what he wished. All and everything. She did not understand, of course, what that might entail.

Poised beside him, she looked and saw into the book. The words were in Latin, and she had no notion of what they said. Her eyes ran across one line that had a large letter of gold and brightest scarlet, showing something that arched backward, like some animal rearing . . . *carnem illam maxime esurio quae adulta et sapida extra omnia ossa gignitur* . . . and out of it a spray like garnets burst.

"My lord—I'm your possession. We are to be married . . . will you take me to your bed?"

He said, and perhaps he smiled, or he did not, certainly he did not lift his eyes, "*Are* we to be married, Meralda?"

It had been her last throw of the dice.

What else could she give him to appease him?

Obviously, it was too late. Or it was meaningless.

He said, "Do you know, however, what coming to my bed might ask of you? There are things I value, there, not always the ordinary things. Not the mundane things, for example, you will have sampled with your paramour, Lorenzo Vai." He paused here, as if for her denial. She made none. Hope had let her go. "The arts of concupiscence are legion, Meralda. I should have wanted, possibly, to educate you in such disciplines. But no longer. You've learned as you wanted. Your quim is undone and I no longer like it."

Still he had not looked at her.

Meralda said, in a fading little voice, "Oh, let me go . . . please, I beg, let me go back to my father . . . he'll see me punished."

"Yes, yes. So he will. But first I have had my say. Your loving enemy, Barbaron, did very well to bring you here. I wonder now, if you will learn anything from *me*?"

Speech rushed out of her. "You killed Lorenzo! He's dead . . . he's dead . . ."

"A fact, lady. Yes. He died last night. I found him scarcely interesting; his death was quick. At a stroke."

She wept. She fell to her knees and the tears seared her eyes—and yet, within the prison of her grief, she knew this was not all.

Standing up now, he closed the book. Perhaps he smiled. Or he did not.

Wrapped in despair, even now she did not see his eyes as he told her what he had done for her, to teach her the lesson of her sin against him.

At first his words dropped on to her like a rain that made a great black tumult, but did not penetrate the casing of her mind.

Then, then the words sank in.

What did he say to her? Oh Christ in Heaven must it be told? It must, for it was done.

He explained to her the Latin in the book she had seen him reading. The passage described the eating of a favorite food, after the carnal act had been completed. This food, the "flavorsome meat that ripened without bone," was Adam's rib. The human penis. There were instructions on the cooking, too, and seasoning. He recounted those. He said that in this one area he had been pleased with Lorenzo, for furnishing an adequate specimen. "I could hardly give you a lesser treat,"

Ciara said, "for your little feast. I was informed, by one who watched, it was the dish you liked the most and ate most of."

Again, night.

About an hour before, the mutilated body of a young man, stone-white from loss of blood, had been flung into the lagoon. (In three or four days more, it would rise again in a canal between Aquila and Fulvia, a foul, pallid fish. There would be jokes among some of the boatmen, that he had been on his way to the basilica, this corpse, to pray. The omission at his groin was put down to the greed of sea-life. He had no other wounds. Presently he was taken to the Isle of the Dead, decently cremated, and buried in one of the tiny ash-graves kept for those unknown. In the Artisans' Quarter, Lorenzo's uncle already thought the boy had run off with some girl. The mother thought so as well, and ever after it broke her heart that he had never told her, and never returned to see her, a thankless and unloving son.)

Now, however, a boat came away from the Island of Eels, There were three men on it, bound up in their cloaks as if bandaged. And a girl.

In the eerie light of the lantern, her hair, very fair and saffron yellow, was ragged and in parts seemed to have been torn out, leaving stripings of old blood. Her nails were torn and bloody too, and on her throat and face were scratches. Other blood, this still fluid and red, thinly trickled now and then from her mouth. Worse than this, her face was more blank than a carnival mask, and her eyes were like things trapped in caves.

But she made no sound. Only now and then she would reach up, and then her hand would fall down again. It was that she had meant to claw her face or tear her hair again, and then forgot what she meant to do.

The trickle of blood was from two small vessels breaking in her throat and nose, with her own screaming. This had happened, probably, when she was shown the naked body of her lover.

Across Aquila, the walls of the night appeared. There seemed only one other landmark there, a strange luminescence rising out of the salt water.

"Church has come up today," said one of the men.

The other only spat in the lagoon. What did he care for churches?

Maria Maka Selena came and went with the tides of the lagoon. It was a phenomenon, standing sometimes only to its nave in the water, at others drowned, all but the tower with its clock and garland of silver maidens. Tonight, those girls were canted, a little out of true, but raised high above the boat, and phosphorescent from the sea.

Meralda gazed up wildly. What had caught her eye, or the things which now passed for eyes?

It was the girls on the tower, the phosphorescent girls with seaweed tangling their limbs, the girls who had drowned in the laguna and yet come up again to watch the moon.

"Sit, you bitch," said the second man, as Meralda rose to her feet. "Or do I thrash you?"

"Let her be. He said not to touch her. She's in enough of a state for when we leave her at the della Scorpias' door."

Afraid of Ciara then, not wanting to go against him, they hesitated just long enough. And Meralda leaned slowly over and down into the lagoon, which silkenly parted and took her, and then she was gone, only one last loosened strand of hair left lying on the water. Finally so strong she was, so sensible, so brave, this child.

BARTOLOME

IT MAY NOT SURPRISE YOU to hear that I had bad dreams the night after Thimeo told me about Meralda della Scorpia.

In later years, I thought it odd, myself, that the most coherent of these night-banes concerned her drowning. One might say, there had been far nastier things in the tale.

To this hour, though, I recall that dream. The water closing over my head, my body—not stifling as you would expect, yet perishing, and feeling as much. I seemed to see through a bulb of obscure glass. And in that fashion I beheld the body of the church of Maka Selena pass, its corners and great door, drifting above and away, and then I saw the bottom of the lagoon, which was inky and cold. Still I remember the cold. And I thought I was crying, and speaking to Meralda, who in fact was invisible to me. To no avail.

From such a vileness I would suppose I should have awakened bawling. No such thing. In the dream, all at once I felt that I need no longer suffer this, and felt myself let go of something, though I did not know of what. And then a warmth stole over me, and I was no longer afraid, and then I glimpsed a mild, green, shining brilliance, almost like a hill, more like an emerald

—but in another second it was gone. It was not for me. And *then* I woke, with a sense more of resignation than anything. Next I got from my bed and said a prayer, as I began to shiver. I prayed that for her it had been in that way, with that gentleness, her end, after the horrors before. But now I think it was something else, something so curious I must come to it in its own season, and not now.

My Uncle Thimeo's house was my home for a further eight years. By which time I was a man grown, and a Master Minore of the guild. That year there was a deep winter, and Thimeo took a chill, and in three days he was dead. This was a blow beyond any other. He had been a father to me and a good friend, and I had not wanted to admit he was of an age to be on the lookout for death.

Rossa and I mourned him, and there were many more to speak well of his name. I put off my doublet in the snow and attended to his grave myself. It was my privilege to see him safe to bed, after all he had done for me.

After that I lived a while in his house by Silvia, but it did not feel as it had. Rossa was too sad and no longer young. In the end, she said she would like to go to her sister in the country. We parted regretfully, but even so I could tell she was glad to be leaving. Since the funeral, she had seen my uncle over and over sitting in his chair by the hearth, seen him with such acuity that she had once called his name, and then he was not there. Perhaps she sensed him sleeping by her in the bed, too. It was not that he haunted her, or perhaps only in her heart. But she was better away, and her sister was a cheery affectionate sort, Rossa would be comfortable. I knew I should not meet her again.

After she left, I too took on a housekeeper, but only for the house, you understand. She was a squinty woman of unreliable temper, known as Strabica. But her batter-bread was the best I have ever tasted, and likewise all her cooking.

Thimeo's house, however, perhaps resentful for Rossa, did not take to Strabica. It shook down pots and shelves on her, and slammed the doors on her fingers— all of which made her temper worse. At last, I sold the place to a man of the guild and took Strabica, and a boy for the other work, to a new house, which stands distant from the City, in the lagoon, on a landspit at the very edge of the sea-wall of Silvia.

Here the weather is often tumultuous, but awe-inspiring too. In calms, it is the most beautiful spot. Black gulls come down into the very garden, to offend the cat. On clear mornings, you can see over to the far island of Torchara. On misty days, it is the ghosts of isles you notice. The sea is like another being, and always murmuring, always talking, sighing, trying to persuade, like the woman you desire above all others.

The waists of female gowns lifted higher two years later, to outline the breasts and leave the rest to one's imagination. The garb of men grew closer to the body, and left the imagination little work. But I was young and fit from my trade, and was glad enough, in my holiday clothes, to be admired now and then. I had not yet taken a wife, or even a permanent mistress.

The Franks or Franchians, who had annexed Milano in earlier years, were recently busy in Italy again, marching to interfere in the kingdom of the Napolitans. Talk predicted they would have all Italy in the end, if Italy did not rouse herself. But she was all a mess of little princedoms then, and even the pope in Rome, Pietus (a conniving but cowardly man), had reportedly bowed the knee to the Frankish king. Venus kept aloof as was her wont, feeling herself mighty enough, and separate. Napolita, after all, was the length of Italy away. (If Milano was much nearer.) Certainly you heard Frankish songs in Venus, sung in Franchian. And here and there, had been a Frankish marriage among the high families, for insurance, perhaps.

That year, too, there would begin another scene for Italy. But also in the drama I would tell you of, though for my part, then, I knew nothing of it. Few did.

PART TWO
Revenge

For as we have candles to light the darkness of
the night, so the cypresses are candles to keep
the darkness aflame in the full sunshine.

D.H. LAWRENCE
Twilight in Italy

BEATRIXA

ONE MORNING, ANDREA, lord of the house of Barbaron, entered his library, where he saw to house business and commerce, and found a man there.

At first Andrea took him for one of his secretaries, both of whom were young men. But then the room's other occupant passed through a beam of light, hung from one of the glazed windows. And Andrea made out that he was dressed in fashionable, quite opulent garments, what any young man of a wealthy family might wear—which was nothing like the plain gown of a clerk.

His hair was plentiful, and worn long, below his shoulders, and the sun fired it up like new gold. It was a mane of hair, too. For a second Andrea glared at it, for he had for some years been without the front and crown of his own.

Then it came to him he did not know this fellow. Who was he, strolling so idly in the sunshine of the Castello's private library, between the gilded books, some illustrated by great painters, some in copper-print, some as large as a four-year-old boy—all costly.

"You there—what's your name?" called Andrea briskly. He waited for the young man to quail. Andrea had now been titular head of Barbaron for eighteen years, *he* was surely known here by sight, and by each of them in the house. Yet among all the great quantity of Barbarons who lived with him in this massive sandstone palazzo called Castle—the cousins, uncles, nephews, sons, and all their adjuncts and hangers-on—this one, distinctive man Andrea did not recognize. That was possible, maybe. Despite his clothing, might the loiterer not be one of the higher servants, one whom Andrea had never had occasion to note before?

If that were the case, what was he doing in here?

"What's your business?" Andrea shouted.

The young man had not answered his first question. He did not answer the second. Instead, not even glancing at Andrea, he stepped around a cabinet of books and disappeared.

Andrea cursed. He strode forward. He had been always thickset in his twenties and thirties, and was bulky now, bull-like. He swung into the space beyond the cabinet, and saw only the empty floor, patterned by sunlight and a design of quince trees done in chipped marble.

For some minutes Andrea thumped about the room, trying to rediscover the intruder. The library was ample but not gigantic. It had only one pair of doors, of carved ebony and not very silent. They had not sounded. Had the damnable rogue got out through a pane of the glazed windows, some of which might be opened? He would then have landed in the fetid Canal of the Triumph below. Ridiculous enough, but there would have been a splash. There had been no splash.

Just then, Messer Oliviotto, Andre's secretary, came in. The doors growled as usual.

"Did someone pass you, going into the lobby?" said Andrea. His color deepened and he was frowning, so Oliviotto took care.

"Why, no, Signore Andrea. No one, that I saw."

Andrea sat down at the table, scowling. He never liked to be outwitted, and those who had played mild practical jokes on him in his youth had soon learned not to.

The secretary assumed his own place cautiously. He began to arrange his accounting slate, pens, ink and paper, taking a great interest in them.

Andrea said, "A man was in this room but he's left it now," looking narrowly to see how 'ser Oliviotto would react. But the secretary only looked as blank as his paper.

Andrea pushed the sense of strangeness away from him and pulled his ledgers forward.

He did not remotely think he had been mistaken. He was even half inclined to admit that something uncanny had occurred. But he would waste no further time on it.

Elsewhere, however, Andrea Barbaron's only legal daughter was about to have a similar experience. Although really in every way, it was quite unlike. Since what Beatrixa would see was, like herself, a child.

Castello Barbaron stood quite high above Silvia, on a sloping street (one of the few Venus boasted) that ran before the southwestern façade, the Triumph Canal stretching at the building's other side. Approachable therefore both from front and back, each face of the house was ornate.

It was a modern palazzo of its kind, not seventy years old, but built on the core of an older house, the original Castello. Masonry ascended, cut by tall windows, clung with carved stonework. Arcades ran across the lowest floor, facing both street and canal, on each arch of which, by night, lamps of vermilion glass were lit.

Out from between the arches there now stepped a little girl.

This was incongruous, somehow: the small, childish figure in its tiny version of an adult high-waisted gown, the mass of the Castello behind.

She was, too, a serious-faced child. A type of introversion in her seemed to have expelled all evidence or chance of prettiness. Fawn of skin, from her swarthy father, her hair was a clouded, curling chaos of black. She held a wooden doll, but the way things that have been forgotten are held.

She looked around, and pointed one set of toes in a minute, silk shoe.

Then a guardsman in Barbaron's colors came from the arches after her.

"M'donna Triche, where is your nursey? Eh, now, you shouldn't be out here."

The child looked at him haughtily. (Her toe-pointing dissembling had failed.) She said, "I am Beatrissa Barbaron" (she could not always quite pronounce her own name, but went on steadily), "and I have things to see to."

"Indeed, M'donna. I understand. Let me lead you back inside so you may see to them.

"Thank you, no," said the child.

She was insufferable, yet not. She was scarcely more than an infant, and normally kept close. The guard smiled gravely, and signaled to another: Best hurry and find the nurse. Then he paced after Beatrixa at a slight distance, as she turned into the alleyway that ran by the palazzo.

Here were kitchen women of the house, standing outside, arguing with a seller of fowls. One said, "Watch she doesn't fall in the canal, or the lord will have your hide."

"My eyes are wide open," said the guard.

Beatrixa went through the arch that marked the alley's end.

Sunlight scalded before her in a sheet across the canal. Out of the brightness, the mooring-poles stood up black, each carved with the Tower of Barbaron. A shrine to Neptunus stood there too, with a fish-head and a wall-flower left in its lap by one of the Barbaron maids.

The guard repressed the urge to call a warning. The paving here was only seven feet across, and beyond the water-steps it ceased.

But Beatrixa stayed beside the Neptune shrine, looking out over the lit water.

There was no traffic for the moment on the canal. The noises of the City were amassed and seemed far off.

What was the child looking at?

The guard thought it ethical to approach her after all. "What can you see, M'donna Triche?"

Beatrixa exhibited vast and stealthy patience. "Nothing. Nothing at all."

But now her eyes were following something, as the guardsman thought, along the surface. In the fierce sun-light, certainly he *could* see nothing, but children were always imagining things. Unless it was a swimming rat.

She had been up on the gallery that ran about the middle floor of the palazzo. The nurse had taken her there to play, for the south-facing garden and the courtyards were at present too hot. Great, dark-yellow blinds had been pulled down anyway along the gallery, where pots of lilies gave off a stupefying scent. The nurse soon fell asleep. Then Beatrixa dislodged the edge of a blind, and peered out at the canal, to watch what boats might pass.

The sun had not yet moved over the house, and no

shadow fell on the water. But then a curious thing occurred. A shadow did seem to settle there, and suddenly Beatrixa was able to see straight through it, and so down, down into the depths of the canal.

Fascinated, leaning between the marble-hipped posts of the railing (as she was told never to do), Beatrixa stared.

There in the water, she could now see a most bizarre and elongated movement, and instantly she took this to be the serpent-dragon which lived in all the canals and lagoons of Venus. But then she saw it was not that, but a slowly twisting current, of a deep, mixed purple-amber, like spilled dyes. And in this flashed a host of little fish, like glinting needles sewing in and out. And then, walking among them, about twenty feet down *under* the water, she saw the other child.

Beatrixa was very young, five or six by then, but she knew humans and animals, save fish, could not stay long beneath water. (The treasure-divers in the Laguna Silvia trained themselves to do this very thing, and might have produced such an apparent underwater child—but Beatrixa had not yet learned of the divers.) Anyway, there was something else.

The child in the canal was a boy, her own age, and very well-dressed. He had long golden hair—even in the water it was gold. And it flowed down his back as if just combed. His clothes stayed close to his body. That is, the current did not disturb them, make hair or sleeves or anything else stream about, as with everything underwater it must. And this Beatrixa grasped, even though she did not know that she did. Also, at that moment, the boy under the canal stopped still and raised his head, and looked right at her. And then he lifted his hand, mildly, waving to her, almost smiling. He had all the beauty of face she did not, but even though he was, as she was, only five or six years old, it was a very male beauty, and almost feral. More, it was the beauty born of some different place. . . . And then she realized, too, that where anyone else would swim under the water, he walked, quite grounded, as one did on the earth.

Beatrixa crept quickly from the gallery. Her nurse never woke. The little girl ran swiftly down the stairs of the Castello, the narrow and the broad. She was winged-footed as the god Mercurius, patron of messengers and thieves.

The lesser left-hand door, to the side of the great one, stood ajar, or she could never have got out. The guardsmen had done this? It was a coincidence, perhaps. Now, as she peered through the blinding light on the canal, Beatrixa thought she could still see the boy in the water, but she was not sure. Then she was less and less sure. And then, suddenly, she did see fully what she was looking at, and a sharp brief cry escaped her.

"Yes, M'donna Triche, now I see it too. A horrid rat. Shall I throw a stone at it?"

She turned to the guardsman and vented (as if she were her father, Andrea) her disappointed fury. "No! Don't dare! You are a wicked godless man!"

"Where do they learn these phrases?" he asked afterwards, ruefully.

From the world, of course. From which all things are generally learned. Unless some other plane intervenes as, in this case now, it had.

Less than a month after this, Andrea went to visit his only daughter. It was the afternoon of the day he heard the story of the Eel.

Going into the big room where the nurse and the child slept, Andrea braced himself a touch. Children, even his own (especially they?), tended to irk him. It was their slowness and gullibility. Even as a child himself, he had felt something of this about other children.

Triche was the only daughter his wife had produced, after a bevy of sons. He was aware this wife had lost most of her looks by then, and was getting on in years—she was thirty when she conceived Beatrixa—and maybe that was the reason why the sons were handsome and the daughter not.

Nevertheless, every time he was confronted by Triche, which was not often, he became conscious that there was something to her after all.

Her nose was certainly too long for beauty, and her face too narrow. It was not even, he thought, precisely a child's face, nor was her hair, so rich and unruly—when it was combed, her screams could be heard over half the palazzo. But her dark, intense eyes might one day be reckoned wonderful. Oh, they *would* be, for she would be the most-marriageable daughter of the house of Barbaron.

She looked, he thought now, like a Roman maiden in an ancient mural. Slender, smoky, from another time.

The nurse had gone out.

"Now, how are you, girl?" said Andrea, bluffly.

And he noted all at once the contempt with which the child accepted this. She was no fool, either, then. Perhaps she would, for a woman, be clever.

"I hear you're out of sorts. But the physician says there's nothing amiss with you. Your mother and your nurse have asked your father to speak to you, therefore I am here. And I am a busy man, Triche. So, be quick and tell me."

All this in a jovial, threatening way. He took slight enough notice of the vaporings of either servants or wives. This though, was another aspect of his duty. His daughter belonged to the house and must be kept in good working order.

"I'm well," said the child. Dismissive, as *he* had meant to be.

He scrutinized her, approving her manner despite himself. She was like him. That would do her no harm.

"You're a minx," he said.

"What is a minx?"

"Never mind." He sat and beckoned her over. "Tell your father why you've been acting so oddly."

"I have never been."

"Yes. Saying you've eaten your food, hiding it, and then throwing it off the gallery into the canal—what is that for?"

"To feed the fishes."

"There are few fish in the canals. They prefer the lagoons." He remembered, not expecting to, the Eel.

Andrea frowned at her, but the child was not intimidated. She said, "I won't, not again." Now she sounded depressed.

"The fish weren't grateful for their dinner?"

"No."

"What about this habit of yours of getting up at night and wandering about the house? The guards and maids have been finding you at every turn. And your cousin-uncle Gualdo found you asleep in the little sala. Why there?"

"I thought—I was lost. Nurse says I walk in my sleep."

"I don't believe that, Beatrixa."

"No," she said. Her respect for his acuteness

peculiarly pleased him. Yes, she was no fool and did not like to be treated as one.

"Very well, if you won't say. But you must stop it all. From this instant. Do you understand, Triche?"

"Yes, Dadda."

Now, astonishing him, a rush of actual elation went through Andrea at being awarded this babyish name for a father. In his forties, he did not suspect himself of any softening or sentiment. But, well, she was his only girl. And so young.

"You're a good child. I know the honor of Barbaron will be safe in your hands. As safe as if you were a boy, and trained to it." He said this to please her in turn. Perhaps he meant it, too. It was the highest accolade he could give her.

And her head went up proudly.

"I am Beatrixa Barbaron." She knew she had received her worth. She even got her name right.

Andrea leaned over, kissed her on the forehead and stood up.

She was very small but that bright glance of her eye was so like his own, in expression if not color. And in the black maze of her curls as sunlight traced them, was a sheen of his own redder hair, what was left of it. All the boys were dun-haired, and fair-skinned like their mother.

"Wave me off from the stair," he said, coy as a suitor.

Serious and concentrating, Beatrixa did so. Even when he reached the stair's bottom, there she was at her door still, sedately waving.

If only females stayed this easy of persuasion, and this wise.

Andrea did not feel altogether too unsatisfied, but through the rest of the afternoon the other thing, which could have nothing whatsoever to do with Beatrixa, recurred in his mind more than once—the Eel.

The story of the Eel—it was not merely an eel—had been told to Andrea by his more pragmatic secretary, Lanto. Which was surprising in itself. But obviously, Lanto, who said he had heard it in the printing-shop from a reliable source, was shocked. It was a shocking story.

"But you judge it a fact?"

"Yes, Signore Andrea. I'd trust the old man. He said he saw two doctors rowed out that morning, and later they came back, with gowns thick in blood. The old fellow lives near Aquila, you see. The wanderliers are also full of the grisly tale."

"They always have something."

Lanto lowered his eyes. He had gone pale, as anyone would, just thinking of it.

"What does the Ciara family have to say?"

Lanto said, "They keep quiet. He was up to his neck in vices, sir. Everyone knows it now. Ever since that affair with the della Scorpia girl—but that was twenty odd years back. I recall they said she was too afraid of his reputation to wed him, and that was why she ran away."

Andrea nodded curtly, a clue that he had heard enough. He did not want to talk about any of it. Especially not that. It was done, long over. But he thought too, *Things surface . . .*

And as they went on with ordinary business, now and then those things kept surfacing also in Andrea's mind, punch them down as he would.

What *had* become of her, Meralda della Scorpia, that he had given to the Lord Ciara all those twenty-four years ago?

In the Palazzo della Scorpia, they believed, as much

of the City did, she had run off with the artisan Lorenzo Vai. But Andrea of course knew otherwise.

He had not cared much at the time. He had assumed Ciara would violate the girl, shame her, and send her back to her own with the brand of slut on her forehead. Something of that sort. Oh, even then there had been gossip about Ciara. But he would not do so very much with a girl of high family.

The wanderlier of their boat, Lorenzo and the girl's, Andrea's men had been instructed to silence. But he had gotten away from them, and maybe it was he who later spread the legend that Meralda and her lover had been tortured and slain on Eel Island for the vengeful delectation of Lord Ciara, their bodies then slung into the lagoon.

In the intervening years, Andrea had had dealings with Ciara only once, a matter to do with Barbaron trade in Candisi and the Levantine. Ciara had been smooth as oil. He always was. And Andrea had given no sign of anything either. But the agreement had gone as if oiled, too.

Andrea did not worry unduly over the girl. No, it was not that. If she had been his intended bride, he would probably have raped, decidedly whipped, and maybe starved her a while, to show her her fault. If she had been his progeny, everything but the rape. A high family, in such a situation, might also be inclined to pack such a daughter off to some scummy nunnery that did not refuse such goods, and leave her there to rot. Thus, it seemed excessive to him only if Ciara had killed her. The manner of her death, though, sometimes that did trouble Andrea. Not then, but as time went on. As Lanto said, that particular lord of Ciara had become known for his depravity. Even the Ciara house had last year seemingly cast him out, for he had spent all his recent hours on his island.

No longer, presumably.

Lanto had told the story quickly, as if to get rid of it.

"He was standing at the landing-stage, soon after dawn. He'd been drinking and playing at—something— and come out for some air, they said. He was looking at the water, and he complained that, despite the island's reputation for netting large eels, he had never seen nor eaten one of them."

And then apparently, one arrived.

"They said it was eighteen feet in length. They thought it the mythic snake from under the lagoons. First just a running ripple they took for fish—then the water exploded and out it thrust. It seized on Ciara at once, and before any could help, it tore into him."

The Eel had taken off Ciara's male member entire, and with it bitten out parts of the belly, bladder, and entrails. Then, in a spray of water and blood, the beast was gone.

"There's nothing can be done for him. He lies shrieking."

"Not *dead*?" Andrea had exclaimed.

"No. No, they said—because of his transgressions he would not be allowed to die. Well, you know how they talk."

"He needs a kind friend," had said Andrea, "to see him through into the Better World." He had thought, *He'll have none of those.*

As Andrea was coming from the Castello that dusk, he heard a voice on the canal, a wanderlier, saying that Ciara still lived. Only days after did Andrea catch the rumor that the injured man had died at last. Could such things happen?

When she stopped searching for him, he came back to her.

She had sensed him everywhere, perhaps mistakenly, and gone looking day and night. A shadow beyond a column or a door—and she would hurry there, but it was only a shadow. Once, the Little Sala, a decorative, formal room, unlit after midnight, luminous with reflected tremblings of canal water, had seemed to conceal him. But he concealed *himself*. She took it to be a game he was offering her, both an invitation and a challenge. Then she supposed, not that she had invented him, but that he was no longer concerned with her, and had gone away. That had made her arrogant. She smarted.

Not for a second did Beatrixa think the boy from the deep of the canal was a ghost. Nor, for a second, did she think him human, or meant for any person save herself.

A child's world, always peopled by miracles and inexplicable laws, gave full rein to this. And she had never been timid.

After she had promised her father not to nightwalk, Beatrixa, alert to the honor of Barbaron, ceased her roamings. Three nights later, waking in the black of a moonless dark, she saw the boy standing across the room, by her chair. It was a lavish chair, made small especially for her, upholstered in brocade and with lions' heads carved on the arms. The boy was examining it. And then he turned and gazed at her.

Though the room was virtually lightless, Beatrixa could see him, and things close to him, easily. His hair seemed itself to give off a sort of candleshine, silvery now rather than gold. His eyes were like that too, though they were dark.

Beatrixa sat up. She glanced across to the corner where the nurse slept behind a screen. Her heavy-sleeper's breathing told all was well.

Beatrixa stepped out on the tesselated floor. In her shift and severely tied hair, she was regal. She stood, but would not go closer to him.

After a moment, the boy approached her.

Something had changed slightly. He was no longer quite her age, but somewhat older, perhaps eight. He was taller than she, and slender, and his velvet doublet was embroidered with seed-pearls. Obviously, he also was of a great and wealthy house, like her own.

For a while they stayed still, looking at each other. He seemed curious, and she returned his stare level-eyed and queen-like.

He said, "Who is that big woman who sleeps behind the screen?"

"My nurse."

"What is a nurse?" he strangely asked.

"She gave me her milk when I was a baby. Now she takes care of me," said Beatrixa, flatly.

"Oh," he said. "A servant." Then he said, "I have never seen one before."

"But you're from a high house. Don't you have servants?"

"Of course." He added lightly, in passing, "But they're not visible."

Beatrixa thought about this. She digested it mentally finding it rather tricky. But he could walk under water, so she could not expect his realm to be like her own.

However, she said, "It is gracious of you to call on me. What shall we do?"

"Why must we do anything?"

"Tell me about your own house then."

"Why should I?"

She saw from this, not that he did not like her, but that he was willful, contrary. He must perhaps be humored, as Beatrixa had heard women say all men must.

But she was not inclined to humor him. Though he

was a creature of otherness, fascinating and magical, *she* was still the daughter of Lord Barbaron.

"I am Beatrixa Barbaron," she announced, and again she had the pronunciation of her name exact.

The boy did not bow to her, or seem put out or impressed. He smiled. His smile was marvelous. It was like a brilliant star breaking from a pale cloud.

She said, slowly, "And who are you?"

"Silvio," he said, "della Scorpia."

The words dropped into her stomach like lead.

Presently she murmured, "You are my enemy. " (For even the children of a house knew who were their foes.)

"Yes," he said. But with no malice. It was simply a fact. He seemed to imply they could ignore it now.

But Beatrixa took a step back from him.

"I won't talk to you any more. It was dishonorable of you to come into my bedroom.

He looked faintly surprised.

Beatrixa went on, "You must go at once. Then I swear by the Lord Jesus I won't call my father's men."

He laughed. A laugh like water.

"Oh, *call* them. See what happens."

"What?" she said, doubtful and unnerved.

"Why," he said, "only this." And he vanished.

A minute or so later, Beatrixa began to cry. It was the reaction to some tension she had not known she felt. And to the supernatural suddenness of his departure.

It was also bereavement. She knew she would never see the boy again, that she had, rightly, dismissed him, and so had given up any chance of their meeting a second time.

The crying woke the nurse, who came fumbling out half asleep, and saw Beatrixa standing there in tears, wringing her shift between her hands.

"What now? What is it?"

Beatrixa sobbed.

"Hush," grumbled the nurse. "What *is* it, child?"

Beatrixa climbed into her own bed. She gulped her tears away into herself and said, "I dreamed an animal was in the room."

"An animal? What animal?"

"From the lagoons," said Beatrixa. Not knowing what she said. Wanting only to be rid of the troublesome nurse intruding on her grief.

"I do think," said the woman the next day to another, "she must have heard some snatch of that gross tale about the Eel."

She was in error in this. And Beatrixa herself had made a mistake. For she would meet Silvio della Scorpia again, although it would not be for ten more years.

BARTOLOME
(The Marriage of Venus)

TWO FURTHER THINGS HAPPENED late that year. One was of great moment, the other of note only to me. This was that I took a wife. I will make no bones about it, the match was suggested to me by my Guild Master. Like the houses of Venus, the guilds also promote their alliances. She was a stonemason's daughter, good-looking and having her own mind. She liked my advancement to Master Minore, and my chance of becoming full Master over the next few years. To me, she behaved as if she liked me for myself. And I was not adverse to her, though she would not have been my choice, if I am honest—as long after, I regret, she one time drove me to say. Her name was Pia, and she and Strabica did not get on. So after our wedding, Strabica went to another household, and Pia hired for us our cook. That woman was, in the matter of the kitchen, to Strabica as some dauber would be beside the great artisan-painter, Leonido Vinchi.

I learned too, even after a month, that Pia liked me only when I let her have her own way. Otherwise she sulked or spurned me. Her liking of me was therefore a trophy she awarded me for allowing her to do as she wished. And so, for the most part, I let her do it. And in this manner, my house became no longer much mine. I mislaid old friends, and had to put up with new ones I cared for less. She was jealous, too. But there, I fared no more dreadfully than many another man.

That winter the canals froze, and the lagoons in places, so there was skating on them. At this season, Pope Pietus (for whom my wife had been named) took it on himself to reform the calendar. That was, he made it regular in the Julian mode, so there were no longer weeks but other blocks of time. (Although few of us remembered this outside of Rome.) In order to have the calendar then in the shape he desired, Pietus found it also necessary to slough eleven days from every year.

To the common man, which I (if not Pia) considered myself, this was nonsensical. Indeed to some it was *unnatural*, and superstitiously, the outlawed eleven days came to be called the Dies Manium. The larger omission of them was to happen in autumn, and a vast confusion it would have caused. The lesser omission, of one day only, was in summer, at the end of the Crab Month, which now had only twenty-nine days. And one day, to be sure, that had been the thirtieth, but now became a *Ghost Day*, and no longer existed.

This eccentricity was reformed back to normalcy by the pope who succeeded Pietus. Yet not before all Italy had suffered one twenty-nine-day Crab month the following summer.

I mention the Ghost Day with good reason. It would seem that, even though restored, once conjured, the single Dies Manium persisted. But we shall come to that.

Having mutilated the calendar, Pietus expired. Many were not astounded.

Ruy Borja became pope before Christ 'Mass.

Much was said of him too, in Venus. That he kept

his mistresses openly in the Vatican was one thing, though that seemed unlikely. That he had admitted to fathering—and maintaining—a family of three sons and one daughter was, however, soon well-known.

Ruy was of Spanish blood, but had lived in Italy since childhood. He gained the papacy both through his enormous popularity and the equal amount of fear he had already inspired in Rome. Plus, evidently, several large bribes. The papal name he took was that of the world-conquering Alexander.

Despite hearing so much of this pope, Alessandro VI, within another couple of years we began to hear far more of the second to eldest of his sons, Chesare.

Pia said to me, "I've heard he is an incredibly handsome man. Handsome as a classical god, and not yet twenty. They say he murdered his elder brother, Juvanni," she added, as if the last were another mark to his credit. To Pia perhaps it was; she had always implied she preferred strong and ruthless men—none of whom would have stood for her tantrums.

Chesare Borja though was more than a handsome face and figure. His physical strength was said to be prodigious—he would bend iron horseshoes for exercise, and had once, before a colossal crowd, beheaded a full-grown bull with one stroke of a sword. More than this, we were to discover his was a military talent, and an ambitious one.

During those next years, Venus took note of Borja as, with papal funds and backing, he swept up the littered bickering princedoms and dukeries of outer Italy. First he regained the Papal States for Rome; next, the whole breadth of the Italian earth rang to the tramp and roar of his armies, and to the blast of the innovative cannon Messer Vinchi had designed for him.

Nowhere did Borja fail, let alone falter. His justice was remarkable. Tyrants he would hang, but to their peoples he was generally benign, providing they were obedient. When they were not, he was merciless. It seemed he should have had the name Alexander, rather than his father. But his own name, of course, meant Caesar.

His goal soon became plain. He meant to conquer and amalgamate all Italy, entire, beneath one banner—the papal banner of the Keys—and one thumb: his own.

The Franchians obviously had had to be dealt with meanwhile, and he had managed even this in the nicest fashion—he was known to have extremely good manners. First, he made an alliance with the Frankish king, then fought for him and his interests, bringing Italian troops into the field elsewhere. After that, Borja used *Franchian* troops to assist him with his own expeditions, weeding them out only little by little as the Italian strength grew firmer. Milano, he let them have (for now, one thought), but dissuaded them from Napolita. That was not too difficult, as the Napolitans were a riotous lot; they had been chasing the Franks out again and again for years. Nor did Borja himself make a move towards Napolita. There was the Spanish influence in the province, after all, and Chesare Borja, like his sire, was a Spaniard. Lastly, Borja had married a Franchian princess, said to be beautiful, although he had stayed apparently no more than three weeks with her. (Pia recounted this, too, with a sly gleam of approbation in her eye.)

Between Napolita to the southeast and Milano in the northwest, inside the following seven years all Italy became Borja's Italy. Only one other area remained outside: the serene city-state of Venus.

"Well, if he were to govern Venus, we might see some order here."

"What order do we lack, Pia?"

"Oh, the prices, for one thing. You never think of it; you are so much off on your man's ventures. And the canals—their foulness and stink in summer—uh!"

"You think Chesare Borja would clean the canals."

"Yes, laugh at me, Bartolo. What do I know."

"You don't seem to know that there might be a war. Venus is too great and puissant in her own right to give in to Borja. And he wants everything, it seems, and may not be content to let her alone."

Borja was not precipitate, though. He was a cunning, clever man, prepared to wait, though still young. With the Franchians not totally dealt from the play, nor the Spanish, he did not seem to want the risk of threatening us outright.

Then came a summer when there was plague in Rome. Alessandro took ill of it and was given up, and then Chesare also fell sick. It may not have been plague, either, for by then these two had adversaries and to spare, and for all the tales of the Borja family's knack with poisons, there were plenty about those who had tried the remedy with *them*. In Rome, there was, instantly, factious rioting. Half the great houses there were out on the streets, intent on seizing power. But even from his sickbed, Chesare gave his orders. His men stayed loyal and the enemy retreated again. In Venus, too, we felt the echo of all this, for any giant edifice, falling, makes a sound heard for miles. If the banners of the Keys and the Bull went down, what would come of it might not be all good, nor all in our favor, either.

At length, an amazing sequel filtered to us. Both the son and the father had survived, Alessandro from being let blood, Chesare from a bath of fever-cooling ice that would have killed a weaker man.

If he had been ambitious before, no doubt this dance with death brought Borja into full wakefulness.

That year ended, and spring came, and then fresh rumors started.

Soon after Pascalis, I was called to a meeting of my guild. Now that I was a full Master, I must always take my place at any convened gathering. But this was to be behind closed doors, as these things are. I told Pia I was going to visit my old friend Simone. She sulked instantly. She had never cared for him.

Simone was at the meeting, too, of course. He was one of the first to speak.

"Can you tell us, Guild Master, what the Ducem proposes?"

We were all dubious the Ducem would propose anything. He was like another that had been, in the time of the invading Jurneians, keen for ducal treats and slow to do much governing. That one had been young, and this one was old, but they were from the same mold in many ways. Their interests were not truly with the City. Ducem Nicolo had even collected a menagerie on his island of the Rivoalto: unicorn-deer, lions, and horses strangely spotted like leopards. When I was a boy I had seen a barge waddling out through the lagoon, with huge cages on it for the menagerie. They were full of something that looked like the clouds of sunrise: extraordinary fowl brought from the Africas. Flame-birds, they were called.

The Master cleared his throat.

"It is less what the Ducem will do, than what the Borja has already done."

At this there was some noise.

The more influential and potent guilds will always get the news before the rest of the City, since they will have a man in every ducal senate.

"Is his army already marching on Venus?"

"Not in the way you mean.

"What other way does an army march?"

The Master, a dry man, said, "It seems we're to have a wedding."

Simone turned and said in an aside to me, "He will get to it, in a minute."

But one of the masons was already shouting excitedly "Has Venus allied with him, then? With the Italian Spaniard—is he to marry one of the Ducem's daughters?"

"There are none left young enough, let alone single," said the Master. "No, it seems Borja has something else in mind, which he has outlined to Ducem Nicolo in writing."

We were fifteen in number, full Masters of the guild, from the ranks of the Settera, the stonemasons, the architects of mausoleums, the Cremaria assistants, the carriers, the makers of graves, and others. We stood listening in silence. Death is generally an easy business, we have all found, compared with life.

During the last months of Spring, there had been some skirmishes on our border with Milano, by the Franchians. None of it had seemed unduly significant. The Franks were wary of Venus, which had not only kept an army of repute since the days of the Knights of God, but which bestrode the trading world to east, west, and south. Though there was no treaty, there had been agreements here and there, and sometimes there were small parties of Franchians in the City, very polite and moderate, miserly in their dress, halting in their Italian, and causing no trouble.

Borja, though, the Guild Master said, had advised the Ducem that the hour was coming when the Franks would stake a claim to Venus.

"As Borja means to, instead," remarked Simone.

"Chesare Borja, it appears, generously offers Venus his protection."

"What—he'll put his troops into the City?"

"A handful are recommended. More to the point, he requests a firm alliance—one that will be noted far and wide. This is for *our* protection, we are to understand and, he has the grace to say, for his own pleasure."

The gathering murmured. Micaeli, Master stone-lifter, said, "So he does *want* to marry into the ducal house—but who? Besides, he's wed."

"His daddy the pope would annul that in a wink," said Simone.

"For *this* wedding," said the Master, "no annulment is needed. He can keep his Frankish wife and have the new one as well."

Borja wished altruistically to save us from the Franks. But also he did not mean to antagonize the Franks unduly. His plan then was nearly frivolous.

Once a year, since the terrible days of the Lamb Council ended, an ancient custom is revived in Venus. It is the throwing of a costly ring into the Laguna Fulvia by the Ducem, standing on his golden boat, while the priests of the Primo sing a blessing. They call it the Marriage of Venus to the Sea—symbol of the City's maritime power.

Borja suggested something only rather different.

He would be married to Venus.

A few of the meeting broke into laughter. It was a funny, a quaint idea—a knot of ribbon tied to a lance of steel.

The laughter withered.

We became pensive, and still.

"What's to be done?"

"Has the Ducem agreed to it?"

"In God's name—what has that fool Nicolo sold us into?"

The Master said, dry and firm as ever, "Remember, Messers, the Italian Spaniard has an army estimated at over twenty thousand men. He has cannon capable of using stone shot and blasting open fortress walls from an extreme distance. He has the friendship, so far, of the Franchians, and the Spanish. It is really only whether he would set us against the Franks, or the Franks against us."

Simone spoke out again. "And never forget either, his father is the bloody pope in Rome."

Who better than we knew what that meant. The holy might of Rome over men's souls—Pope Alessandro would only have to warn us that he could remove our dispensation for burning the dead, to cause tumult and despair in any of Venus's citizens who were believers. Which, to some extent, almost all were. It was no use saying only the credulous would be afraid. And even if only the credulous were, there were enough of them; it would make for havoc.

The Ducem, for all his failings and flamingoes, must have thought so too.

He was that very moment agreeing to welcome Chesare Borja and his wedding-party into the City.

One of the reasons Pia scorned me was, I believe, that I gave her no children. Occasionally, I noticed her playing with some neighbor's baby or infant, and then it was another Pia I saw. I am certain, too, the fault was not in her body, but in my own since, in all my several earlier hot affairs, no woman had ever claimed to have borne me a child. Nor in any later connection, either.

But when she learned we were to be at the "wedding" of Borja, and herself in a new gown, for a time she liked me very much. She did not mind that we had had little choice but to attend.

Every guild was to be represented by its Guild Master, and the seven Settera Masters, plus one full Master from every internal section of which, in our case, there were seven, and all their families as well. The head of every merchant family of the City was also summoned to attend, and all the high families in particular were expected—whatever their disputes with each other, which were to be put aside as for the marriage of a great prince. (Already the poets had likened Chesare to the war god Mars—in myth, the lover of the goddess Venus.)

One did not know whether to laugh or shudder at it all.

But it was to be a great pageant, and what City of Italy does not like those? (I have heard the Franchians think us vulgar, but then the Italians think the Franks mean.)

Contrary to the usual procedure, the generous bridegroom was to pay for most of the show.

The day dawned fine.

All week there had been arrivals in the City. Small packs of Borja's troops, standing in boats as they were rowed to their stations, looked disturbed without their horses—or the ground—under them. But they were all in holiday mood and many in holiday clothes. They minded their manners, as they said Borja always did.

There was no argument anywhere, and the wine-shops and brothels did a hearty trade.

When we left the house early, not an hour after daybreak, the crowds were already fomenting everywhere, jamming the alleys and the narrower waterways, whole families squeezed into wanderers and other craft. Every window space, every balcony, and also any possible roof, was freighted with people. The quays were thick with the crowds. From the galleries and windows of Venus, by Ducal decree, drooped cloths in both the lion colors of the City, white and gold, and the colors of Chesare Borja, gold and scarlet, and ropes of spring flowers also poured over the sills.

Everywhere, one saw also the motto of the City, *Peace to you Venus* (never more apt than now). But also there was Borja's insignium, *Either be Caesar, or nothing*.

We, being favored, were to be among those to watch the entry of the bridal procession from a balcony of the Palazzo Bene, one of Nicolo's other houses, which overlooked the last mile of Chesare's journey.

The canals here are very wide. But all the route had been devised to employ the larger channels, and both of the greater lagoons.

It was noon before they reached us.

I had considered how he might manage it. He, too, was used to streets, not water, but Borja was a showman as well as all else. A Caesar might have envied him.

Great stages had been assembled and these, besides having oarsmen, were dragged through the water by nothing less than brawny gangs of swimmers. They were attired as the mermen of Neptune, and some as merhorses, fish-headed beasts, and other fabulous monsters. How they handled both their work and their costumes in the chilly spring canals was a wonder.

First on the stages came some troops, splendid in their armor, with tasseled banners, so the people cheered—yes, cheered. And they were a brave sight, picked for their swagger and looks. Then came musicians on a barge that was like a ship from a dream, with gossamer sails and gilt chains that hung in the water. These men played loudly and well, the chitternas wreathed with sparkling silver, and the rebeccas from the East twined with blossom.

After the musicians passed, four remarkable things, which set the crowds cheering again. They were meant as a compliment to Venus, no doubt, for they demonstrated the City's mystic Zodians, Cancro the Crab, Scorpio the water-Scorpion, and Pesci the Fish, here shown as Venus has them, one in the other's belly. They were huge floating models that seemed alive—the Crab waving its blue pincers and the silver Scorpion its tail and foreclaws, while the little fish swam about the larger one's openwork inside. All three burned with gilding and glass gems; and their supporting understructures, or the men inside who worked them, were scarcely ever visible. Fourth of these prodigies came the legendary serpent-dragon of the lagoons. This really was an astonishing creation. Nothing could be seen of any workings or supports within its awful warted head and body, at least the length of ten men lying prone. As it writhed along through the water, there were even some screams from the banks.

When these apparitions were past, there came some lords under a gold sail, the wedding guests. Dressed fantastically and gorgeously, their jewels scorching one's eyes, they were a marvel in themselves. More musicians followed, giving off a popular song of the City. The crowd put words to it—and at the end began to cry

"Borja! Borja!" As anyone might have known they would.

Then there was a stage with girls who seemed in a floating garden, their setting equipped even with trees (in pots) and arbors of roses, while doves constantly flew up and then fluttered down. In the middle of all this, or so the exclamations next informed me, was Borja's sister, the Donna Lucretza d'Estro, who had been brought with him as an attendant for his "bride." (So complacent was he, he had thought it no risk to include her.) From the balcony I saw only a slim slip of a young woman seated side-saddle on a blanched palfry trapped in red, two guards standing by to keep it steady. She, too, wore scarlet, and her long, crimped hair was a curious peach color in the sun. Later, I was able to see her more closely. And then I pondered. Lucretza Borja had been married herself already three times (d'Estro of Ferrchita was the latest—the other two were dead). According to some she was also the leman of her brother, and father. But she looked like a virgin, pure and delicate, like unmarked snow.

After the ladies, some more impressive soldiery went by, and then a floating barge with crumhorns sounding. And then, Borja.

He was the only one not to be wearing his own or the papal colors. He wore the most costly black velvet, Venus velvet—I could tell even from the palazzo balcony. It was quite plain but for a pair of golden brooches shaped as the Keys, to hold his sleeves. His linen was the whitest I have ever seen. Other than this, his hair was an unusual dark copper shade, that flamed out in sunlight (giving him, after all, his colors) and deepened out of the sun, so one could, in shadow, take him for a dark-haired man. He was clean-shaven then, though in later years he would affect a narrow beard, as certain painters have depicted him.

The stories were not lies. I have to say he was the best-looking man, bar one, that I have ever clapped eyes on. And the other, anyway, was yet a child.

Behind Borja stood two cardinals sent from Rome, in crimson, to help wed him.

And these three alone were on the barge, with six oarsmen, but it had been made like a chariot, not of a Neptune, but a Caesar. And I thought at once of the mural I had glimpsed before even I saw it, in the della Scorpia palace, Caesar being offered the wreathe of an emperor.

At the back of Borja's chariot came a train of boats with wedding gifts for the City: golden boxes and silver trays and artistically arranged heaps of all kinds of things—books, swords, astrological instruments, casks of wine. Also, there were three or four more gossamer ships with girls and music; and a confetti of sweets in tinted paper, and even gold coins, were thrown in a shower at the banks. Some of these naturally fell in the water. Then men jumped in from all sides to retrieve them, and soon the canal was a whirlpool that nearly upset one of the lighter vessels, but not quite.

There was a continual yelling now of Borja's name. I judged the women were mostly sighing, too. I did not glance at Pia, but from the edge of vision, I had seen her lean forward and heard her catch her breath. Well, small wonder. I confess that I later thought, when I had looked at him across less space (he lost nothing when seen close) and at Madonna Lucretza too, that maybe only their looks were the reason for the talk of incest. Some would always reckon that two persons of such glamour, brought up in proximity and living under one roof, would not be able to keep their hands off each other.

Just past the Palazzo Bene, was a slope of open garden with a topiaria of trees, and the landing-place. Here
it was the bridal procession had to come to land.

The neptunes and their creatures disbanded and
swam ashore, leaving the boats to be rowed in and
moored by the oarsmen. The crowd fell away from this
costumed horde at first, then began to touch and pat
them, amused, while the swimmer-actors frolicked and
shook water off themselves. The smiling crack troops of
Borja then began to take a hand in holding the people
back, as the Ducem's guards had not entirely managed.

Borja's party landed neatly. The musicians formed
up, playing and, between them and the soldiers, the
crowd at a correct distance, the lords went up through
the garden. Next followed, in a cloud of her ladies,
Donna Lucretza, riding her pale palfry and minus her
husband, and then Borja, looking neither left nor right,
but smiling a little, just as his trained men did. One did
not know what that smile meant, though it seemed affable. Last came all the marriage goods borne in display,
with another tidal-wave of sweetmeats and money flung
to all sides.

The Scorpion, Crab, Fish, and the serpent-dragon
they left to disport themselves in the canal, which kept
the crowd tickled a long while.

The pageant had meanwhile swept on into the
Ducem's palazzo. And we were called from the balcony
to go down.

Nicolo's great sala had been thrown open, a chamber as
big as most guildsmen's houses.

The columns were of decorative marble and the
ceiling painted with scenes, and everywhere were the

banners of Venus, the Ducem, Borja, and the Papacy. Flowers, some of paper and brightly dyed, erupted from urns. All of this, with the costumes of everyone assembled in their finest, and the conflicting house colors of every high family in Venus was not, it seemed, enough.

The Ducem had thought fit to bring with him some of his menagerie. There was an ivory-hued horse with charcoal spots and a grey mane and tail; and there a lion, snarling, just held on a chain by the muscular arms of two jailors. Five or six peacocks paraded up and down, spreading their fans of eyes at the women, and now and then shrieking in their unnerving way. A rosy flame-bird had been brought, too, and stood on a marble tank at the room's center, stone-still, perhaps frightened, or only indifferent.

Borja had arrived. Courtly presents were exchanged. I was not surprised to see the spotted horse brought forward, in its silver bells and saddle of Spanish-work, and presented to him. Would he get the lion, too? It seemed not. His sister stood by all this while, with that immaculate completeness you find sometimes in women of lofty rank. She was limpidly calm, and mildly agreeable to everyone of the nobles they brought before her. She had a pretty voice, too. I heard it. (His was also excellent. I had been told he sang well.) But what either of them thought, God knew.

The heads of houses were presented, with certain of their kin. There were so many of these that each greeting was a swift process. I, from my corner, saw Como della Scorpia—an aging man mismatched to a sagging young man's face—and his cousin, the coal-haired Lady Caterina, whom I had seen all those years before, at my first grave-funeral on the Isle. She was now turned sixty, but looked not so very different, not even her hair, since it was a wig. A young woman, too, was brought forward. She wore a somber gown, but her sleeves were in the della Scorpia colors, yellow, gold, and brown. She had that pale yellow hair. It seemed her husband had been a Franchian with the Frankish king's armies, and later served with Borja—but the man had been killed at Fensa.

I saw the Barbarons, too, generally separated from the della Scorpias by the length of the long room. Where they needed to cross each other's paths, they did not speak to each other, and indeed would not. There were other families who behaved in this way to one another, and in Rome, doubtless, it was the same.

Beatrixa Barbaron did catch my eye. I was very taken with her, perhaps more so than with the exquisite Lucretza. Beatrixa was about sixteen, and not beautiful. Her face had a half-severe, classical quality. She reminded me of one of the more youthful Roman goddesses, Hestia, perhaps, or a young Juno. But her dark eyes were very splendid, and her hair like no hair I had ever seen that was real. It was such a mass, so black, glossy, and densely shaped, falling far below her waist, it reminded me strangely of the foliage of some tree: a cypress, the most. It was ornamented only with a little cap of silver spangles, each the size of a grape. She wore the Barbaron blue, and had a small white dog on a lead, which was virtuously behaved despite the flamingo and peacocks, and the lion. She stayed to one side and was not presented.

We, needless to say, Pia and I, were also not presented. But the Guild Masters, Borja chose himself to walk among. Our own Master later said that he was a perfect gentleman. He spoke to everyone courteously, and to the point, but not overlong, and with charm rather than condescension. The Master added, to me,

"But I would trust him no farther than a spade's length."
This is a jest of the guild. It means nothing middling—it
means the subject of it, to be trusted, would have to be
dead, and lying down.

That day was a long one of standing about, admir-
ing our betters. First it was in the Ducem's sala, then at a
Mass in the chapel. There, some of the guild-members'
wives and daughters fainted, as some always do at the
stateliness and incense. Not Pia. She was never the faint-
ing sort.

The marriage was in the afternoon, and before that
we sat to a dinner for all the guests of the Ducem and
Signore-donno Chesare.

It was laid out on vast tables. Although this was a
lesser feast (the more lavish was to be that evening, when
such as the guilds and merchant families were gone), it
was impressive enough.

There were all types of foods, several of which I had
never seen before, such as the preserved eggs of a certain
kind of mouse found in the East—if it was to be believed.
And also oysters that had been bred in tanks. Besides
these were presented pheasant sausages stuffed into
baked fowls, tarts of chestnuts boiled in sweet wine and
sugar, whole spring lambs, and enormous mescalaras of
various fish. The centerpiece was a blue-black shining
fountain of squid, cuttlefish, and octopus, lying on beds
of herbs and sliced fruits scattered with ice, and glazed
by a honey and white vinegar sauce, the gleaming dripping tentacles cascading from one tier onto another. The
dish was easily nine feet high, but not for long. The
guests had grown hungry.

In the City, tables were put out in many of the great
squares for the populace generally, and loaded with
roasts and cakes. There were also plaster fountains

supplied at Borja's expense, which would play wine. Some of these had been formed like cows, the liquid spurting from their udders, which caused glee. Years later, you would still hear people refer to this exotic day, not as a marriage, or the penetration of Venus by the warlord Borja, but as "the day we milked the cows for wine."

When the dinner ended, some hours later, the wedding party was rowed over into Fulvia, to the Primo, in the Ducem's three barges. A train of other craft followed. In fact, only the nobles were obliged to attend Borja's marriage, and of these only the men, and the Guild Masters and various Setteras. The rest of us might do as we pleased—which would be to attend, of course—but we must take our places in the crowd.

Pia did not like this. She said her new dress would be dirtied by the rabble. But she would rather have jumped in a canal, I believe, than miss the spectacle.

He was not to have his mystic wedding in the Primo, nor in any church. The ceremony, such as it was, would take place in the basilica square above the lagoon. Borja had himself determined all this, it seemed in order not to offend religious sensibility. But even so, the two cardinals were there, with the authority of a pope.

The Primo Square was a solid wall of people, with just the area cleared, and held by guardsmen—Borja's and the Ducem's—before the doors of the basilica.

We, Pia and I, found ourselves a spot on one of the platforms put up for the guilds, and so after all she did not have to rub sides with any slumdwellers.

In the brilliant sunshine, the basilica seemed magnificent, picked out by its mosaic, gold, windows, and carvings, and with the huge pale dome above. The lagoon glittered, and a million jewels. The crimson and scarlet, ochre, gold, white, and plum-red of the devices and banners, the velvet cremisi of the carpet laid for the dignitaries, filled up one's eye with splendor. Black gulls flew overhead, and white pigeons rose from the roofs, all catching the sun on their wings, every one with a flash like a sequin.

The old story came to my mind, another flamboyant drama that had been enacted here, or so Rossa had insisted. It was the legend of the saint, Beatifica, whom Rome had never recognized. My uncle always dismissed Rossa's version as a popular fantasy, but when young I had always liked it best. She had said that, once the invading Jurneians had got through into the lagoon, and their ships massed there a thousand vessels deep, the saint had come out of the basilica, riding into the square on a red horse, the Knights of God in their mail about her. (When I was older, Rossa had told me, too, that some said Beatifica had ridden naked, yet so luxuriant was her hair, it had clothed her modestly.) "And then," Rossa had said, "she raised her hands to the sky, and begged fire from Heaven. And God sent His fire and the enemy ships were burned, everyone, to cinders."

Where, I thought, was Beatifica now, when Chesare Borja, conqueror of Italy, stood here, marrying himself to the City and State of Venus, while his troops prowled smiling in the garrison?

Aut Caesar aut nihil. That is not a man who will stop at a little resistance.

But anyway, the miraculous relic of the saint's heart had disappeared some five or six years earlier.

I saw, but did not hear very much of the marriage. The Primo Square is a sounding-stage, and things can be picked up far across it. But the crowd made a lot of noise, shouting for the Ducem, and for Borja, and for Venus, as if all this were the answer to our prayers.

Though a spectacle, it was the oddest sight, too, of course. There were the groom, the functionaries, the witnesses, even the queenly maids of honor—and the cardinals—but no bride. The bride was all about.

There seemed to be questions and responses, as is normal in a wedding. As the bride did not speak, however, her replies were assumed. All this the people of the City, and everyone, even Ducem Nicolo, who looked perfectly sanguine throughout, accepted with no qualm. He acted as the bride's father indeed.

Then the "couple" were blessed by the cardinals, and boys from the Primo paeaned out a beautiful *Gloria* as might be sung at such a high wedding, had it been one.

When this had concluded, and also the cheering and cries of *Borja! Borja!*, the bridegroom spoke directly to the assembled crowd.

For this, they grew quiet, and I heard his words.

He thanked us, and said that Venus should have his protection and his particular love from this day on.

"And to this end," he said, in his fine, trained voice (he was to have been a priest, they said, in his youth), "I will now set upon the flesh of my wife, this ring."

Even from that distance I saw it blaze. It was, I have been told, a circlet about the size of a child's bangle, but wider, heavy gold with a blood-red carbuncle large as a quail's egg.

Still, I wondered how he could put it on her hand. But Borja was a magician, and had thought of everything.

Up the Tower of the Angel, which stands beside the Primo, up there they went, the Ducem and Borja and their immediate court. They were a while climbing the stairs.

The Angel Tower looked all a structure of air and light that afternoon, the sun going over now behind it and the sky like gold leaf, and shining through all the galleries, and every pleat of stone or angle of brick limned too with gold. And then it grew flat and dark on the effulgence.

On the topmost gallery the wedding-party presently appeared again.

Borja was first. I heard someone say later, he had run up all the stairs like a boy, so fit he was, so eager and so sure.

Emerging to stand upon the tower's very top, against the flaming sky, he showed us again the ring. He was black now in silhouette, but once more the ring shot fire of its own.

How small we must have seemed to him, if we had ever seemed anything else, a sea of tiny faceless creatures such as might be hauled in a net from the lagoon. But much of Venus he would see too, from such a height and the sun sinking, the courts and spires and walls of her, that ran, among the arteries of water, up on the land, and the other way to the lagoons and the sea, and those all clad in her ships, that have assayed the whole known world.

Into that map of power, Borja cast his ring, away and away. The metal and the gem flashed fiercer than the sky now. And the people gasped at the magnificence of his wasteful, extravagant gesture. I have said, the Franchians call us vulgar.

For months, years even, men searched for that Borja ring. It was worth a fortune. Now and then somebody claimed to have found it. No one who did so could prove as much, nor ever grew rich.

The anecdote I liked best, and one worthy of Rossa, though I got the tale elsewhere, was that a magpie had caught it on the wing, and carried it to some nest in the heart of the City, where it still lies.

But Borja had married Venus in the sight of men. He had given her his ring. She was his wife, and must obey him now.

After this, the sunset began, and they rang the Venusium.

There were to be other entertainments about the City until midnight, and still later. The Ducem had arranged these. We had heard of processions of demons and angels, jugglers and shows of peculiar beasts, and comedies played on stages in the squares. All that, and the tables were loaded up again with food, and the plaster fountains endlessly gushed wine. Pia was afraid it would grow rowdy, as it did. She wanted to go home. I could see she was in an odd mood, between an excitement at what had gone on and a sullenness that, for her, it was over. I felt rather sorry for her; she seemed such a child, and I intended to make her evening as comfortable as I might. Then, as we were getting off the platform, a man appeared before me, smartly clothed in the colors of the della Scorpias.

"Sir, are you Messer da Loura, Master in the Grave Guild?"

I said I was. As we do, on such occasions, I wore my guildsman's finery, with the badge on my shoulder. He had hardly needed to inquire of my status.

The man nodded, and asked me politely if I would come with him; the Lord Como della Scorpia wished a word with me.

I raised my eyebrows. "Isn't it the Master of the Guild he would rather see?"

"No, ' ser da Loura. You."

These things happen. Favors are wanted, where the Guild Master is not to be directly involved, to do with future burials, or long-shut tombs. Normally, they are seen to more discreetly.

But argument, of course, was not in it. I sent wide-eyed Pia home with the family of Crespe, who would see she got safe to the house. Then I followed the della Scorpia steward over the square, one of the della Scorpia guards making our way for us.

Some great palaces owned by the Primo, along the Blessed Maria Canal, had been given over today to the use of the noble houses, way stations, to save whole households going home before the feast that night on the Rivoalto.

We crossed a courtyard and went up an outer stair to the second floor. The sala was full of people, servants and so on, and then we turned down a passage and came to a sitting room.

I was let through the door, and next found myself alone in the small chamber with Como della Scorpia.

He got up immediately, glaring at me, but some men behave curiously in such circumstances, when needing to ask help from an inferior. I bowed, lifted my head, and stood waiting.

"You are Bartolome da Loura?"

"Yes, my lord."

His glare sagged, like the rest of his face and body. His eyes were watery and bloodshot, and the last light from the broad, fretted window was not kind.

"Well. Your name I found out simply enough. Now what I want to know, and so I've sent for you, is your father's name. And your mother's name."

I was jolted. After a brief hesitation, I told him.

He shook his head.

"No, you are wrong, I think. Somewhere or other."

I said, "My lord, my father was a butcher. It was my uncle who took care of me, however, and brought me up. I was apprenticed by him to my guild, which was also his, when I was seven."

Como looked impatient. His spoilt eyes fixed on me.

"Your uncle and your father don't count in this, 'ser Loura. Somewhere some other has been at work. Your mother was called as you say?"

"Yes, my lord."

I had begun to see where we were going, but I could not think why.

"You are not your father's son, Messer. Not in a thousand years.

At this, did he anticipate my anger? I almost grinned. I had often wished so myself. But not in the way this man meant, for he was telling me, it seemed, I was a bastard, the son of another man.

"Does your mother still live?"

"No, my lord."

"While living, did she tell you anything . . . interesting?"

"No, my lord. She was not often—" I paused. "She was not often well."

He scowled now. He said, "I have heard only sensible things of you, Messer da Loura. So I will be plain with you. I saw you across the Ducem's hall today. I had never seen you before. You bear a great resemblance to one of my uncles. Not only in your face, the color of your hair, but in some of your mannerisms. He, too, is dead now. An upright and abstemious man, as I hear you are

thought, also. Shall I speak his name? It is, you understand, in confidence. But in your work, you're used to
keeping secrets, I believe."

"I will say nothing of it, if you wish to tell me, my
lord."

So he told me the name.

I must put it down here, now at last, for it has a
bearing on my tale.

The man that supposedly I so resembled was
Justore della Scorpia, who, all those decades ago, had
been the hard father of Meralda, she who drowned herself in the lagoon.

"Justore had a mistress," said Como then. "Being as
he was, abstemious, as I told you, we took it that he had
limited himself to her. But maybe not."

Then he fell silent.

At length, I said, "My lord, I swear to you I've heard
nothing of this ever. To my real knowledge my mother
was, and now that she is elsewhere I shall speak frankly,
a sotten drunk. She would have appealed to no man very
much, and to an abstemious man less than to another.
This was true at the time she conceived and bore me.
Evidently my father, also a tosspot, was not particular.
Besides, if he'd thought she strayed with any other, he
would have killed her. He was jealous, usually half mad
with drink, and generous with his fists."

It had seemed necessary to say this, as things stood,
but I would rather I had not had to. I was a man young
enough to be proud. To drag all that muck before him
did not please me.

This he seemed to see, despite his manner. He nodded to me and said. "Well. Master da Loura, I too can
keep a still tongue. We have exchanged our secrets."

After which, again, a silence.

It was getting dark now in the room and no one had brought candles. Outside there had begun to be some noise—shouts and other sounds—but one expected it on such a day. My mind was fully engaged with what he had said.

We had, by then, one of those new mirrors in the house, of Venus glass. It was Pia's, and if I had looked in it twice I doubt it. For my own self-examination, I used my uncle's old looking glass, which was of polished silver. This gave back enough to see my doublet was properly laced and my face clean. What did I want with more? So, I had not ever really studied myself to know if I was like any other, let alone any man in a higher walk of life. Therefore what he said was probably a fact, that is, concerning the resemblance, or why else had he said it? He seemed to want nothing from me but discretion in this single matter he had broached.

"I must tell you, sir," he said now, "if you had made a claim on me, and on the house of Scorpia, at this point, I'd have thought you a more canny and less honorable man. But you have pushed me for nothing."

"Because I don't think I am due anything from you, my lord. Nor do I go in want."

Como sighed. He said, "God keep you so. But if it should change, you may come and speak to me. I won't forget what I say. I shall send it you, written down. You can read?

"Most men in the Gravemakers' Guild can read."

"Very well. Now I thank you for your time, Messer, on this unlikely day. What is that shouting out there all about, I wonder? Has someone murdered Borja?" He looked to see how I would take this. Seeing how I did take it, he smiled slightly, and so did I. "He is a handsome man, Borja, and accomplished. A great soldier. He is never revenged on anyone, only exacts justice. You'll have heard his motto."

"I have."

"He quoted to the Ducem today, at dinner, 'Severe circumstances and my kingdom's newness, force me to act comparably, and to guard my frontiers far and wide.' Perhaps you know the source of that in the Latin?"

"*Res dura, et regni novitis*—I think it is from Virgil, my lord."

"Dido's words, on essential cruelty. We are his friends now. Let's hope he is never out of sorts with us."

Outside and below, the yells grew abruptly very loud, and now both of us made out the clash of swords.

Then there came a hammering on the door.

As I took my leave of him, he was dealing with urgent news.

It was full dark by now, but torches and noise flared over the wall. Servants showed me out by a side way into an alley, to avoid the skirmish which had spread along the front of the building. It was with the Barbarons, of course.

Despite the trouble, Como's letter of pledge came for me two days after. I have it under my hand as I write this now.

BEATRIXA

"Do you want a quarrel, 'ser?"

"I? No."

"If you *do*, 'ser, like a quarrel—then I'm for you."

They were young men, beautifully got up, hair curled and in their best clothes, three in the yellow on chestnut of della Scorpia, and four others in Barbaron's deep red and blue. Higher servants from both houses, no more. Yet they had steeped themselves in house honor, had been trained to it from infancy, and that meant, too, in its feuds. And now, meeting each other like this on the pavement above the Blessed Maria Canal, they had strutted, sneering, laughing behind their hands, until words had broken out. It was a fact, the three had come looking for trouble; the four had had no choice but to be where they were.

Alongside lay the palace to which many of the Barbaron family had retired, until the feasting began on the Rivoalto. The building loaned to the della Scorpias was some distance along the canal. But even this had not prevented a collision, since the three della Scorpias seemed to desire one. They had been drinking—most of Venus had. They were full-blown with ceremony and pageant, mixed suspicions of Borja, water-monsters, and gorgeous sights. They were not themselves, or they might have weighed matters first.

The Barbaron men, too.

"How is the old Scorpion, your lord? A tippling old sot he is, yellow as his flag and your hair—" this from the most tipsy of the Barbaron pack.

"Our lord does well enough," came back, "not fat with sins like the Lord Andrea.

"Sins? What sins? No one need sin; old Como sinned enough for all the City, once. Now that he can no longer lift his cock save in two hands, that doesn't make him virtuous—only impotent!"

"Lady, come inside," said one of Beatrixa's women, who was standing next to her on the broad step. They were low enough down the stair, they could see across the yard and straight out to the terrace where the young men had gathered in the dying sunlight. "Lady Triche—come away."

"Don't be a fool," said Beatrixa. "*You* go in and tell someone. Our guards should be there, by the gate, to stop this."

"*They're* off drinking," said the woman.

"Never mind. Go fetch somebody."

The woman did as she was told at last, hurrying down the stair and away under the arches of the palace.

Beatrixa, meanwhile, also gathered her skirts and descended the steps.

She could see quite well the young men were spoiling for a fight. Sometimes it would happen, in the alleys of Venus, even once on the canals, where two Barbaron men had been drowned.

"Give us our ground!" one of the della Scorpias shouted now.

"What, that ground you'd steal from our lord? No one has it, through your tricks. It lies there useless, and the graves of good men pile up on each other—"

They were speaking of the disputed burial ground on the Isle of the Dead. These words startled her. Half the time, she had always felt, none of them remembered any more why the two houses were supposed to hate and fight each other and did it only from some inner taste for violence. But apparently, too, they learned the original motive by rote. Dredged up into the overcharged dusk, it became a cue.

Suddenly, swords were out. She saw the flash of them, and moved forward even before she knew what it signified.

No one had come from the arches. Everything looked dark, and not even a voice had been raised indoors.

Slender and quite tall, in her cypress cloud of hair and her stately festival gown, its bodice stitched with lit- tle Barbaron Towers in gold and silver twisted thread, Beatrixa left the gateway and stood on the paving in the fallen light.

Her voice was low and vibrant for her build and her sixteen years. She used it coolly and clearly. "Put down your swords. This must end at once."

It was not that she was unthinking. Only that she was rational and brave. She had known where this was going, and no one else had come.

The authority in her voice did check them for a moment. They looked at her, and one of her father's men—a youth not yet her own age; she knew him—cried to her, alarmed, "M'donna Beatrixa . . . stay back . . . mind the blades—" As he did this, trying to protect her as she had meant to protect them all from each other, a della Scorpia man, taking the opportunity as if it were the most natural of actions, skewered the boy on a sword.

He went down, and the blood splashed Beatrixa's

skirt. Now, none of them paid any attention—they were fighting in earnest, dancing and yelling.

All light seemed bleeding from the sky, the world.

She leant over the boy—he was already dead. Her heart went cold. So quick, and all was *over*—

Then the flailing blades he had warned her against made her step back.

She had not heard anyone approach. In the next second, when a pair of hands took hold of her arms, she thought her father's guards had finally arrived. Yet, turning, she saw, in the light of the torch they carried, they wore the wrong colors.

"Here's a choice dainty. *Beatriche* did the oaf say?"

"That's the old one's daughter," said another of the della Scorpias now grouped about her on the pavement. These were young nobles of their house; they ignored the underlings who were still fighting.

Beatrixa said, "Yes, I am Lord Barbaron's daughter. Let go of me.

"What shall we do?" said the first one, who continued to hold her.

He, too, was well-liquored. She did not bother to struggle; she could feel, even in his cups, he was strong.

Another, also sopped, announced, "There's a boat there. Let's take the lady to some quieter place."

Then she resisted. But it was of no use. So she shouted in her clear, dark voice. She sounded almost male—it was not the scream of a woman.

None of the Barbaron servants came to her aid—not amazingly; one more had gone down, the two remaining were fighting for their lives.

By then three of the della Scorpia upperlings had bundled her into the boat, and pushed the panicked oarsman off into the water.

Another of their number sprang into it with a whoop.

One rowed, in fading afterglow, up the choppy black canal toward the Laguna Fulvia.

If she had hoped, on the lagoon, where there were already a multitude of lights, to attract attention and rescue, it quickly became obvious to her she would not be seen. Or, people *would* see, but take her for one more dressed-up celebrant, either making a fuss from flirtatiousness—as many were—or vexed by some annoyance that was her own business. No daughter of a high house could be in the position in which Beatrixa now found herself. Therefore, she was fair game to those who had her.

This, they realized, apparently.

She knew well enough they would be sorry for their behavior, scared mindless at what they had done, once sober. But while the spirit of the wine lasted (and they had a wine-skin with them), they were certain it was a witty move.

They told her why, when they had maneuvered past the other boats, the mass of sails and oars, lanterns, laughing crowds, and gotten into one of the mostly unlit waterways leading through to Aquila.

"There's a deserted island some way out. It has a bad name from someone who lived there. He did some terrible things."

"She won't know. Shall I describe them?"

"And there's a church that comes out of the lagoon. A girl of our house threw herself into the water there. So the story goes. She did this because the evil villain on the island had raped and tortured her. Rather than come back to our family in such ruined disgrace, she took her life, and now she lies in the wet sea-mud, unhallowed at the laguna's bottom—not even in a bed of earth."

For a moment, they waxed maudlin.

Then one of them said, "Listen, Beatriche, daughter of fat Andrea, the one who betrayed her—*sold* her—to that evil lord, Ciara—that devil was one of yours. He was a Barbaron."

"It was Gualdo Barbaron did it," said the youngest one, "so the story has it."

"Story? It's no story. It is God's veracity."

"Well, Beatriche," said the very strong man, who still kept hold of her with one arm, his free hand clamping both of hers (so long ago had she lost sensation in them that she ceased to feel the pain of his grip). "Well, what do you say? Are we just? Are you ready to pay us for poor Meralda della Scorpia?"

Beatrixa had once before heard this tale, or a snatch of it. How these had learned so much was questionable. Perhaps, over the years, Ciara's servants had blabbed, or unseen watchers. Or it had grown, as sometimes the real facts do, out of thin air, out of vapor and the night—a fabrication that is ultimately the truth.

In any case, Beatrixa did not speak.

Then one of them cuffed her.

It was the most glancing blow, but in it was spelled her doom—and theirs. If they dared do even this, they would do all, rape, torture, murder—like the other woman's —Meralda?—until the wine and its fire ran out.

So she said, quietly, "My name is not Beatriche. It is Beatrixa."

"Your name is *Barbaron* and it stinks. But you do not. You smell of rose and ambergris.

"If you harm me," she said, though it was not really worth the attempt, "you will cause such an eruption in the feud between our houses, my father won't rest till everyone of your kin is stone-dead, and every stone of your house beneath the sea."

They chortled, and drank.

Beatrixa sat, silent. She might escape death at their hands if she was patient and cunning. She had her own profound notion of honor, which did not necessarily exclude dying, but which did not invite it wantonly. But she was glad her captor clenched her hands so, for otherwise the men might have seen them shaking. And she did not want to give them that.

That year, the spring tides had only filled the church of Maria Maka Selena two-thirds of the way up the pillars of its nave. In the dark, far from shore, it was an eerie sight.

The moon was rising out of the sea, only a quarter moon, narrow-waisted as a girl. But the church shone with phosphorescence, and the nacreous face of its dead clock was another moon, this one more bright.

If they had passed the island they had mentioned, Beatrixa had not noticed. That was stupid, and she upbraided herself. She needed to be aware of everything, in case it might assist her.

"Well, Dario, shall we go inside?" (Dario was the strongest one, who held her, though less brutally now.)

"The house of God?"

"No longer. It's Neptune's house now."

They laughed again, continuously pleased by their own style.

And the boat was rowed in at the carved door, which gaped from the water like a cave.

Weeds curtained down, palest brown and sleek

azure in their own luminescence. Then the church opened out, its whitish columns, ringed by other floods, balanced in water, seeming to go down and down beneath it, both in actuality and in phantom reflection. The roof, decorated with metal stars and indigo, was only some twelve or thirteen feet above their heads. Dull-glowing angels with trumpets leaned out.

Everywhere, peculiar small, bluish lights floated about in the water, like lamp-wicks in oil. What caused that? Perhaps some tiny sea creature giving off its own radiance.

Beatrixa saw that flower heads and scraps of colored paper from the wedding confetti had also wended in here, as they had across all the lagoons.

Her captors were quieter now, disturbed by the drowned church despite their bravado.

She wondered where they would tie up the boat, or locate firmer ground, in order to do their worst to her. She could see no suitable landing-place.

This seemed to occur as well to them.

"Light another torch."

The second torch was lit. Fresher light came, and at once the colors of the church turned to bronze, swart blue, sharp silver. The reflections hardened in the water and, trying now to observe everything in case it might help her, Beatrixa now stared deeply down into it.

"Shall we do it here, Dario?"

"Let me think."

"Look, the altar's above water too—it must be raised up. It's broad, too."

The youngest one said, uneasy now, "Should we go back to the bad island? Take her there, as Ciara did with our girl?"

Abruptly Dario let go of Beatrixa's hands. For an

instant she felt nothing, then the agony of blood running back in them.

"Row for the altar. I'll have her there."

"But . . . it's the *altar*, Dario—"

"Do you think this place still sacred?"

"I've heard the fishwives come here to pray—"

Let them. God isn't here any more. We'll confess tomorrow."

No one was amused now.

Beatrixa understood from their tones that the church had sobered them, not to realization of their colossal crime, but to a deadly earnest. For, yes, she heard her death in their voices.

As the boat started on, she got to her feet.

Dario lurched up beside her and, turning, she spat into his eyes, then thrust as him with all her might. She, too, despite her slenderness, was strong. He staggered, could not right himself, and crashed into the thick blue oil of the water.

Immediate pandemonium broke out. Dario splashing and calling, showers of liquid, the oar extended for him to grasp, the boat floundering, two others pulling at her, cursing, howling. And she thought, *I must go in now. I must go in and die because there is no other way out*—

And in that moment, something—dreamlike, impossible.

There beneath her, she saw, as if only through tinted air, the floor of the nave, the bases of the pillars. A man was kneeling on one knee there below at the foot of the long stair leading to the high altar. Although she had mostly forgotten, although she had not been reminded for most of the decade during which she had grown up, although she had never seen him in this adult shape— she knew who he was.

And the moment she did, pulled and wrenched this way and that in the careering boat, she saw how his golden head had lifted. He stood, and then he raised his face, and through the sea she beheld him, the man who had been the child under the canal.

The fragment of inattention had of course given them complete mastery of her again. Dario had wallowed back into the boat, swearing and hawking, and now he hit her across the face, so that she almost fell. The boat, upset again, nearly threw them all in the water.

"You bitch . . . you slut-whore . . . *true* Barbaron harlot—"

She was stunned. Not from the blow.

She could think of nothing.

Then the surface of the water parted, as if for the ejection of a great fish.

All motion otherwise, apart from the rocking of sea and boat, ceased.

They had turned to look. They had become statues.

Up from the depth rose the man. He emerged fluidly and simply, as if born upward by some smooth machinery. And then he was there, above the water. And they saw, the four della Scorpias and Beatrixa Barbaron, that he was standing now, feet apart, easy, as if upon a tesselated floor—*on the water itself.*

His hair was not wet. It hung around him dry, dense, and shining, to his waist. His clothes were not wet. And so it was not difficult for any of them to see what he wore. His fashionable doublet, which clothed a slimly muscular body, was deep chestnut, his hose and shoes the palest and most couth of yellows. On his breast, and embroidered in thick gold along his sleeves, was a scorpion that held a flowering branch in its claws, worked in a very elaborate and fetching pattern. The colors and emblem of the della Scorpia house from whence, those ten or so years ago, he had told Beatrixa he came.

The youngest of the men in the boat spoke hoarsely. *"What is it Dario?"*

"By Jesu . . . how do I know . . . some trick. It's some trick left from the Borja pageant . . . it's not real—"

"Good evening, sirs," said the unreal thing, standing there in perfect equilibrium on the sea. "My kinsmen, I believe."

"It talks!"

"It's a *trick*. He's standing on something under the water, just below the surface."

"Oh, do you think so?" said the man on the sea. And he sprang forward, a vast leap, and stood beside the boat now, exactly by it where the water was deep, deep, or the boat must already have grounded. "You are in error, gentlemen."

One of them fainted, plunging straight down into the boat as the slain boy, Jacomo, had done on the canal paving earlier that night. The boat swung. And *he* stood there, not inconvenienced at all, steady, relaxed.

"My name—" he said, when the boat had righted itself again. "I am Silvio della Scorpia. And you have there a lady who is not of our house or family. Give her to me."

What happened then resembled no human activity. The three conscious men hurtled from the boat. In the water, they at once began, with much thrashing, to swim away, out of the church, even while one cried that he could *not* swim, the other two hauling him with them. It was the instinctive flight of beasts. The man who had fainted revived at these sounds, bent over, and vomited into the water.

Indifferent, Silvio della Scorpia watched this, only stepping aside, as someone would on a street, to avoid the regurgitated mess.

"Well," said Silvio, once the retching had stopped. "Do you want to be off, too?"

And the last man also slid into the water, and feebly pushed himself away.

After this, only Beatrixa remained in the boat, standing, her hands loose at her sides, the bruise on her cheek even more vivid against her pallor.

Silvio della Scorpia stepped into the boat with her. "Shall we sit down?"

She sat, and he beside her.

Two tears ran from her eyes, that was all. "I thought I should be killed. By their—attentions, if nothing else."

"Yes, it seemed likely."

"How is it you are here?"

"I come and go," he said, "as I want."

"I can see that," she said. "What are you, that you can come and go in such a way?"

"What do you think?" he said.

It was all a dream now. Perhaps she had perished, perhaps they had killed her after all, and this was some hallucination at the edge of death. The boat was moving, softly, quickly, without an oar. They glided into a side-cave or chapel of the church, next through and along a corridor all shimmering with candles or moonglow or water or some other element not belonging to the world. . . .

"I don't know," she said, "what you can be. I remember you from when I was a little girl. I remember . . . your face, and your hair."

"Did you never look for me before?" he said.

"Yes. I looked everywhere. I waited always, for a year, more than that. But you never came back. They tell children that such beings don't exist—or they say they are demons of the Devil."

"I'm a demon, then. For I *do* exist, as you see."

"No," she said, "I don't believe you do. And yet you are here."

The boat flowed through a skeletal arch and came out on the lagoon.

The broken ring of moon was higher, colder. There was no sign of the della Scorpia men. Maybe they, too, had been drowned, like the girl they had spoken of and had thought to avenge.

"What do you want?" Beatrixa asked.

"What I have. And one more item, perhaps."

"No, I meant what was your purpose?"

He smiled his beautiful smile. It filled her with a great calm, and also an ache of longing—for what? For what? She wanted in that instant to touch him, but surely he would be insubstantial, or—like the water, unable to be grasped in any way.

"My purpose," he said, thoughtfully. She had not supposed he would reply. "I am at play," he said.

"Then you played at saving me."

"If I'm a minion of Lucefero," he said, "I must have done it to get something from you in return."

"My soul . . ."

"Do you think you have one?"

"Yes."

"You have something," he said. "I would not call it that."

"Is it—" she waited. She looked away from him, "Is it what you are? That something not a soul?"

"Oh, Beatrixa Barbaron, how skilled you are in argument."

She turned, and now he was no longer a man, but the recollected child again, sitting there by her, as she had seen him last. And then that too was gone, and in the boat with her was only a core of radiance, a blue-green, white-golden light. And she put her hands to her mouth, and in that instant he came back, a young man perhaps a year or two older than she, and dressed in the height of elegance and wealth and the dyes of the della Scorpia blazon.

"Don't be frightened," he said, gravely now. "I didn't want that, not with you."

Then he reached out and took her hand and held it a moment, before gently letting it go.

"You may be touched then," she said. "How did you know what I thought?"

"I didn't know. I don't read your thoughts, Beatrixa. I'm not God."

"Do *you* credit God?"

"Yes. I credit God. Though what He is I have no idea. To answer your question, on my wanderings . . . I've never met Him."

She regarded her hand. It tingled still from the crushing Dario had given it. Nothing else.

Beatrixa knew that, though she had touched Silvio, and though he had felt solid, and alive, *tangible*, he had not felt like anything she had ever known. Not of flesh, certainly not of that. But not either of any other material—stone, silk, leather, wood, glass—not even like an animal's skin, the flesh of his firm and well-made hand. Not even water—or air. What then—what? Not even . . . earth.

"Are you dead?" she said to him.

"Do I seem dead?"

"You are of the spirit. I don't know what you seem."

"Let me tell you, then, how you seem to me," he said.

She sat in the boat, waiting again. At last she asked, "What do I seem like to you, my lord?"

"Like music," he said. "You seem like music played low and sweetly and well, in the first dusk, when the stars come out."

Something moved inside her, pain, that was not pain.

She thought, *I do not know what manner of being he is. I've never believed properly in devils, though I think there may be a Hell. In Heaven I believe, and in the spirit. Is he from Heaven?*

There was a slight tremble against the boat and she looked up.

They had reached an island. The island the others had talked about?

Silvio stood, and stepped off on to the landing-place. He stretched out his hand to her, and she was afraid to touch it again, but she took it. And he seemed to lift her up through the night, without any strain to her arm, and set her down on the island.

But still she did not know what it felt like, to touch, to be touched by, Silvio.

"They said this was an evil spot," she said.

"It was, but it was happy once, too."

"Why have you brought me here?" she said.

"So you could feel terra firma under your feet for a moment," he said.

She nodded. She said, "But Venus is all built on water."

"And the seas," he said, "flow over other lands, far below. Earth is always at the bottom of it all."

There was the vague bulk of a house above. He did not take her there. They walked aside into a wild orchard of budding pomegranates. In the mythology of the Greeks, the pomegranate was the fruit of the dead.

An old bench leaned among the trees. They sat

here, a little apart. She thought, *Who has sat here before us? Are they gone . . . so quickly gone, like poor Jacmo who died today . . . and are they then . . . like Silvio?*

For a while she did not say anything. The lagoon sipped at the shore. Across the stretch of it was a dimness like a cloud, all that could be seen of the fierce torches and the lights of Venus.

"What shall we do now?" she said.

"This is very like that first time we spoke. Why must we do anything?"

She turned and looked at him. He appeared precisely like a young man, so cruelly handsome, so fine, so alive.

"What do you want?" she said again. Her heart drummed in her throat.

"What I have," he said, as before. "And one thing else."

In fear, she looked away. Then, arrogantly, she looked back. "Which is?"

"Not yet. I don't mean to tell you yet."

"It's so terrible?"

"In part. And so much mine for the having."

She stood up, and walked off through the gnarled nets of the trees, and then of course he was simply standing in her path, and he said, "M'donna, you must return to your City."

Then the boat came to that end of the orchard on its own, and where the wall was broken now, they went through, and she thought, what would it have mattered anyway to him, if the wall, had been taller than a house and made of iron?

I shall be damned for this. To converse with a thing not mortal and not divine.

Then, in the magic boat, close to Silvio della

Scorpia, whom already, for she had never been a fool, nor timid, she knew that she loved, Beatrixa fell asleep.

A spell. Or only her exhaustion.

When she woke, she found the boat had come to rest against a shadowy quay. This was a side canal off Fulvia. She was alone.

Between walls, she could see the torches that lit the great front of the Primo, and the dome aloft like the full moon. A bell began—how late, how late—it was the Prima Vigile they rang, first watch of morning.

Nor was anyone about nearby.

She got ashore awkwardly in her heavy skirt. Bewildered, as other girls had become that night, she instinctively strayed toward shelter. To the palaces by the Blessed Maria Canal, where her house had arranged to sleep that night.

Beatrixa . . . felt herself now also to be a ghost. Though she passed among groups of late revellers, no one seemed to notice her. When she reached the gateway of the guest palace, she came against the guardsmen in a group, and when they saw her, they started, as if she had suddenly appeared from thin air.

"M'donna—did you go out? You never did. Have you come from the Rivoalto . . . no, you never went there—"

"No, no," she said, "I was here all this while. I came out of that door over there. I'm just taking the air in the court."

The oddest dialogue. Which, as the night wheeled on towards dawn, was reinforced by a most curious aberration.

It seemed her father had sent word she should not

go to the evening feast on the Ducem's island. Andrea had taken over only two of his sons, and his wife. After the fighting earlier, which had spread from the Barbaron bivouac all the way to the temporary accommodation of the della Scorpias, a number of other houses had kept their womenfolk indoors. Della Scorpia had, it seemed, avoided the Ducem's feast entirely. Once the fracas had moved from servants to masters, and their guards, both of the warring families had sustained losses.

If Borja was put out by gaps at the dinner tables, no one could say. But the Ducem decidedly was not best pleased—perhaps he had wished Venus to look united. (To add to his irritation, apparently, his flamingo had also escaped.)

After the fray was curtailed, no Barbaron had thought to search for Beatrixa. Why should they? Only her maid knew where Andrea's daughter had been when the trouble began. And the woman had not spoken, thinking her mistress had sensibly retreated indoors, as she, the maid, had advised her to. By the time the maid had determined that Beatrixa was nowhere in the palace—and her search had been belated and sketchy, besides—Lord Barbaron had gone over to the feast.

"I was frantic, madam," said the maid, who had been.

"You were also too afraid you'd be blamed had you told anyone, let alone sent my father word. Where did you think I was?"

"Well . . . M'donna . . . you know you go off sometimes . . . I thought—"

"You are worthless to me," said Beatrixa. Her face, which was no longer bruised, was instead like a stone. The maid shrank in horror. "If any violence had happened to me, which is what you suspected and were too cowardly to report, I might have died."

Beatrixa now found herself trembling. In this state, she did not trust herself with the woman. Nor did she want to reveal to anyone what had occurred. The opening so wide of the old wound of feud was already serious enough If her father were to hear that she had been abducted, not to mention the abductors' plans—God knew, God knew. . . .

But oh, she was so tired.

"Get out. I won't have you in my service. Send another of the girls to me."

"But lady . . . what shall I do if you do this . . . ?"

"Be thankful I am alive to do anything. If I were not, it would be worse. Go to the stewardness. Tell her I will speak to her about you tomorrow.

"Lady . . . *no* . . . I shall be thrown out in the alleys—"

"It is what you deserve. But I won't tell her that. I shall say you are very splendid, but that I am tired of your chatter. She'll reprimand you and place you elsewhere in the house. Mend your ways. Never serve another of my family as you have dis-served me."

But I'm not fair. Thank God she did not speak.

Later, before the mirror, Beatrixa remembered how Dario had struck her. And she could not find a bruise. Could it be he had *not* bruised her? Nor was her dress stained from the salty, splashing water—or from the blood of Jacomo, as she recalled. Had . . . his touch done this? What else had it done?

Her white dog sat at her feet, watching her, uneasy. "All's well," she said, to reassure him. But it was not.

She had imagined everything, or dreamed it. Where then had she been to? What had become of her? What *would*?

EUNICHE

The palazzo of the della Scorpias had been young three centuries ago. For the last hundred years it had taken on a look of age and sallow weathering, yet it remained defiant. Its Scorpion escutcheon was cut deeply into the facade, its banners were hung out. As with the newer palazzo of its enemy, Barbaron, a gallery ran around the middle story, but was framed by the horseshoe-shaped arches of the East. The columns of the ground floor had capitals of acanthus leaves. Beyond the great door, its vestibule contained the marble staircase mentioned previously, and the mural of a Caesar, these now dulled by some further years of existence.

Yet people wear worse.

Far inside the hive of the house, which was now once again in mourning, Euniche stood in a long room, overseeing, *watching* the antics of others. Her hands and lips were folded. She was still as a statue, and in the heartless spring sunshine, her shadow stretched black on the floor.

Once, a generation before, Euniche had been the maid of Meralda della Scorpia. But Meralda had vanished from the scene in veils of sinister speculation. How then had Euniche, one of the foremost agents of Meralda's downfall, clung on? More apposite, how had she arrived at this moment as a thin, stately woman past her fifty-second year, once wed, once widowed, and clad in a gown of thick brocade, with a gold chain over it, and small pearls in her ears?

You might read it all in her face. Oh yes. Where Euniche had been harsh and uncomely at nineteen, now her unnerving mask was carved, like the stonework on the palazzo, with her own escutcheon.

She had learned early, on Meralda, what she liked best—to get power over others. Euniche had even purely rejected the riches of bribery in order to have this. But in the end, through her wiles, her spying, her insidious and useful and trustless assistance to all her superiors in the house of the della Scorpias, she had come by the riches too. At first sorry for her—she was ugly and beneath them, but so willing to please, to fetch and carry, and subtly to flatter—they grew to rely on Euniche. For Meralda's disappearance, they did not blame her. Euniche had rushed in good time to the ladies of the house, crying that her mistress was gone and could not be found, and although Meralda had acted so strangely just before, it had not been a maid's place to question her behavior, till now. And Euniche was plainly ignorant, as were they all, of Meralda's conniving nature, or her schemes. . . . Even when certain rumors of Lorenzo Vai surfaced, no stigma became attached to the upright and obviously distressed Euniche. She had misjudged Meralda's character just as they, the great ones, had.

Then Euniche was given a place with another daughter of the house, an older and more obedient one. And in this context Euniche learned, by her watchfulness and the use of her disgusting, slithering brain, so much—that soon she gained even more power, and also a jewel, and later some money.

At length she was looked on as a chaperone of the house, dedicated to her charges and the family, a loyal retainer of some standing. And so in her thirtieth year she fastened on a man, a lesser steward, and by means of her prospects and her stash of coins, elbowed him into marrying her. It was a childless, loveless awful union, that ended after a while when her husband made off with death. Thereafter Euniche was a widow, and wore black like her shadow. Of all dark things, she truly was a reminder of night, or of the grave.

Now there she stood, with her snake's face.

And all around, the angry misery of these high ones. They had lost a son of the Lord Como—not to a sword-cut, it seemed, but by drowning, and the body not recovered. And even in the lower caste, there was grief. Underlings had also died. A guardsman, and a personal servant of Como's. And more.

Avid for all such news, Euniche had looked so very sorry. She loved to be around the tears, listening, nodding with such sympathy. She had done everything she could. Lapping up their hurt like blood.

"Euniche, will you go down to the courtyard, and find M'donna Caterina's little passionaria? She laid it by and forgot, and no wonder."

This came from one of Como's brother's granddaughters, a haughty girl Euniche had her eye on, and so always liked to run errands for.

"At once, lady."

Euniche descended by a back stair to the palazzo's yard.

The house crowded this area. The court was well-like, deep but not particularly large or airy, and overhung by an inner gallery above. Even so, an acacia tree, currently bare, grew in a plot at the yard's center, supported in summer by terra-cotta vases of roses and spindly hollyhocks.

Caterina's little handbook of saints was on the bench. It was expensive, hand-painted and hand-written too, by the Priests of the Sorrow. And here it lay, carelessly forgotten.

Euniche picked it up. She opened the passionaria at random, idly curious, yet as always instinctively on the lookout—spying now upon the saints.

She could not read the Latin, of course.

But there was the most startling picture painted there. Against a blue sky, a fiery angel dived earthward, its face enraged and snarling, its sunset wings spread wide, and in its hand a flaming sword.

Above, over the courtyard, there came the sound of wings.

Euniche lifted her head. She did not yet glance up. She knew that this sound was utterly inappropriate.

Birds constantly flew by. Pigeons and sparrows, the ferocious soaring gulls from the lagoons. Those wings did not have this sound. These hissed and clattered—and then another shadow threw night into the court.

Euniche looked up.

She gave a thin whine, and the passionaria slipped from her hands.

The angel dived. Straight out of the ether, out of the steely spring sun.

It was redly pink, like coral, but the undersides of the vast wings were also sable, and the flaming sword had a jet-black tip.

Euniche shrieked—but no noise left her.

The angel fell directly upon her, she thought, and she felt the flames of its blush-black wings sear her face—

and then it smashed with a lashing shatter of small branches into the acacia tree.

Euniche crouched on the ground. She did not know what had happened. She felt her face; it was not burnt off. She fancied she had soiled herself . . .

But it was *not* an angel. It was only a bird—a pink improbability of one.

It hung there in the tree, the wings half folded, black one side, coral the other, its long neck like a serpent, and with a sword of a beak. Its eyes, though, were red, and stared down at her, soullessly, like pins.

Then it propelled itself out of the cradle of ripped branches, and plummeted to the courtyard floor.

Euniche got up. She stood with her arms held out as the bird held out its wings. Then it closed its wings. Its legs were long, lacquered stilts and, raised on them, it was very nearly Euniche's own height.

Euniche did not pray. Had she realized that she no longer had a right to? No, for she would pray often in the church, asking all sorts of blessings for her masters.

She began to back away, and the bird of flame began, like a dancer, to come towards her.

This was very slow. It was measured—yes, a dance.

Then she turned and ran, stumbling on her skirt, tearing it, leaving the pricey book, trying only to get back into the house. At the side entry under the gallery, she threw herself in and, turning, thrust shut the heavy door. *It* had almost reached her—a mass of flames and night—almost, but not quite.

She lay against the door a moment. Then she scuttled off, down the passage.

Outside, Ducem Nicolo's flamingo rose ponderously up again and lit upon the railing of the internal gallery. There were windows all along the wall, the shutters of only one of which had been undone, to let in the sun and air. One, obviously, was enough. The flamingo stepped through.

Dario, a member of Lord Como's band of nephews, was walking glumly through his ancestral house.

He and his friends, all save poor Grasotti, had had a lucky escape. And he had pondered if, after all, what had happened in the drowned church might have been an ill dream. But no, it was real.

What then had that creature been, that seeming man, who rose out of the water and stood on it and was not wet, and sent them away with a power of fear only something unnatural and unhuman could wield?

It seemed later to Dario that the being might have been some emanation of the della Scorpia clan itself (it wore their blazon). It had, then, risen to correct them in a fatal error. For what they had done in drink, grabbing old Barbaron's daughter—and what they *would* have done, which, sober, did not bear thinking of—would have brought down God knew what disaster on the della Scorpia House—and principally therefore, on Dario.

You could not fight even the most repulsive enemy with such weapons. Rape of a high-born woman was beneath a proper nobleman.

As the headache of the wine faded, so Dario's uneasiness grew more insistent. They had sworn not to speak of it, he and the others who got away. Grasotti, though, had gone down in the lagoon. They had said subsequently, he had been caught in the fighting by the canal, fallen into the water and, unable to swim more than a few strokes, sunk before they could reach him. Como had brought divers from Silvia to try to find the body. (The nephews had already attempted to, of *course*, hence the wreck of their clothes that night.)

Grasotti, the fat one, had been only a bastard got on a girl of the house, but Como had recognized him. Como was honorable about that. He had been a child of Como's old age, too, which probably made the old man feel it more.

Meanwhile, there had been no word of Barbaron's daughter having gone missing or suffered any insult. She, too, must have escaped the apparition, though one could only conjecture how. Then she had decided to say nothing. Who knew why? Perhaps she had liked Dario a little. And believed he had not meant what he had threatened—as, unarguably, if it had really come to it— he had *not* . . .

Dario paused in his self-deceptions.

He was in the passage that connected the sala to a generally neglected room. The passage was not well-lit, having no windows, but from the room itself a bright wedge of sunlight ran out of the half-open door.

There was a sound in the room. What was it? A woman s gown, he thought, sweeping back and forth. The servant-girl Fiora maybe, opening the shutters to air the room's fustiness.

Well, nothing wrong in that. Why then did the sound seem so ominous? That, and the way a shadow abruptly blotted up the sun on the floor. . . .

Dario had been going to that room. He sometimes met Fiora there. If they were quick, they could have some fun, squeezed in the great cupboard, with no one very likely to intrude.

"Fiora?" asked Dario.

Who else could it be?

But it was not Fiora, for although she had opened

the shutters, she had then been called to and detained in the attics by her duties.

"Come now, what are you at, girl?"

Something scraped the door open wide, and now it sounded like a sword.

Dario backed away. He cursed himself and stood his ground. What a ninny he had become, since that night in the church.

No one heard his shout of terror. The walls of the ancient palace were dense.

Dario fled down the passage, through the sala, through an annexe and another corridor, and all the while the thing ran after him, holding out its wings as far as the space would allow, its neck stretched forward. He knew it was a bird. He knew that much. But though he had seen it, at the Ducem's dinner, picking about around a fountain—he had forgotten, and now anyway, it was not the same. Dario knew it was too large for any bird. And surely neither was it merely animal, but some terrible, feathered golem invested by a sorcerer s will.

The flamingo chased him to a flight of stairs. Running down them, he lost his footing. He was not badly hurt, but he had banged his head and felt dizzy. Trying to regain his feet, he saw the bird was gone.

Then, Dario began to think that he was under a bane, or had been driven mad.

Euniche's own room—such was her standing, she had had one to herself since just before her marriage —was also in the attics. She went to it, as soon as she had collected herself a little. This was necessary. She needed to change her soiled private garments, her shift and curtella.

Coming up through the house, she met some of the ladies, and had the sense as usual to behave fawningly. She also met Donna Caterina, who stared at her coldly but seemed not to recall the mislaid passionaria, nor that Euniche had been told to fetch it.

I must say I was taken faint, Euniche thought.

Already, her devious, practiced mind was working on the problem. Should she tell one of the men to go out and chase off the bird, or even capture it? By now it might have flown away. That would be better. Not to tangle herself up with its peculiarity. She had found this was always the best course, to avoid much overt participation in anything other than virtuous service.

Dario could have warned Euniche that a sorcerous will that directs a golem does not hesitate in pursuit of what it wants. Does not, for example, let the golem fly off.

Like a ray of rosy sun, dawn or sunfall, the flamingo picked its way through the house.

Conceivably the Eel had been supernatural, if the story of its length and vigor were true. (And there had been many witnesses.) The flamingo was a fleshly reality. It did not therefore pass through walls, vanish, and reassemble. But, as Dario had partially fathomed, it had been possessed, and was moved by, an intelligence not its own.

So it followed a route upward through the Palazzo della Scorpia and, now and then, when people approached along a corridor or from a doorway, it drew back into concealment.

If any sensed its presence, that was another thing. Some did, and flinched aside, hurrying on nervously into other areas of the house. Or some stood, looking about, *half* seeing it—a bleached carmine shadow among shadows that were brown or black. Or hearing a rustle of dust lost among other lesser noises; a stirring like a creeper, a woman s dress . . . feathers scraped softly on a wall. Once, the fieriness of a pink chrysolite passing over her vision, a girl with two or three gowns in her arms for sewing, had turned, startled. For what had she glimpsed? Nothing was there, only the sunbeams and the shed powders of the house, flickering against the plaster, a maroon curtain which hung straight down from its rod.

For all who almost saw it, only Dario did see. Dario, and Euniche.

Euniche was going to see it again.

Reaching her chamber, Euniche shut the door. Then she stood quite still, regaining her poise.

What had happened had been a silly business, except that the creature was undoubtedly savage, and she had been sensible to avoid it. Now that she had time to think about it, she guessed the bird came from the Ducem's menagerie on the Rivoalto; she had heard he kept exotic fowl, along with his horses, deer, and lions. The wings of those birds were clipped, but sometimes the vital tufts grew back and then they could still fly.

That she had mistaken the great bird for an angel of retribution, Euniche had, in her frontal mind, forgotten.

The room was dim, for it was not big and the window was small, and closed by its opaque glass pane that she had no wish, now, to throw wide.

Even with the window closed, she noticed a fishy odor in the room, come in, most likely, from the canals.

There was another stench, too, and hastily Euniche began to strip off her gown, and next the dirtied curtella, and the rest. She bundled these away. She would wash them herself, later, because she wanted no one to know about her lapse in control.

Naked, thin, and scrawny, her breasts shriveled and fallen, Euniche did not look less fearsome. In youth she had quickly learned to take no pride in her body. Only her brain did Euniche hugely respect, and this lack of self-regard, coupled to such intense vanity, showed in every line of her, clothed or bare. She was both states horrible, appalling.

Having wiped herself with a cloth, she went to a chest that stood by the bed.

Hers was a broad bed, and it had a frame—it had been the couch of her marriage. A piece of curtaining hung down around it and, as Euniche went by, the curtain shifted.

Euniche stopped. She looked sidelong.

The flame-bird stepped daintily out into the room. How the scrap of curtain had concealed it was debatable. How any of the curtains, shadows, angles of walls had done so, also unsure.

It was too big for the room.

And Euniche suddenly far too small.

Yet there they posed, the ugly, fearful, evil thing confronting the beautiful, fearful, thoughtless thing which was being moved like a figure on a chessboard.

Then Euniche gaped her mouth and spread her lungs to get enough air to scream.

In that instant the flamingo struck forward with its long serpent's neck.

The bill carved like a blade through the middle of Euniche's face, and down her body to the root of her belly. She was undone in one faultless seam that instantly offered up its scarlet lining.

She was not dead. Her windpipe had been scored but not severed; her heart had not yet ceased.

As she toppled over, she made a clucking sound. She lay helpless on her back, writhing when able, watching for some while as the flamingo tore her in ribbons, and the ribbons into threads.

When it ended, her eyes were fixed, holding in each of them the image of her coral death.

A day went by and no one knew where Euniche had gone. At last another woman went to her room—Euniche had always discouraged this.

The door was shut and, getting no response, the visitor lifted the latch and glanced into the dimness.

"I never knew she had such colorful clothes—for some festival perhaps, when she was young. Deep red and pink—left there in a heap on her bed."

What this woman saw was not clothing.

Later, the smell made another investigation necessary. And then, they found her, what was left.

"Is this house accursed?" Como's steward had cried, tried beyond patience. Afraid to admit his fear.

"Rats must have done it, sir. Rats, from the canal. She died, and they got in and found her—there is the tale of the old Lord Alberdo, who died in his bed and—"

"The window was shut," said the steward.

"Not the door, though. That stood partly open."

The flamingo had made Euniche into a nest, upon the bed, and there it had sat, as if to warm an egg of its own kind, its black legs tucked under and folded behind it.

After a day had passed, however, it left her, lifted

the latch of her door with its bill like a curved sword, which had killed Euniche. It went through a passage or two, still unseen, and soon found an exit to the outer City and the water.

Perhaps it fed from the lagoons. Presently it flew back to the gardens of the Rivoalto. It came there by night, and if any had noticed it, they, too, would have thought it an angel, a vision of some other world—or the wine-bottle. Its wings had been clipped and had stayed clipped. How it could fly anywhere would be a mystery.

Altogether there were twenty flamingoes on the Ducem's island. Eventually it was noted that twenty remained. Ducem Nicolo had other worries. Nobody told him the mislaid bird had come back.

SILVIO

FROM THE ISLAND, the lagoon stretched away in all directions, its water like pale green silk. No other shore was ever anywhere visible.

It was a warm, soft day of clear light. The days were long, and always like this. The sky was turquoise blue, crossed only by a few lambent, creamily-golden clouds. The sky had also a tint of green sometimes, which, after the slow riot of sunset, would intensify. Prolonged glowing dusks hung over the island, holding the copper, viridian, gilt, and amethyst of a peacock's feather. The nights were calm and sewn with large stars.

As he climbed the island, walking up through the groves of myrtles and lilacs, which were flowering, Silvio stopped and regarded for a moment an obelisk which stood among the trees. It was made of the finest marble, smooth and white with translucent veins, and all about it the island's grass had been scythed to velvet.

He imagined this obelisk was a monument to his dead father. Though unmarked, it had always been here. Sometimes he had seen his mother come down through the groves and linger beside it. But he had never asked her what it signified. There was so little about her he did not know, this seemed not to matter.

Now Silvio went to the marble, and walked once around it. That was all he did.

Violets were growing in the grass at its foot. Silvio leaned down and plucked some up for the woman in the house. Then he went on.

His mother's palazzo lay at the apex of the island. A hill pushed from the slope, and cypress trees ran along its shoulder, casting their royal shadows. Then the building appeared.

The palace was of three stories, with a gallery running around the middle floor, and with Byzantine arches. In the sun, it burned a vibrant apricot color.

Silvio had known the palace all his life. He had grown up in it through a swift, bright childhood to the prime of a young manhood that did not change.

And his mother, of course, neither did she change one jot. She was still the slender and beautiful girl he had seen from the first. Yet, despite this, they were mother and son, very definitely that.

He had never missed or been curious about his father. Silvio knew everything about him. He was aware, too, of how his father had died, and why, although his mother had never spoken of it, or even obliquely referred to it. Silvio, also without reference, understood what she herself had suffered.

They did not need to discuss such things. Nor need he tell her what he had done, would do. She did, however, undoubtedly know.

Yet now, for the first, Silvio was a little perturbed. For something in his game had subtly altered.

It had happened, if he were honest—and he had never felt the need to be anything else, with himself— when he had met the child-girl in the Barbaron house. He had set out to meet her, impatient, since she took so long to grow up (unlike himself). *After* meeting her, he had been restless for a while. He had not gone back. And the minutes had dripped down and become years. Then he glimpsed her again, and she was suddenly grown. She was a woman.

He had intended . . . what? Perhaps it was not planned, exactly—he preferred to improvize. It did not signify, anyway. Fate, the current which brought to him everything he wanted, had brought her in the rambling boat, along the filthy and turgid water of Aquila. So he came out once more to meet her, Beatrixa Barbaron.

Silvio thought of a bird. A bird appeared. It was like a flamingo, yet its hues were more startling, damson, crimson, and flaming orange. It was positioned at a pool, feeding, its head curved over oddly to do this, as he had seen the other one do—the other flamingo that he had removed from the Ducem and sent visiting in the della Scorpia house.

Everything went on as it should, as he wished. As his mother wished. Everything. And so, why perturbation? Silvio put his doubt aside.

Looking up, he saw his mother had just come out on the palazzo's gallery. She wore a white gown, her hair dressed ornately, with polished jacinths.

She had not noticed him yet. She always smiled the instant she beheld him. Her exquisite face lit up like the beautiful sunrises, and made him at once glad and happy and strong.

He was her life, he knew. She, his.

Of course, she was his mother, and he, her son.

The flamingo rose suddenly into the turquoise air and flapped away over the cypress trees, a flaming rose in the sky.

PART THREE

Love

She is coming, my own, my sweet;
Were it ever so airy a tread,
My heart would hear her and beat,
Were it earth in an earthy bed,
My dust would hear her and beat,
Had I lain for a century dead;
Would start and tremble under her feet,
And blossom in purple and red.

ALFRED, LORD TENNYSON
Maud

BARTOLOME

IT WAS EARLY SUMMER, and the month of the Twins, before Chesare Borja took his official leave of us.

The Ducem had got up, for a farewell, a grand mascera on the Rivoalto, with actors to depict Madonna Lucretza as Beauty, the female Twin, and Chesare as Valor, the male. In Venus, these Twins stay also emblems of the goddess Venus, and her lover Mars, the god of war. Borja was reportedly pleased by this, though I heard he had slept poorly on the island. They said anyway he was more prone to work all night with his maps of conquest than to slumber or entertain women. (Half the rumors of him speak only of his lusts, worse than his father's; the other half, of his miserly abstinences.) Presently he was gone, however, and his fair sister with him. But they only crossed the River Lungo, to her husband's city of Ferrachita. And meanwhile, the agreed portion of his troops, with their commanders, remained—both in the City garrison, and in those garrisons at Veronavera, and out on the island of Torchara. (I also heard that the wig of the boy actor who had been Lucretza in the mascera, and which had been dyed to that same marvelous peach shade as her own natural hair, sold for fifty gold duccas in the Setapassa. That, too, may be a lie.)

In any event, my mind was full of my own affairs. I had been puzzled and a little disturbed by my interview

with Lord Como della Scorpia. This slight anxiety was
not decreased when I learned the outcome of the fight
along the Blessed Maria Canal, and how one of Como's
lower sons had drowned. To add to the upheaval, Pia
became ill with a congestion, and was put to bed for a
week. Some of her closest women friends flocked in and
out to nurse her. Their kindness I did not doubt but,
when at home, I was glad of any excuse to be away again.
Pia's doctor then told me of an apothecary's shop near
the Gardens of Diana, which dealt in Eastern spices and
herbs known for their help in sickness. There I went, as
soon as I could. It was a longish way.

I left Pia propped up and telling cards with one of
her friends, and I remember how, her cards obviously
being no use, she thanked me so prettily, and said to her
companion I was a good husband, and a saint to her.
This stabbed me through, I confess. As if somehow I
knew what was to happen next.

Oh, I cannot deny it. Here and there, since the
fourth year of our marriage, I had known other women.
Not many, but a few. And spring and early summer that
year had woken up in me some sleeping lion. I had recognized it, and paid it no heed, for I was well into my
thirties by then, and expected nothing that way.

The Gardens of Diana lie behind Fulvia, uphill.
They were once a property of a prince of Venus, but now
his palace was pulled down. Instead some classical statu-
ary had recently been dug up there, notably a Diana with
her hounds, old as ancient Rome.

The apothecary's shop lay in an alley across the
Centurion's Bridge, on the Neptune side—that is, the
pagan side.

I entered it, and told the old man's assistant what
had been recommended. Then the apothecary himself

came out, peering from a seeing-lens fixed in his right eye. "Yes, she will need galingala, nutmeg and ginger, cloves . . . and powder of pearl, I think. She has had no trouble when eating a fish with a shell?" I said not, and off he went to make up the dose.

There was another in the shop—a servant, I thought. Now he turned to me and said, "Are you a gravedigger, sir?"

"I am of the Grave Guild."

"You're a Master, I believe."

"Yes."

"Well then, might I make bold and ask if you will come with me to my lady. Her house is only up by the Diana Gardens."

This was once a choice area, now rather less so.

"Is your mistress near death?" I asked sternly. I was not in my guild wear, and wondered how he knew me, and if some trick was afoot.

"No! No, no, sir. She is very well."

"Why am I needed then?"

He lowered his voice. "It is to do with a certain situation. She has written to your Gravemakers' Guild, it's true, but then no one has yet answered her letter. I know you, sir, from the day of the Borja wedding."

"How?"

"I saw you, sir. I saw you with the men of the della Scorpias, crossing the Primo Square."

Again I thought this might be some curious ploy. But why should it be? It sounded like the sort of business I had supposed to be Como's own—some matter of tombs or other grave arrangements.

He looked honest enough, this fellow. And he had been buying a tincture, the kind a woman might use for her eyes, perhaps inflamed by weeping at a funeral.

"What is your lady's name?"

"Flavia Tressi," he said.

No loud trumpet sounded, or bell rang out. I own I thought it a noble-sounding name, that was all.

Maybe all this was, too, once my medical errand was done, an excuse to put off going home.

The Tressi house stood on the south side of the Gardens, rising up from a narrow, weedy canal. We entered the door, and presently I was shown up to her private room.

This caught the sun, and so did she. She had been sitting at a desk in a much-carven chair, on a silk cushion—but the silk was faded, like the painted walls. Still, it was an attractive room, a woman's, but not cluttered or full of small fussy items. I saw mostly books, and pens.

And she? She was no longer quite young, about nine and twenty, I thought (in fact, she was somewhat older), and of a lithe, full figure. She had an olive complexion, a quantity of hair the shade of dark honey, and showed no signs of tears or unhappiness.

The instant I saw her, I knew. I can say nothing else. Indeed, I do not properly see how to explain myself, or what occurred. This meeting with a stranger was like meeting again someone well-known to me. And yet, at the same second, an excitement came with it, almost a fear. Later she told me, it had been the same for her.

Of that she gave no sign, and nor did I. Practiced dissemblers, both.

"Well, madam. Your man told me you need some service of my guild."

She said that she did. Her voice was low, and pleasing. I sat down, and I remember to this hour the bowl of winter-stored apples on a table, and the scent of them that mingled with her own.

She told me what she required. It will do no harm to speak of it, now. Her husband had been a cloth merchant who had worked at his commerce in the City. He had been a good deal older than she—she was married to him at thirteen—and, two years before, he had died. His body had been duly cremated and placed in an ash-grave on the Isle. "But, you see, that hadn't been his true desire. And he asked me that, should the other ever become possible, I would arrange matters for him."

There had been some family dispute—she did not tell me what—which had barred his remains from the family vault at Veronavera. Now her husband's sister had written to say that the one dissenting member, who was getting on in years, had at last bethought him of pious charity, and withdrawn his veto.

"Therefore, Messer da Loura, I should like the grave here opened so I can remove his ashes, and inter them where he had always wished."

I replied that there would be some formalities, but that I anticipated no obstacle at all, and I would take it on myself to see to everything for her.

She thanked me very much, and then a little maid came in with a jug of bitter walnut-milk for us—which is the only sort of milk I have ever liked to drink.

Well, I stayed a while, and we talked of other ordinary things, like old friends, or new ones who do not want to separate, and then I drew myself together and took my leave of her. I told her, at her room's door, that her act was very worthy, and heard myself say it and felt a fool; and then, to my horror, I blurted like a very boy that not all widows would be so honorable, after the death of a husband so much the elder.

But Flavia Tressi thanked me, as if I had paid her a compliment. Then she said, "He was very generous to me, you know. He taught me a vast amount about his trade, and he also taught me how to read and write. I never loved him, 'ser da Loura, in a romantic way, but I was fond of him, and I respected him greatly."

"Of course, madam. I spoke out of turn."

She went on, as if I had not said this, as if I had every right to know all her affairs: "Besides, we must surely honor the promises made to the dead. Oh, not in case they might take umbrage or grieve—I think, neither. But how could he have rested when *alive*, if he'd thought I would not keep my promise to him after he was dead? And, too . . ." she hesitated, then said, "though he may not now remember, or care—something may. Some part of him . . ."

I was left speechless by this philosophy, so sensible, so kindly, so strange.

Then I parted from her.

And outside, as I was rowed across to the lagoons, my blood seemed full of the sunlight and I thought, in shame and wonderment, *I am in love.*

My wooing of Flavia Tressi was not in the common way, then. I would visit her as I arranged for the opening of her dead husband's grave. If our hands touched, it was over guild papers or the deeds of burial.

But we talked of other things as well, though none concerned the two of us together. (I regret to say, when I mentioned my wife Pia's improving health, I was sorry to catch no reaction in Flavia beyond polite solicitousness.) Our talk, though, told us a deal about each other. Of our lives, and what we knew. Flavia's intelligence and learning quickly impressed me very much. She attributed them to her husband's teaching, though they were evidently, too, the result of her own good mind. But unlike many who are clever, she was not chilly. Nor was she dustily dry.

I do not know if she was then beautiful. Which is, of all of it, perhaps the oddest thing. I recognize, as the next man will, beauty or its lack, in others. But she—I could not take my eyes from her—even when we parted, I could not, for she moved constantly across the floors of my mind—and yet, if she was lovely or not I cannot say. I might exclaim, I should have loved her if she had been cruelly deformed or raving mad. How can I know? She was as she was. Yet, too, I think if I had first set eyes on her and she had been dead, even then, I would have loved her, and hopelessly then, but still, always.

It began to be that the evening would come on as we spoke. Pia was well again, but my house stayed full of her friends—they all thought me off on guild business, as I had been. As the light went, candles were lit, and Flavia would invite me to a small supper alone with her. And then one evening, the night also came on, and she took me up to her roof. And there she showed me the stars through a series of ground lenses, which she said her husband had commissioned from the Glassmakers' Guild. What a sight, those stars, blazing and huge, and luminous shadows near them, which she said were the ghosts of other stars, or so she thought. But also I saw the faces of the planets—Mercurius, and Jupiter, and even Venus—and they are not as we see them with the naked eye. But I will not say any more of that, for some of you may think such gazing blasphemous. Although neither she nor I thought so.

Flavia said the ancient races had watched the stars as we did that night. And there on her roof, among the pots of herbs and flowers, I said, "Why do you put apothecary's drops into your eyes?"

She turned and looked at me, and said quietly, "I read a great amount, and sometimes they're tired."

"I don't believe you," I said. "Your eyes are brighter than the stars."

And in that moment I could have thrown myself off the roof. For who was I, a man past thirty-three years, to say such words to her? And what words, too, so false-sounding and worthless (though I had meant them): your eyes are brighter than the stars—

But she said, "They are so bright then, because I have been looking at you."

I took her to me. And to me she came.

After a pause I said, "You recall that I'm married?"

"Of course. At our age, we must be married, or bereaved."

Then she led me down into the house again, and into another room, where her bed was.

DIONYSSA

BORN LATE TO HER MOTHER, she had also been wedded late. She had stood at the altar at nineteen years of age. And then her husband had taken her away with him, to the Frankish lands, and left her there for safety when he joined Borja's armies. Yves de Mars had been slain only last summer. A year ago to this day.

It had not even been war, only some plot of Borja's enemies at Fensa; some fighting, a scatter of casualties, but one of them—him. Then she had come back to her own, the della Scorpia's, in the City of Venus. She had not wanted to go on living in Frankish lands, an Italian noblewoman, a widow who—there—must wear white to mourn, like the Frankish queens.

So. Late to birth, late to her wedding. Early to widow-hood.

She was yet young enough to miss a husband, they said. But had she loved him? Like all such marriages, it was made for policy. Or had been, then.

Dionyssa de Mars sat in her chamber in the Palazzo Scorpia near Aquila, playing Franchian songs on her viola-lute painted with marigolds. She also sang in Franchian. What had she had to employ her all that while, left among the bluish, dripping woods which ringed Yves de Mars's fortress-house, but to learn her husband's language, and a few suitable songs.

> *Sweetest, keep the promise*
> *That long before you made me,*
> *Since never will my heart seek*
> *A new love or another lord.*

"Is she sad?" the della Scorpias asked each other now and then.

The whole house groaned under its misfortunes—the bastard son drowned, the hideous devouring by rats of an upper servant—life was well-endowed with horror. Not to mention inconvenience. Who was to chaperone the younger daughters, now that Euniche was gone? Who would be the butt of the young men s jokes, now that Grasotti lay under the water?

> *And if I am blessed with anguish*
> *I shall be consoled by gentle thoughts,*
> *And only wish to honor*
> *And enoble you the more.*
> *Sweetest, keep the promise—*

"Dissa must feel the cold now at night."

Dionyssa wore a black gown, unrelieved by color, and her pastel yellow hair was today partly caught back under a stiffened velvet hood, in the Frankish manner. The melody faded in the otherwise silent room.

Dionyssa laid aside the viola.

A moment later, her door opened without a knock. It was her mother.

Donna Caterina glanced about the chamber, and took in Dionyssa apparently as part of its furnishing. She had never approved of this child, visited on her so late (she had been thirty-six). Caterina approved of little anyway, except God.

"I have spoken to Como," said Caterina. She pursed her lips. One sensed, she approved least of all of him. "It is not the first time. One has to remind him always."

Dionyssa, who had risen from courtesy, looked at her mother.

"I mean," said Caterina della Scorpia, "I've spoken to him, again, on the subject of your remarriage."

Dionyssa lowered her eyes.

"Why did you do that, Mother?"

"Why? Because you're young enough to wed again, and to bear the children which your last husband was unable to give you, being so seldom," her lips now seemed quite hard, a curious thing, for lips, "at home."

"I don't wish it, Mother."

"No, perhaps not. But it is wished for you."

"By whom?"

"Your house. What else? You are marriageable. If not in your first bloom, now as a widow you have those estates de Mars gifted you in Franchia."

"Very well, the house of Scorpia wants me to remarry to secure another alliance. Is this necessary, Mother? Surely—"

"Never more needful than now. You've seen how we are treated. How the beasts of Barbaron have used us, and this Ducem, whose father showed much favor to us, does nothing. Yes, we must ally with strong friends, Dissa. They are no longer afraid of us, those Barbarons. They think us old and toothless. But they're mistaken!" Her eyes sparked, and she stood straight as an iron spear topped with a black wig.

Dionyssa regarded this, then again she looked away.

She had been brought to the attention of Borja, at the Palazzo Bene, and this had initially seemed only correct, for Yves de Mars had been one of his captains. But later Dionyssa had seen that, by doing this, too, general attention was drawn to her: to her comparative youngness; her widowhood, her ownership of Frankish land; her connections, however tenuous, with a conqueror.

Caterina had lost her brief fire. She sat down in a chair and plucked at the scrolling relief on its arm.

"You are absurd, Dissa. What was that man to you? He was not an Italian—he was a foreigner Como gave you to, to further some foolish aim. And here you sit about moping. Yes, it may give you an allure, and is a cunning way to show how faithful you are. But no one else is here now. No one else sees."

"No."

"You must put yourself into a prepared state of mind. You must be ready."

"What did Lord Como say to you?"

"That he was agreeable. You were too young to be alone And *I* say, I won't have you a burden to our house. You're no parasite. You shall be useful."

Dionyssa thought, angrily, secretly, *Why did I never conceive a child? That would have made me more awkward to sell again. And I might have argued for my freedom, with a child to tend. But here is my only choice now. Another marriage, or some nunnery.*

She had nothing left of him. There was a little portrait, painted on wood—but it did not look like Yves at all. She had the lands—they were so far way, even when she had been among them. His family had not liked her. She could not stay there. They hated it that he had left her land, and tried always to take it from her, and gladly she would have let them, but she was also a della Scorpia, and well-schooled. She must keep everything, in the interests of her own kind, her house.

No, he had not been an Italian. Yet he had spoken her language fluently, and elegantly. He had taught her a little Franchian—she was later able to obtain more.

When she had been with him, it did not concern her that they each talked the other's tongue with an accent, or in what country they were. Now that he was dead, she sometimes wondered *where* she was, for pieces of her seemed to have been taken away with him, but he had left her with nothing.

Caterina was saying something else. Ah, it was about the viola, that the pattern (Frankish) was not well-painted on it. But now she was getting up. Praise the Christ, she was going away again.

It had never been possible to debate with her mother. Dionyssa's mighty self-control had been learned in childhood, holding down her urge to rage and battle that resulted only in punishment. She had learned to speak without emotion, and to deceive.

"Think of what I've said to you."

"Yes, mother. I will certainly think of it."

Como was slow, as a rule, about such arrangements as betrothals. He left them to others, as in the case of another daughter of this house, the pitiful, mysterious, lost Meralda. Como would be tardy. Nothing would happen immediately. Yet, probably now, it *would* happen.

She had been frightened, meeting Yves on that first occasion, when they had put her hand into his. She had believed herself plain, and that he might be vicious. But his eyes had been dark and full of humor, and his hand had been warm, and he had said, "They never told me you were so charming." And she had believed he thought so, and been glad to be thought charming by him, and suddenly her fear had melted from her, and she knew herself happy. But it was not only his kin who had been jealous. God had been jealous too. He had seen them shining in their garden and plucked Yves like a flower and thrown him away, and left her behind to wither like the grass.

BEATRIXA

THERE EVEN IN THE BACK of her child's chair, the Barbaron motto had been carved. Carved small, it was true, and between two birds. But the birds sat on a tower-top, and the motto ran from their beaks and read, *Vita gaudemus, in morte nil timemus.*

Beatrixa lowered her candle.

She stared about.

The big room was unfamiliar, as if she had seldom seen it or any of its furniture, although she had slept here since her twelfth birthday; she could remember having them bring the little chair, despite being unable, any longer, to sit on it.

Disgusted, she thought, why inscribe such words on a baby's chair? *Joyful in life, fearless in death.* How could one be either, unless one was a fool?

Beatrixa walked to her mirror, which was of Venus glass, and looked into it, and saw herself standing there. She wore her shift and an overgown of velvet for the night, and her hair was loosely plaited with a velvet cord, to save her from its violence. When she was a child, too, the nurse had threatened her that, if she were bad, her own mass of hair would come loose and strangle her during sleep. "I wish I could cut off my hair!" Beatrixa had announced, terrifying the would-be terrifier, who then tried to hide from her for weeks any sort of implement which might be used in cutting, including the supper knife.

That tyranny, the nurse's, was long gone. At least now, Beatrixa might do as she wanted behind the closed door of her bedchamber. Why, she had even brought her lovers here, and been possessed by them too, her own strong, narrow hands providing their unreal but vividly imagined love-making and the delirium of physical release.

Who had there been?

A captain of the palazzo guardsmen—alas, he had died last year of a sickness—and a companion of her cousins, from the Strotsi family—but only once, he was unworthy—and others, very many; she was profligate with her affections, then. Even on one night, when she was fifteen, she had fictionally brought into her bed an older man glimpsed in a wanderer on the canal... he had been blond-haired.

How did she know what a man would do with a woman? She had listened, observed. Intimations were all around. Besides, she was well read, and now and then had come upon some unvetted reference, in Catullus, for example.

All this was a sin, she knew. She had never revealed what she did, to a priest, or to any other. In the beginning, this was because she did not *think* it a sin. Then, when various dubious warnings were cast at her (by the nurse, her own mother, and the very priest who heard her confessions), Beatrixa was taken aback at their ridiculousness, their unwisdom. For how was *this* sin a sin at all? However, she had inferred enough not to deflower herself, which might otherwise, perhaps, have accidentally happened.

And now. Her tingling blood would bring her thoughts of only one man with whom to slake her body.

Save, he was no longer a man, but one of the dead.

She turned from the mirror and paced to and fro. The white dog, which had been lying by the window, got up and began to pace with her.

"Well, Leone," she said to it, as they stalked up and down. "Well . . . shall we run away, just you and I? Shall we?"

The dog wagged its tail.

If only they might—yet, then, there was her father.

Beatrixa liked her father, loved him. It was he, indeed, who, by allowing her to read where she wished, had assisted her to think as she would.

She supposed she must always have been impressed by him, to some extent, he was a powerful and dramatic figure about the Palazzo Barbaron. But Andrea had won her over personally, too, not with constant attention, of which many of her female relatives provided too much, but through intermittant shows of firm interest, treating her as no other did. Once, when she was thirteen, and again a year later, he had taken her with him to Veronavera. There had been the usual ladies to care for her, of course, and she had had to travel in a slow carriage drawn by mules. But at the castle, a smoky, towering cliff, Andrea had spent time with her among the echoing chambers. He had shown her, in the Hall, the battle honors of the Barbarons, from the time of the Crusades. And the library in a turret, and the physic and fruit gardens enclosed by the great walls. He had had her taught to ride as well, on the hills above the river. And when she said she would have preferred to do this astride, like a man, he nodded, not shocked, but added, "You must wait for that Triche, till you're wed. Then, why not." She had thought at the time it was considered improper for a maiden to ride other than sidesaddle. But by now she knew that astride a horse, also, a girl might lose her maidenhead. Preposterous. She balked at such a precaution, yet saw its meaning.

For Andrea had infused her too with the awareness of house honor. And somehow, even before Andrea gave her much notice, Beatrixa had been concerned with the honor of the Barbarons.

And now, too. Now she was a woman. Still, she was proud of who she was, and of her name, and fastidiously kept up the duties of her position.

But she had ceased much to value them. It was because she valued Andrea that she stayed within the strict palisade of her station, and tendered it due homage. And she knew this as well. And sometimes it made her half afraid, for what if—what if she ceased to revere and love her father? Oh, this could never be—but if—if this were to take place—or, if he were to die. . . .

Which brought her again to death, to the dead.

It was madness. Silvio was not dead. Was not a ghost. He was—a dream, one more lover she had conjured. A contrary one, an enemy. And if others had seen him too, and they *had*, no matter. He was gone now.

The dog called Lion bristled, and a soft growl rumbled in the engine of its body.

Beatrixa saw, across the room, in the mirror, the reflection.

She spun about.

An old man was sitting in her other chair, the adult one. His head was covered by white hair and he leaned it on a hand like a winter leaf. His face was fallen and deeply seamed, and out of it gazed two ink-black eyes that gave a silvery light. . . .

"Silvio—" the name came out of her like escaping life. And then, stupidly, "Why are you old?"

The old man said, "I believed you would prefer

me like this. A feeble dotard. Too decrepit to lay a finger on you."

Her heart stopped in her breast.

She said, "You told me that . . . you couldn't read my thoughts."

"I can't read them. I have come up here on other nights, since our last meeting in the church of Maka Selena. I've watched you sleeping, dreaming. When you dream, sometimes you speak aloud."

"What do I say?" she whispered.

She knew, if it were so, what she must have said. In her dreams she had not denied herself the vision of Silvio that, awake, she refused.

And he, reading her or not, said nothing now.

"Why are you here?"

"That song again. I am here because I like to be here. I must tell you anyway, Beatrixa Barbaron, you could not have me even if you would. I mean, you couldn't lie with me in the carnal mode, thigh to thigh—"

She felt her cheeks grow hot, then cool.

"Since you're a ghost," she said acidly.

"Am I a ghost? Do you think me a ghost? What do you think me?"

"A trickster."

"Yes. But not with you."

"It's all one. A cat is still a cat, even if you dress it in a mouse-skin."

"The old riddle. Answer this one then: I have me a wolf from the plain, and a ewe-sheep, and a bag of fragrant clover. And I must take them over the lagoon, from one side to the other side. But my boat will only hold myself and one of these other things at one time, the wolf, the sheep, or the clover—or go down. How then am I to transport them? For if I take them one by one, two of them must stay together on one shore or the other, without me. And though the wolf will not eat the clover, the sheep *will* eat it, or if I leave the sheep with the wolf on either shore, the wolf will eat the sheep."

She stared hard at him. This lively old man, sitting up now, eager and alert with his puzzle, offering it to her. He had said, he liked to play.

She replied slowly, "There is something like this in Pliny, and in Babrius too." She frowned, remembering it with care, and she was a moment like a solemn child, posted there in the body of a young woman. "You must first take the sheep across to the other shore and leave it there. Come back for the wolf and leave that on the other shore—but return with the sheep. Then leave the sheep on the first shore again, and take the clover across where the wolf is. Then return lastly for the sheep once more."

"Perhaps," said the old man. No, he did not look so very old now. His hair was much longer, fuller, and of a ripening shade. "Or, there is another way."

"None," said Beatrixa. "It's a problem of logic, and has only one answer."

"And I, it seems, have only this one small boat. But also having foresight, I understood that one day I would have to transport a wolf, a sheep, and a bag of clover. So then, I chose a wolf-cub and a lamb, and brought them up together, feeding them by hand, bedding them in the same pen. Farmers will do this, and then keep the wolf as a guard dog. It will guard the sheep with its life, let me tell you, and the sheep will run to the wolf in any tribulation. In addition, I shall have made sure the sheep has often had a taste of clover, but before ever I allowed this, I had sprinkled the clover with something sour no sheep would care for. Soon my sheep had no wish to sample any clover, thinking all of it tastes foul. Thus, on the momentous day, I can take any of my three possessions across the lagoon, leaving any other two of them alone together. The wolf won't eat the sheep, thinking they are brother and sister; the sheep won't eat the clover thinking it will taste, as ever, bad. While I can do as I want."

"This is a parable of forethought, then. Or of manipulation by cunning," said she with asperity.

"How stern you are." (He was no longer old. He had been seventy, forty, thirty. Now he was young, two or three years her senior, and his hair was like a flood of molten gold.)

"You are not *meant*, Signore Silvio, to alter the rules of logic."

"Why not? What am I, sweetheart, if not the proof that logic will not always apply."

"Oh," she said.

He smiled. His beautiful, overwhelming smile, that dissolved her bones, weakening her, so she sat down on the stool by the mirror.

"I'll tell you something else," he said. "Have you heard of Beatifica, the saint who brought the saving fire?"

"I've heard of her. The Church—"

"Confound the bloody Church," he said mildly, "listen. They burned her in turn, as a heretic. But her heart would *not* burn. It was saved in a golden box and kept in the church of the Lullaby of Tears, La'Lacrima. Here it worked miracles. The lame walked, the blind became able to see, and the dumb to speak. Have you heard of *that*?"

"Yes. But the miracles were long ago."

"Belief grew less strong. And then, some years back the box disappeared. It was searched for, but never found—like other things in this city of water."

"I have heard that, too."

"Well," he said, "I know where the Box of the Heart is." She looked at him. She scarcely heard what he said at all. "I've seen it, Beatrixa Barbaron, sweet wolf never trained to love us, we poor della Scorpia sheep. I've seen the casket with the heart of a saint."

She shook her head,

"Your della Scorpias are the wolves," she said flatly. "Where is the casket then?"

"Under Silvia. In the mud. Deep down. *You* are the wolves."

"Our emblem was once an eagle. Now it is a tower. How is the casket there?"

"Probably stolen. By one whose boat would only carry a single item, and had too much in it, since the heart of a saint would weigh a great amount—and the boat sank, and the casket went into the salt-mud. The Silvia Lagoon was once a marsh. I was named for the Silvia Lagoon. I'll tell you now why I am here."

He got to his feet, and crossed the room and stood above her. She gazed up into his face, and was blinded, and even the Heart of Beatifica could not have helped her.

"Go to your father," said Silvio della Scorpia. "Say that you have something to ask."

". . . and then?"

"Then ask him this: When was it that he met with Meralda della Scorpia."

"I don't understand you."

"*He* will understand *you*. He will go flaming red and mad, or white as stone."

"Why—why?" She too had stood up, and as she did so, he caught her against him.

And she felt, the length of her flesh, the pressure of his body that was not, and could not *be* flesh, or anything

of the world, that truly she could never have or be possessed by—and she seemed turned to snow.

"I said, Beatrixa, I would give you a question, not
answer one."

"Why are you so adamant—what has he done, my
father, that you want to—to drive him mad?"

"Ask. He may tell you. If he doesn't, his *face* will tell it
all. Be prepared for him to strike you, too. That's nothing to
you, is it? You're brave. Meralda was not. She had not one
hundredth part of your courage—nor of your good luck."

His face, too, told her everything. It was like a
demon's—handsome, not foul, and the worse for that.

"Am I to have heard of Meralda della Scorpia?"

"Have you not? I think you have. If so, perhaps you
can put it together alone. But ask him anyway, Andrea
Barbaron, your lord and father. *Ask him.*"

And in that terrible moment, he shook himself free
of her. This rejection of flesh was as she had once heard
a lightning-strike described. Scalding yet cold, glittering.
He had killed her—yet she was still standing there,
drained of blood and life.

He was her enemy.

As her eyes cleared, she saw that he was gone
once more, had vanished into air, as a spirit or devil
always could.

She went to the Castello library in the morning, quite
late, at the time when house business was usually being
concluded.

Sure enough, Lanto and Oliviotto were collecting
up their papers, and the ledgers were being put away.

Andrea Barbaron turned around, saw her, and
grew affable.

"Good day, Triche. How are you?"

"Very well, my lord."

"You look a little pale. Some early peaches came this morning from the garden at Verona. You must eat some."

"Yes, Father, then I will. Thank you."

"And look," he said, coming towards her, nearly jocular, "these books have arrived, too. *You'll* want to see them, I expect."

The secretaries were bowing, going out.

Beatrixa stood straight in the summer light of the windows.

Andrea gazed back at her, narrowing his eyes. When he did this, a crafty, porcine look came over him. He was very heavy now, a bulkily-muscled, fat, high-colored man in his high-colored mantle of Barbaron red.

What do I know of him? Nothing. Lord, Father—these were titles.

"What is it?" he said.

"I have something to ask you."

"It must be no joking matter, this something."

"I think not."

"Come, sit down here at the table. Drink this wine."

Don't be kind to me. Because, presently, all that may end for ever—

Yet, why should it? Demons lied. It was their faculty. They *lied*.

He pushed the goblet towards her. In the crimson glass, the Barbaron tower, hatched with gold. What had they ever talked of, her father and she? Cerebral topics, or frivolous meaningless things—

Yes, I will ask, but not as you would have me do it, Silvio della Scorpia, my enemy, my devil.

"There is an old story, Father. I heard it in childhood, oh, I forget where I heard it. But unsuitably, it's begun to unsettle me. I say unsuitably, not because it isn't a horrible story—it is—but because it concerns the house of our foes, the Scorpion house."

Trying to scan his features, her own eyes flickered. She steadied them.

Andrea thought in turn, *I have seen eyes like those behind a drawn sword.* (And, she saw him think it.)

"Don't prevaricate. You're my daughter. Speak out."

"A high-born girl of that house, Meralda was her name." His face had not altered, nor his color. He simply waited.

Beatrixa looked away from him, and took a mouthful of the wine he had poured for her.

She knew the tale, who did not? And she had already been reminded by the threats of the della Scorpias who abducted her. Originally she had heard maids' chatter, one stormy night when the sea had roared and the lagoons churned. Meralda, betrothed to an evil lord, had fled with her lover, some artisan. Had been betrayed or caught. Tortured, murdered, discarded into Aquila. Down in the salt-mud, like the Casket of the Heart.

She had *not* heard from the chatter any mention of Meralda's betrayers. (The servants would have kept one rumor at least that night away from Beatrixa's honed, childish ears.) While the della Scorpia louts, sitting by Beatrixa in the boat, had accused another—Gualdo.

But Silvio—what had he intended? What did he mean?

Ask him: When was it that he met with Meralda della Scorpia. He will go red and mad and white as stone and strike you—

If he is the one—if he did this, my father, gave her to such

*an end—if he says that it was he—how will I ever look at him
again, or, if there is one scrap of a soul in him, he at me, his own
daughter, if, if he did this thing—*

"Meralda, yes," Andrea said. "I've heard of it. Much
of Venus talked of her, for a while."

"Yes, *that* story," Beatrixa said.

"Well, I'm surprised it stays with you. Yes, a grim
affair. But it's done. Thirty years and more, done."

"Perhaps."

"What does *that* mean? Come, Triche, this isn't like
you."

Beatrixa gathered herself up. "Then, my lord, let
me ask you—" she began. She stopped. The breath of life
seemed to leave her. She stared, rigid, beyond Andrea's
bolstered shoulder to where, across the sunny room,
Silvio stood beside a cabinet of large, gilded books. The
light caught them, and him, and all the embroidered
gold of his doublet and his hair. "I—" she said, "I would
ask you, sir—" And Silvio shook his head at her. He
raised his hand and touched his own lips, as if sealing
them, then again he shook his head. His face was
unnervingly grave, as she had most often witnessed it.
Not as she had beheld it last.

"What can you see?" Andrea turned sharply, looking behind him.

"There is—" she faltered.

"What? There's nothing—what is it?"

"There is nothing there," she said.

She stared on at Silvio, whom Andrea could not see,
or was not permitted now to see. Silvio had begun to
laugh. She could *hear* it, this male, musical laughter. And
Andrea could *not* hear it. But then Silvio reached out and
pulled all the books from the cabinet, flinging them
down. They fell with a crash on to the floor.

"Blood of Christ!" Andrea lunged up from his seat.

"Who's there?" he roared. He strode over the room, lurching slightly, huge against the light, and as he went he *passed through* Silvio della Scorpia, who stood there laughing at him.

Andrea halted. This, something of this sort, had happened before. He glanced down at the fallen volumes, and saw his shadow thrown there from the sun and beside it, a second shadow that, even as he observed it, faded like moisture on a hot stone.

"This room is haunted," Andrea said. He was not greatly unnerved, only somewhat startled. "It's gone now. What did you see?"

"I don't know. But yes, it's gone."

With a grunt, he bent and picked up one of the books, carried it back to the table, and slapped it down there.

"These things happen," he said. "It's a new house, but the foundations are old."

Beatrixa said, "You believe ghosts come back to haunt us." Her voice was faint, soft. Andrea thought she had had a fright. And on top of the other thing: superstition, tattle. She was a woman, after all.

"No, Triche. I don't think they haunt us. But I think there are ghosts."

"How can there be? After death we sleep, to wait for Judgment, and Heaven or Hell—" Did she plead?

"That's the priests' version," said Andrea. He felt gloomy suddenly, out of sorts. There had been a coldness in the sunlight, where the phantom must have been, and it had touched more than his books. "Now, to your other matter. What did you mean to ask?"

Her color had returned, he saw. She was not swooning or carrying on as most women would.

"I simply meant to ask you if it were true," she said.

"That story of Meralda? That Ciara slaughtered her? God knows. I don't, Triche. I don't know. But Ciara gained a name afterwards that reeks like a three-week carcass. And Meralda—" he paused.

Silvio had prevented her from asking. But even so, did she still see it in her father's face? Something unspeakable, something long ago, which he had done?

"Meralda's at peace," said Andrea Barbaron weightily. "That's all we can hope from death. Peace in Heaven. Or peaceful sleep in ashes or a bed of earth."

But Hell, she thought, *what of that?*

S I L V I O

A WOLF AND A SHEEP lay side by side under the cypress trees, among some clovers, and watched him with tranquil eyes as he went past. When he looked back from higher ground, they were no longer there.

The dusk had begun. The sky was a peacock's feather, violet, Tyrian blue, and emerald.

Now in shade, the palazzo continued to glow from its memories of daylight, and even as he approached, his mother's servants were lighting the candles and the lamps, so the windows each became a single recurring day.

"Mother, tell me what I am?"

"Mine," she said. "And your own."

"You," he said, "are a mighty sorceress. If I hadn't known it, my books would have informed me. You are great as Melusina or Cleopatra, or the goddess-women of the barbarous northern world: Grania, Morcandia . . . and I am your son. So what am I?"

"Whatever you desire."

"That I know. Are there no limitations?"

"Oh," she said, "none."

"There you're wrong. There are some after all."

She sighed. She lifted one hand a few inches, and

the unseen musicians started to play. Delicate note trickled to note.

He sat on the floor of the chamber, resting his head
against her knees as she leaned back in her tall, carved
chair. Sometimes his mother stroked the hair from his
forehead. Her hands were scented with bergamot, and
she was younger than he. But that was usually the case.

The room was full of lampshine, crystalline yet
warm. When he was a child he had sometimes tried to
count the lamps, which hung down from chains of silver
as fine as eyelashes. It was never possible.

Silvio sank into the state of quietness, almost trance,
that was habitual to them both when together. They did
not really talk to each other very often. And yet, they
communicated, without words, by some process he had,
formerly, never considered.

But this, too, had happened with Beatrixa. She had
believed Silvio able to divine her thoughts. That was not
what he did. It was more as if she breathed into him the
meditations—not of her brain—but of her body. Though
he had seen her dreaming, too. And once, when asleep,
she had spoken his name.

From the first, it had no longer been simple, none
of it, with *her*.

She was to have been his pathway to Andrea, the father.
To allow him to damage Andrea in ways other than those of
a demonic eel or a flamingo-golem. To chastise him, rather,
with scorpion whips of the psyche. And then, and then—
Beatrixa. The arrogant, fierce child . . . the severe and grace-
ful, restrained woman, whose silence lay about her, even
when she spoke the most, like folds of a samite curtain.

Their unseen slaves came floating round them now.
They poured white wine into cups transparent green as
the waters surrounding this island.

Silvio thought he had drifted asleep. He was so comfortable, nothing need concern him. What he was, what he felt, or must do. That had never been his, none of that rubbish to which a human man was shackled.

And yet, he had prevented Beatrixa, at the last second, from asking the deadly question. He had wanted to save her from that. Why was this? He knew why it was.

"You are a sorceress," he said again to his mother, out of his half-trance. "Will you give me what I most dearly desire?"

"I'll give you anything."

"I wonder if you can."

"What is it?" she said.

"A woman that I want," he said.

"Oh, that would be easy. For either of us to do."

"No, mother. Not a woman of that design, not like the birds that come and go, and the animals. Not a creature we make for ourselves. Not like those. This is a woman who is really alive and lives in the world we have left, you and I, a woman of mortal flesh."

He felt her shift away from him. Her caressing hands were gone.

Silvio also shifted, and looked at her. Her eyes had stretched wide, and she was so much younger than he, three years or five, his mother.

He had never until now imagined, seen, her afraid. Was she afraid? Was this her terror?

Silvio felt a sense of abject loss, a despair coupled incongruously to fury. Had he felt such an emotion ever? Even working out their vengeance, surely, he had never felt any of that.

She said, "What are you talking of? You speak as if we were dead—"

"Mother, we are."

She rose from the chair. A razored gleam came from her, like sun striking on ice.

"Not as you mean it. Say nothing else. Say nothing."

She was walking away from him, over the silky lagoon floor that was like the glass of the goblets.

Was she fearful cracks would appear, and let the water through? Or the roof would collapse, or the sky?

He was sorry to have dismayed her. He was angry. He thought of Beatrixa, and a darkness flashed through his mind. If he was not of her clay, also neither was he of the clay of the mother who had borne him. He was, then, unmatched with anything he had ever known. He saw it now.

But his mother was gone into the dusk beyond the door, and the sky in the windows was all emerald now, like her name.

MERALDA

WITHIN ONE MOMENT, a million years—

And in the four minutes, the amount of time it had taken, less than a single second.

. . . I beheld . . . the church of Maka Selena pass . . . drifting above and away . . . I saw the bottom of the lagoon, which was inky, and cold . . . I remember the cold . . .

All confusion assembled into this chaos.

A sensation of falling down and down. Of heaviness, suffocation, blindness, and the roaring of the sea, and salt, the scorching taste of the salt. And—

—not fear. Or the fear only of the body and the mind. Something other—

—more unthinkable, less human—

Then

I glimpsed . . .

The drowning creature experienced her own expulsion from the flesh, but far away. Some different part of her was aware of it more immediately. And this part gazed back, and outward, and down—or *up*—and saw the dying girl, floating in her skeins of hair, only a doll. But there, embedded in her like a gem, was another something, which was not yet anything much, not yet truly sentient, not yet two days old in its forming, but clasped in the death of her: the seeded child inside her womb.

And, though mostly already dead, she, or the other incorporeal filament to which she was returning, took note.

Not one life then, but two, both of which *drowned*.

I glimpsed . . . (Bartolome, seeing too, if not all, in his boyhood dream fourteen years after. But how . . .?)

What lay beyond the world? Heaven, they said, or Hell.

Some choose Hell.

Meralda chose Heaven, or its shimmering shadow.

. . . *A mild green . . . a hill . . . more like an emerald—*

This was what her name meant, Meralda—*Emerald*.

Out of the depths she came, out, upward, or deeper down, carried on a rush like wings. And in this flight, she left behind her, in the lagoon, all her horror and her hurt, or meant to, along with her body and its death. But the child—her's, Lorenzo's—*that* she took with her.

She awoke on a shore. The sea was going in and out, but gently, more like the rippling of a lake. It was a lagoon, of course, and behind her rose an island, lavishly green in the glassy morning water.

The time was just after sunrise.

Meralda thought birds would fly across the sky, and then she saw the birds, flocks of them, making eloquent swirls and featherings against turquoise blueness.

Presently, Meralda got up.

She was quite dry, her clothes comfortable and pristine, her hair decoratively dressed. She felt, at first, tired and almost disorientated, as sometimes happens on waking up. But this was already fading. The air, with its scents of clean open water, and the flowers and trees which grew along the slope above, refreshed her like an elixir.

The way up from the shore was easy. A green path. Myrtles grew beside it, and tamarisk, giving a cloud of scent. And in the shrubs, as she would have expected, small birds flitted and hopped about. But they were of wonderful colors, primrose, cobalt, and flame, and somehow she had known they would be like this, too. Perhaps she had looked at such a scene illustrated in some book?

The island seemed familiar. Seemed nearly recollected. And she knew her way.

Further up the slope, lilac trees grew, and when the land folded outward—for the island was large—orchards of apple and damson. They were in blossom although, from the fig trees, the ripe fruit hung out its green pods, and peaches showed, too, like pink velvet globes.

When she hesitated to sample any of these, despite beginning to want them, something happened.

Someone went among the trees, and gathered up some of the fruits, then brought them to her in a little silver basket.

This someone was not visible.

However, from it streamed such an emanation of benign things—kindness, innocence, a wish to serve, lovableness even, and love itself—Meralda was not afraid or unnerved, even with the basket bobbing there in front of her seemingly unsupported.

She had been waited on all her life, before. If she had forgotten all that, or pushed it from her remembrance, nevertheless, certain fundamentals obtained. (For this reason she had found herself well-dressed, and been pleased to; nearly relieved.) But in the past she had been bullied, also. *Harmed.*

Now, here was a servant. A kind and loving servant, to whom she might entrust herself without a qualm.

And though she could see nothing of it, yet in a way,

she could. She did think she almost saw it, in fact, by use of another mechanism than sight. What it actually was she did not know, nor contemplate. Such questions did not matter any more. So much at least she realized.

The ethereal servant accompanied Meralda over the island, and sometimes (how?) showed her things: A natural fountain sparkling on stones, a wood of beech trees, grapevines with bells of olivine and rubicelle, bees and butterflies. Everything was beautiful, flawless. Not a blemish on it—*new*. And also, strangely, an air of incredible antiquity hung about the island. But age lighter than the atmosphere, like an ancient woman with wings.

There were animals, as well. Spotted deer came and went through the poppies, white birds fluttered around the trees, and a peacock walked across Meralda's path, his fan trailing like a train of jewels. There were no intransigently fierce or dangerous animals. She might have been alarmed at those, although here they would have done her no damage—and that she knew also, in a way, or might have done had she thought of it . . .

At the height of the island, the groves and woods centered in a garden. Here the trees were sculpted into a topiaria. Statues held shells dispatching spangled water, roses cascaded from urns of porphyry. Also there was an avenue of tall cypresses, which led to the house.

Never did she ask herself to whom this palace belonged. As with the rest, she was half familiar with it. This was, more than anything perhaps, a feeling of coming back, of return.

It had a look, however, the palace, of the Palazzo della Scorpia that stood, a million years and a moment away, in the City of Venus. But it was altered, youthful now and hotly-colored, among the wine-red roses.

When Meralda went into the house, it was lit with

sunlight from all its windows, which sometimes had glazing, and sometimes did not.

For the night, wonderful lamps like pearls of fan-
tastic size were suspended high up from silver threads. A
manmade fountain—although what man?—played, as in
the garden. There were no murals on the walls; there
could have been. But the della Scorpia murals had never
meant anything, or they had meant only awful things,
being emblems of house power. And so the palazzo of
Meralda rejected them and contained nothing to discon-
cert, as the island had no tigers or lions.

Indoors, the invisible servants flocked about her, as
the birds had flocked about the risen sun.

How welcomed she was, how lovingly taken care of.

Standing in the middle of this transparent, glimmering of force, Meralda put one hand for an instant
against her body. She rested the hand over her belly.
When a small girl, she had seen a lady of her house do
this, and enlighten her attendants . . .

Meralda spoke aloud, as she had to the servant met
outside.

"I'm with child." Solemnly she added, with no trace
of grief or panic, "My lord is dead. I will have a monument set up to his memory. In the future, his son will be
your lord, when he is a man."

Some items do linger, at least a while. The oddest of
life's customs, splinters, or even granite blocks, of eti-
quette and ritual. And love, love stays. What else, in such
places as these?

At the palazzo in Heaven (for so it will be easiest to call it),
Meralda grew up. And as she grew, so did the child she
gave birth to, early in the sixth month of her pregnancy.

She should have been afraid, but now she had no fear. Fear had been jettisoned in the lagoon, out of which she had brought so little—but so much: the name of her lover, Lorenzo, some dreams, her baby, and her soul.

Curious, in a way, that here she accepted Lorenzo's death—had spoken of it at once and, within another day, seen an obelisk (which should have been the work of months) erected to his loss. But then, if she had not allowed Lorenzo to be dead, Meralda would have needed to recreate him from the brilliant air. Which evidently she could have done. Thus on the level of her consciousness where this was known to her (for it was, though it was also hidden), she resisted indulgence of such a fantasy. For of all and everything, Lorenzo had been to her the most real. Since he was not automatically here with her, she would not fashion his image. After all, she thought herself still alive, and while in a magical world, still a *physical* world.

Demonstrably Heaven must have many mansions— once, we were told so—and they cannot be physical— maybe they are only the more absolute for that.

To Meralda, however, the island was built on earth. Somehow, and somewhere.

Nevertheless, she had no trepidation as she carried her child, and she was perfectly right to be unafraid.

When the hour came, she felt him move in her, without pain or upheaval. She went to her bed in the palace and, lying down between its slender posts, let the gentle invisible servant-spirits hover over and about her. Until, still with no pain or even any effort, they drew from her (apparent) body, in a mingling only of slight pressure and excited urgency, a baby. It was unmarked by blood or slime or any soiling, and it was male, as Meralda had known it would be.

There he lay, smiling, delightedly kicking, thrilled to be at liberty, among the unseen, careful hands. He was still attached to Meralda, but only by a birth-cord like a thin, silver rope. When this was bloodlessly severed, he drew his first breath, this newborn child of the afterlife, and broke out not into crying—but laughter. Laughter.

Silvio, the son of Lorenzo and Meralda—oh, what was he, what would he be? Another soul that loitered in this sumptuous mansion-waiting-room—or, something else? A ghost . . . what can a ghost be, if a soul need not remain? As Bartolome would say, we must come to that.

Only this should be believed of Silvio. He arrived in that wondrous otherwhere equipped with none of his mother Meralda's preconceptions or devices of forget-fulness. He came with his *own*. And like the Snake, Silvio, with his acts of play and vengeance, would introduce truth, shame, and evil into Paradise, and the knowledge of death.

PART FOUR
Heaven

Oh, it is then . . . that you are on the border-
land of Death's amazing kingdom, where
everything moves twice as fast, and the colors
are twice as bright, and love is twice as gorgeous, and sin is twice as spicy. Who but the
doubly purblind can fail to see that it is only
on the Other Side that one can begin to agree?

MERVYN PEAKE
Gormenghast

BARTOLOME

ONCE WE HAD BECOME LOVERS, Flavia and I, we met whenever we were able to. Which meant, of course, that I would visit her house. For a guildsman Master, in most trades, there are plenty of excuses for being away, and in mine none more. What with genuine business then, and the affair with my mistress, I was seldom at home.

At first, Pia seemed quite content with that, then she became fretful, then she turned abrasive. We exchanged unfriendly words, and afterwards I was sorry—not for my adultery, let it be said, since I could no more have regretted that than I would regret drawing breath—but to have upset my wife, to whom, under the circumstances, I owed extra fair-will. It seemed the strangest and most perverse thing, that I should be hurtful to Pia, at a time when I was so happy.

In fact, I had never stayed a full night in Flavia's bed, returning to my house often by the midnight bell, or at the worst, before Prima Vigile. Flavia and I would have preferred to remain longer together and to meet more frequently—generally one, at the most two days, in every week, were all we had. Then, it seemed to me a sacrifice we made for Pia' s sake. But, really, no doubt I was indulgent enough to myself. Even today, however, I cannot say I am contrite, or would do anything differently. Rather, I wish I had been yet more selfish. Truly, indeed.

The month of the Twins was gone. The Crab month had started, very warm, and with it the fetidness of the canals, drenching the City in a rain of stinks.

"I have a vineyard and a little house, Bartolo, at Veronavera," Flavia said to me, one baking noon as we lay on her sheets, the window shut despite the heat, because of the reek of the water below. "It's in the hills above the town. We could be cool there."

"If only," I said, "wishing could take us there."

She had spoken of the house once before. It was a property of her late husband's, but until the breach over his resting-place was mended, she had not had the heart, she said, to go.

"Now I would like to. Now and then I was there with him, and he taught me about the vine-stocks, and how to judge wine." (She was certainly adroit in that.) "The vineyard is well managed, but I've not seen it for five years. Besides, I could attend to the reburial of his ashes in the vault, as he had wanted. There is every reason to go." And then she added, straightforwardly as was her way, "If I went to Veronavera, Bartolo, might you come with me, and stay a short while? Would such a thing be possible?"

I thought longingly of it.

Then I said, I did not see how I could. Pia and I had already quarreled about my absences. How could I distress her further by a wider lapse?

"Alas," said Flavia. Then she kissed me. "Poor Pia. Never mind. I'll be gone only a week or so. And I will bring back food for a feast, apricots and cherries from the orchard, and one of the best chickens to lay eggs for us. And the nicest wine.

This was how she was, Flavia. Even that evening she sent me homeward early, and gave me besides a white rose in a pot to give to my wife. Another woman might have put poison on it—I had heard of such antics—but Flavia, though she was adept herself with herbs and healing potions, had nothing of that malice in her.

"What do I say to her," I said lamely, standing there with the rose. "I've never taken her a flower before."

"Then you should have done so, sir. Be off with you, and tell her it is a peace-offering, because you are most content when she's smiling."

When I reached home, Pia seemed pleased to get the rose, and never asked what I was up to, but at that time she was rather distracted. Someone had brought word her own father was sick, and he would have no one to nurse him but her.

I was astounded by this stroke of fate, for the stone-mason, now retired and pensioned by the guild, lived out on the islands of Myrrhano, where the best glass in the world is made.

"But Pia, do you feel you *must* go?"

"Yes," said Pia. And I saw a glint in her eyes that told me she meant to pay me back for our disputes. "When he is ill, no one can do anything with him except me. So I haven't a choice. I'll be gone at least fourteen or twenty days.

"What shall *I* do?" I said, woebegone (nor can I exonerate my villainy), "left here with that cook of yours—"

"Oh, you'll do very well. Go out with your friends as you always do, in any event. Let them feed you and see to your comforts."

"Pia—"

No. I must put my husband behind my father this once, Bartolo."

And so she went. And I told the cook she might do as she liked, I intended to visit my uncle's old house-keeper in the country. As a lie it was not such a stretch, for Rossa lived only a few miles beyond Veronavera, though I knew I would not be seeing her.

As for the guild, I arranged that I myself visit Verona to superintend the matter of the Tressi vault. It is not always unusual for a Master to take on such a task, and no one looked askance, while since these grave exchanges are normally not noised about no one would speak of it, either.

It was at Veronavera that Flavia told me of the dream she had had of me, when she was six years old.

But I had been surprised by her already, before that. I had arranged to meet her, as I thought in her carriage, where the Veronavera Road properly begins, beyond Venus. As I waited there then under a tree, up rode a well-dressed young man with his servant, and hailed me.

"Your horse seems a good one, sir," said he. "Better than mine, I'd think."

I wondered if he was a ruffian and meant to try to steal the horse, which I had hired. The servant, too, had muffled his face oddly, I thought, as robbers sometimes do—

Then, something in the look of the servant, and next in the angle of the young man's head, and his eyes under the unruly fringed locks—he had even a little beard too, and moustaches, in the Franchian or Spanish manner—made me suspicious.

"Who are you?" I asked.

"Is this civil?" asked he.

"Well," I said, "perhaps not, as I'm impatient, waiting for my dear friend, a lady, who is late."

"Yes," said Flavia, for it was she beneath the small, round, masculine hat and mass of loose hair, with the moustachios and beard stuck on (and her servant trying to look like someone I had never met, "and here I am."

"Is it *you?*"

"Come now. You guessed. I saw it in your eyes. Don't be shocked, dearest one. It's safer for me on the road, and quicker, too.

So we rode on to Veronavera—I, this youth who was my mistress, and Flavia's servant.

It was a glorious day, and out of the City it smelled already of fields and wild flowers, ripening grapes, and pleasure.

We broke our fast in the garden of an inn where there were goats grazing under the quince trees. When evening fell we found another, and slept together, she and I, all that night in the clean rough bed. There she said to me, "This is Heaven on earth, my love."

Because it was summer and the road was easy, on horseback we made excellent speed. By noon of the following day, we reached the hill country above the town.

Veronavera is old as Venus, a Roman outpost in ancient times. The Roman fort is there yet, now with extra walls, to hold the garrison—which included during that time the recent addition of the soldiers of Chesare Borja. But we did not think of them. The River Adza lay miles off below, a milky coiling, with the red-stoned town all along its banks, towered and sun-kissed among gardens of dark trees. Here the hills rose and fell, and beyond, across the gulf of distance, hung the smoke-blue cliffs of the mountains. Between these two vistas, I could make out a rocca-castle, also quite far off, yet gleaming in the sun. It was the Castello Barbaron.

The Tressi house was small, but the vineyard and orchards ample.

No sooner were we there than Flavia was off about her estate, greeting everyone and embracing some, even the men. None seemed put out by her appearance. Later on, she explained to me it was her own husband who had suggested it to her as the safest and fastest mode of traveling. "He saw to it," she added, "that I learned to ride both sidesaddle and astride. He and I often journeyed like this. We found it amusing."

In the evening, though, Flavia took off her disguise, and was a fine lady in the cool, scented garden, amidst its arbor and oleanders.

As I was coming down the stair of the house that dusk, someone passed me, which is the only way I can describe it, though no one was there.

The stair was narrowish and turning, and the light almost gone from it, but I found I had drawn back to let something slip by and, as I did so, I caught a faint perfume. It was only a moment or so after that I seemed vaguely to see a woman—but in my mind only, the way you might recollect someone just glanced at a minute before and now gone away.

When we had dined, and Flavia had shown me all the garden again by starlight, I mentioned this phenomenon to her. She nodded and said, "Ah, that is Jinevra. So I call her."

"And who is Jinevra?"

"A ghost, what else? I've seen her myself now and then, and rather more decidedly than you did. She wears a light-colored, long-waisted gown, and her hair is dressed high and veiled. Her face, I'm less sure of, but she is smiling always. There's nothing horrifying about her, as with such things sometimes there is."

"We are told," I said, musingly, "that there are no ghosts, since all souls sleep, or else they progress directly to the other world."

'Oh yes," said Flavia, as if all this were the most ordinary of subjects. "But a ghost is not a *soul*, Bartolo."

"What is it, then?"

Flavia pondered a second, as she would always do when thinking how best to tell me of something in which I was unversed. (As I have said, she was extremely clever and well-read, which I am the first to avow I am not.)

"Great happiness or great anguish or hurt can leave a mark behind them, Bartolo. The way a shoe is worn to the shape of the foot that always dons it. Or as a blow to the flesh may leave a scar. These wearings and scars are on the skin of time and of the earth. And sometimes still we see them, though not always, and not always very well. The one I call Jinevra was happy in this house, and has left the impression of her happiness. But I know of a terrible house in a village near here, where no one can live, and they must pull it down, so full is it of something dreadful left behind."

I cannot say if I believed what she said, although I was always inclined utterly to believe her in everything.

But anyway, I smiled and said, "But I've heard stories, Flavia, of ghosts that speak and hold conversations, or others that throw articles of furniture about a room. How can that be, if they are only such scars, such memories as you say?"

"These aren't ghosts of the same kind. Yes, I've heard, too, of such happenings. And—you must allow me to say, I have now and then spoken to a ghost myself."

"You're a witch. I've always suspected."

"Some would think so. I've a kind of facility for see-ing ghosts. Some do, and others not."

"Well, and what did you learn from these different ghosts?"

"Usually, my dear, that they were lost and wretched, and wished only to be elsewhere. Either to be alive again, or in Heaven, where their souls had already gone."

"Now I'm lost also, Flavia. What do you mean?"

We sat down in the arbor, and Flavia told me what she believed to be the truth. I remember every word.

"When we are to be born, and the flesh we are to in-habit is growing in our mother's womb, our soul comes often to visit and regard it. It comes so often that the child will stir and shift about, and so the mother thinks her baby is already ensouled, which in a way it is, the soul being always so near to it, and to her. Some women speak of sensing a guardian at such times—what they sense is the soul of the child itself, watching over itself-to-be, and them. At last, the soul claims its flesh entirely. Then, or soon after, the child is born. Before that, how-ever, the visiting soul has made for itself, within the shell of the child, a potential for its life. Which is, if you will, the *physical* soul, or character, it will come to have. For through this character, while alive, the soul will learn what it wishes in the world. Now, Bartolo, this personal-ity may become so overbearing during a lifetime, that it can hide all remembrance of the soul from the mind. Indeed, the physical soul may often end by becoming far more insistent and vigorous—though far less strong—than the true soul which made it. Or how else is the earth so full of wrongdoing, confusion, wickedness, and mis-ery—for no soul is ever capable of those states, unless a physical character rules it, hiding from it all it has been, and will be again. Only death finally separates the soul from its other lesser self. And at death even, for a time, the soul may still think itself the physical creature it was, slave to the passions and sorrows of the flesh. This passes. This passes, then we relearn the greater passions and joys, and are free, and that is the real Heaven."

"But you say, if I understand you, that what I would call a ghost—I mean, that tribe of ghosts which talk and appear to live independently in this world still—they are the phantoms solely of a man's *character*—what he has been, while in the flesh?"

"How else do they seem," she asked, "but as pale or extravagant copies? They cleave to what they have had—or have wanted to have. They try to live on always as they were. Or as they meant to be."

"But the soul's gone—"

"Yes, Bartolo. No soul is ever trapped in such a way."

Perhaps it was the wine, or the night, or being with her like this, and knowing how brief would be our holiday, but melancholy stole over me. I said, "Poor godforsaken things, then."

"God forsakes nothing," she answered. And kissed me.

Much later, when we were still in bed, she told me how she had dreamed of me when she was six years old, and I also six, for I had already learned (she did not obscure such things) that she was of an age with me.

Flavia said she saw me lying on a bare floor, and that I had been beaten, and there was all about an effluvia of rage and violence and hopelessness. "I knew you," she said, "as I knew you again when first we met last month. I might say, I don't know how I knew you. But I remember there was, too, in the dream, a man, who lay

in a chair snoring, and by him an empty wine-bottle—
no, it was a skin, the kind they sell in the markets." I said
nothing. I had never told her of my drunkard father and
his drunken wife. "I took you in my arms," said Flavia.
"You were so thin and cold, and you'd been vomiting.
But you were like my brother. I told you everything
would soon be well, for I felt it would be."

Before I could stop myself, I said to her, "It was. My
uncle rescued me from that Hell."

She asked nothing. She said, "Of course. Forgive my
trespass, Bartolo. But I do see things, sometimes. I don't
frighten you?"

"I could never be afraid through you, sweetheart."

"I'm glad. For I wanted to tell you how I'd seen you
before. We were intended to meet. I think . . . it was a
plan we had made, before we were born, you and I."

With this I did not concur. I thought we would, had
we planned it, have arranged things better, so both of us
had liberty to join our lives as one.

There was to be one more suprising moment. It
seemed then largely irrelevant, among the earthly joy of
our lovemaking, the constant magic of her company, the
brevity of our days and nights together.

I had gone alone to the town to see about opening
the Tressi tomb. She had told me they would doubtless
hear, in her late husband's house, that she had now a
lover, but she was no longer a girl, and providing it was
not made too obvious in Veronavera, nothing would be
said. In fact, I had sole dealings with her husband's sister, a sprightly old lady with only praise for Flavia. (The
fellow who had opposed the burial here was apparently
now too sick to see me.)

"It was," said the old woman, chattering to me merrily enough, "all such a foolish business. To blame Flavia for another's sake, and then hold my brother responsible." She must have seen how I became alert—anything to do with Flavia naturally interested me. Then she told me what, plainly, was not any secret, except I had never heard it.

The Tressi anger with Flavia's husband had arisen from an initial annoyance at his marrying Flavia, then a girl of decent family, well-dowered and only thirteen.

"I was the one who said to him, Messer da Loura, that he should consider her bastardy no obstacle. She was born inside wedlock, as many are who aren't at all the children of their legal fathers. And besides, the legal father had recognized her and made no trouble about it, giving her his name until she wed my brother and became a Tressi."

Who then had been Flavia's actual father? I did not ask, of course. But the old lady, bright as a polished sequin, told me without prompting. (I believe she was quite proud of it.) My Flavia was the daughter of Andrea, Lord of House Barbaron.

SILVIO AND BEATRIXA
(The Ghost Day)

Tonight, the moon had risen, which it did not always do. Over the lagoon it blazed, its face here and there flecked by lavender traceries. Where the white reflection seared the water, eels were leaping, hundred upon hundred of them, like an endless cracking of liquid silver whips, breaking the moon-mirror into a thousand pieces.

Silvio stood watching the eels.

He was far from the palazzo, far off across the island. Here everything was dark, but for the moonlight, and fireflies of green and gold which danced in the stone-pines above him.

His mother must have wanted the moon to rise. He had not thought of it, yet there it was.

He had always known certain areas of the island altered, now and then, as he or she moved over and through them. Besides, he and she saw things a little differently. For example, the gardens which clustered about the house were not quite the same when Silvio looked at them, as when Meralda looked. She, of course, invested them with all the aspects of gardens she remembered. And he, with elements which he had recently seen, in the other world of mankind, the world which living men assumed, despite their prayers, was the only definite one.

Their unmatched images of the island had never bothered either of them. Or, they did not cause *him* any anxiety. But perhaps Meralda really did not like there to be apparent discrepancies.

Though she would, from the first, admit that any animal, plant, or inanimate article might be summoned by wanting it, she still seemed then to credit these apparitions with reality. And they were *not* real. None of their world was. At least, only the *stuff* from which it had been made up—only that was real. Yet this malleable material—what it was he did not know, nor did he greatly care. To him, it was usual. He was accustomed to it.

The world outside, the arena of humanity, that fascinated Silvio much more. And charmingly in that world, too, he was also a magician. He might come and go, manifest and vanish at a whim. He might still move objects, and even creatures, as he willed, there as here. Even human things, he had found he could sometimes influence. And he had been able to punish them, which was what he had desired the most.

Until now, Silvio's dual existence, here, there, had stayed a glorious, complex, and enjoyable one, seemingly limitless, lacking no stimulous, threatening no accident nor mishap.

His earliest memory was of lying in crystalline air, supported by invisible and loving arms, and seeing everywhere beauty.

He remembered how her servants had placed him delicately against his mother. Her hair, the color of lemons, had shone and smelled of carnations. He had not needed to suckle, nor to weep. They had slept, Meralda and he. Within three or four days, he could talk to her.

Childhood, as birth, was for Silvio all benign. He was adored, but it was more than this. No one was ever angry—or had need to be. No one ever chastised—or had cause to, since nothing seemed beyond any of them and there was no unsafety. Therefore, nothing need be denied. Nor did anything ever distress Silvio. If he ran and fell, for example, it did not hurt. He swam in the lagoon simply by one day jumping into it (fearless; fear was unnecessary). He could rise into the air as effortlessly. His youth had been filled with flying, winglessly, over the island and the waters. It was only after he went among mankind that he took up the habit of walking with any regularity.

Maybe in his flights he had been looking for other land. He had seemed to sense other places existed, some-where. Certainly he did not want to invent them, as God had had to do. Did not want the responsibility of that. It was not that he grew bored with Paradise either, only that he was full of *life*. Yes, there is no other word. And, full of life, he began to search for whatever symbolic food would best feed his hungers.

Silvio knew all of Meralda's history. Had done so from before the third or fourth day when he began to speak to her in a child's small voice, and with the dia-logue of a far older person. Generally what he said was always adult, and too, then, it had always the flavor of a feral childishness.

"One day I'll find them and kill them," he announced to his mother, when he was probably ten years old, an age he had reached in a few months, or the equivalent of that seeming time.

Meralda had gazed at him, half frightened, her girl's eyes open wide. "No," she murmured, "we must forgive our enemies . . ."

From this peculiar slip into instructed formula, he saw (at ten years or ten months of age) that he should not say such things *aloud* to her.

Nevertheless, he had believed that, just as she had grasped his complete knowledge of her, and had known precisely whom he had meant when he had spoken of killing, she also knew everything he later did. How could she not? They were two who were yet one.

Now, on the slope above the lagoon frenzied with moonstruck eels, Silvio was no longer utterly sure of this. For he and she were, essentially, not of the same essence. It had nothing to do with gender, or time, or that she was born on the earth and had left it, or that he was born out of the earth, and often went back there. It was to do with that psychic difference which now he could not ignore. That she was spirit—and he, some other form, *not* spirit, yet spiritlike, and sorcerous. More so than she, perhaps, though he had called her the Sorceress.

Silvio shut his eyes for an instant. Then he looked again, and the lagoon was still in the moonlight, the conjured eels were gone.

So *he* must seem, appearing, disappearing, in the physical world of the City.

To Beatrixa, he must seem this.

A ghost. A magus. Fearsome.

As he had grown up on the island, Silvio began to lust for the things he would have had, had he been born to Meralda in that physical "real" world. A mixture, they were, of what he might have expected had she borne him to the Lord Ciara, and Silvio become a nobleman—but also of the advantages he might have reckoned to get from the scrambling life with Lorenzo Vai.

So banquets evolved on the island, great dinners full of aristocratic people (apparitions) who fêted Silvio, and musicians who played and sang—and phantom realistic armies, and horses to be ridden that were entirely equinely solid until he was done with them, and hunts and games and various tests. All of this. Then, too, princely books came, and Silvio, looking through their convincing but illusory pages, saw that he could not read a line.

Then he went to Meralda, and said she must teach him. She was no scholar, but she knew a little, and this she rendered unto her son. Who, like some fiery sun birthed by a paler moon, took to the mystery of written language as he had taken to speech, and thereafter taught himself. Even the Latin of these recreated books he fathomed gradually, totally. His mind was not human. It was not spirit. Yet somehow it was able to come at both these conditions, and apparently outstrip them. If Meralda was no scholar, Justore had been. Some unrecognized trace of her father perhaps, informed her uncanny child.

As for the books, how did he get them? He, who had seen nothing at that time of the world of humanity. It was as if everything which Meralda had ever glimpsed, or been told of, was there in Silvio, too. And so he could make use of it. No wonder he had believed so long they were each other's alter-self. He was the man Meralda might have been, had she *been* a man. Bold for her timidity, and without nervousness—for how could he know such conditions, being and living as he did? The seed of her possibility, which had never been allowed to flourish, became in Silvio a healthy, towering tree.

In the end, stretching for more knowledge and more of all things, he had come to desire the world that they had left behind. To crave physical books, animals that were of flesh and blood. Humans, likewise. Women.

Women, he had had by then. He was sixteen, mostly. (How much time had that taken? It seemed a year or so. But it might have been less, or longer. Did time, anyway, even exist on the island in the green lagoon?) But the women were dream-women, lovely and enticing, and soon abhorrent to him. And, like the books, they somehow issued from the inner ideas, the meager acumen of Meralda, to which he was then very subject—and, too, they resembled her somewhat. And so they were like sisters—incestuous. To Meralda, incest would have been, of course, unlawful and obscene. And Silvio was not distinct from her in this. He turned in distaste from the visual consanguinity of his invented courtesans.

His desire for the world built in him, like a pressure. He became, not dissatisfied, but restless.

But that was to be expected. At sixteen, as a young man of good family (or a soldier, or an artisan's boy), he would be on the lookout for new adventures. Of ways to uphold the honor of his house, or burnish his own name. (Were these Meralda's expectations?)

Silvio would go and sit a while beside the marble obelisk that demonstrated his father's loss.

In that era, Silvio, too, had been called Lorenzo. Meralda had named her son after his dead father. And Lorenzo-not-yet-Silvio had mused on his restlessness, by the obelisk. Then he would spring off the island, and dive deep down into the supernal lagoon.

The lagoon, here, was endless. In all directions, or downward, there was nothing else.

Silvio-Lorenzo floated, careless, not requiring to have air until he should emerge again, even if that were hours distant.

Light-filled in its bottomless depths, the lagoon stayed an emerald for a great way, and then it changed to a green sapphire. Silvio (Lorenzo) allowed himself to tumble down and down, through the pulsing sapphirine, to a matured violet-purple deep, a kind of blackness that was not black.

He stared around him, disorientated finally by infinitude and beauty. But most of all by the immaterial.

A score of occasions, he must have done all this, and felt in this way.

In the real world (as he later discovered and understood), more than twenty years had passed. Silvio-Lorenzo, who had grown to the age of ten in ten months, and to sixteen in a couple of years, had also been on Meralda's island for over two decades.

It happened as everything for him did, easily, at last.

One second, he drifted about in the Heavenly lagoon which was purple-blue and sweetly odoured. And then, a sort of gushing and spinning—the water stank and was full of mud and darkness, and a vast fish—larger than himself, he thought—thrust by him. And at the touch of it, like a raw, blind flash, he and it both recoiled. It was a real fish of the real world. It was physical, corporeally alive.

Silvio, who never had, now felt terror, of a kind. He struggled as if he were drowning, and choked, and then pulled such idiocy out of himself and flung it away. The urge to cry out, almost to weep, convulsed him for another moment. (These were, the fight for breath, the lament, normal components of birth into the world of Man. But Silvio's birth had not been of that order. He did not know.)

He circled, half lazily, half dazed, in the putrid gloom of the alien water. He saw that by sinking down and down in one world, he must have risen up in the other. And he supposed, since Meralda had drowned herself in the lagoon called Aquila, that this was where he had broken through.

But sending himself upward again, through shoals of pallid fish, through clouds of filth and strange weeds, through shards and shapes, as his head burst the skin of the water, he did not find what he anticipated.

The Laguna Aquila, which Silvio's key to Meralda's memory had let him see in his own mind, was not as it had been. For one thing, a heavy mist draped over it in thick folds, and a dead, grey twilight.

When he had swum in the other lagoon by the island, upon leaving the water, he had never been wet. Now he was not, either. And, just as always, he was able to lift up into the air, until he stood on the lagoon's back. It was, today, very still. He knew such a lagoon was not frequently like this. Nor so empty.

Venus and her waters were always riotous with traffic. Not here. Perhaps then he was far from the land, from the islands of the City and her internal shipping.

Silvio walked through the web of mist. As a rule, he would not have done this, but flown. Yet in the world of Man, already he walked, although he walked on water.

Presently a wall surged from the fog.

It was grey, like the rest, but darker, and not very high. On top of it there sat a thing which Silvio knew from his mother's trove of recollection: a cat.

The cat was nearly colorful in its monochrome. It was white and brown with a sort of gilded striping and dotting that ran through its fur. And it gazed down at him with nacreous eyes.

Then, Silvio noticed that he no longer trod over the water. He was walking now, and had been a little while, on a sandy raft of shore that ran out of the mist as the wall had. Some hag-like trees, deformed by sea winds, scraped against the stones.

There was another shadow beyond the wall—other walls, those of a small house. Even as he looked at it, the atmosphere shifted like a gauze. He saw a shuttered window.

Silvio now flew up to the wall-top, and the cat hissed, its hair standing on end, and jumped away.

Beyond the barricade was a garden of salads and herbs maintained for a kitchen, and in it a pear tree grew, less haggard than the trees outside, in the shelter of the wall.

"Well, seen a ghost, have you?" said a female voice.

She was addressing the cat.

Silvio stared down and so beheld his first mortal woman.

She was a squat one with crossed eyes and angry hair.

In that moment, Silvio realized that he had made himself invisible, in order to hide from her, when she should glance his way. Which now she did.

And then, as she squinted up at the wall, Silvio saw, too, that, although he was *not* to be seen, nor did she *see* him, yet somehow with her unruly eyes she made something out.

He had concealed himself not from any unease. (Already, he guessed himself master and mage in this concrete but absurd place, so dull of color, so lurid with potential.) No, it was a playfulness in him. Nor particularly a tender playfulness.

Then the woman spoke to him. "Who is it?"

Silvio could not resist answering, though he made sure she would not hear. "Not any lover of yours, lady."

But she frowned. She had not caught the words, not even the voice, he thought. Nevertheless, she knew that something sat on the wall, and it had insulted her.

"Away with you, Sinistralo. This is a Christian house."

Evidently she suspected, also, that he was male—an unlucky spirit of the left-hand, devilish side. (The word she used had a Latin root.)

Silvio grinned.

Then a boy ran up to her through the mist.

Heaven

"Strabica—what are you looking at? There's nothing there."

"Nor is there," said the woman. She grunted, as if to emphasize Silvio must now indeed be off at once. Then they turned back to the mist-shadowy house, and vanished themselves in the vapors.

Perversely, Silvio made the cat return to him. He had known he could. He smoothed its rough, real fur, which did not feel as it looked, or should, but seemed of pure otherness, strange, nearly frightful (as later he would find all fleshly things did to him.) The cat, too, felt some obvious horror at his touch, and growled, though it could not bring itself to escape until he let it go.

Silvio did not then realize this, but the boy and woman were perhaps servants. The only servants Silvio had so far come across—were not visible.

What he had learned, and swiftly, was that despite his powers, when he himself was invisible, a few mortals would always detect him anyway, sensing, hearing, or seeing enough of him to know he was there. It was their gift: second sight.

Silvio went from that house, and left it lying out along its isolate spit of sandbar and shingle. He went off to see the City of Venus. He duly saw it.

A revelation. Better than his mother's limited recollections, and the shades of the recollections of others filtered through her. How it had bloomed, the City, like the whole world-in-little, from the fog . . . its colossal geography, like cliffs afloat on a sea of glass; the tiny details intricate as the scales of dragons.

Here, in this besmirched earthly Paradise, Silvio was as ever able to do as he pleased.

Coming and going where he would, *how* he would. And from his initial excursion (which itself lasted days, nights) grew all his avarice for the physical impedimenta of Venus. And, too, his culminating gluttony for revenge.

Meralda's father, Justore, was already dead. But three others remained, like matured fruits on a tree. The evil Ciara; the jealous bitch, Euniche; and, maybe more unspeakable even than they, since he had had no true reason for what he did, Andrea, the fat man, who had handed Meralda over to her death. Silvio did know almost everything. He knew about the letter Euniche had sent to Barbaron, though how he knew it Silvio did not bother with—Meralda had *not* known. (In a similar manner, possibly, Silvio grasped he had no jurisdiction over the already-dead.)

Silvio saved Andrea for the last. To this end, Silvio went often to the Palazzo Barbaron, watching the lord and his household, gloating. There were the excellent books in the palazzo library, besides, which Silvio delighted to read, and the sunny gardens and courtyards. Soon he came across a little girl, also. She who was Barbaron's sole legal daughter.

In the beginning, Silvio paid her no more attention than he gave to any of them. She interested him because she was *alive*, and he liked to dislike her, since she was the child of his enemy.

Silvio della Scorpia—that was the title Silvio had now put on. He had become partisan with revenge, and took up the name of his house. The name of *Silvio* he gave himself, however, once he knew the name of the lagoon (Silvia) from which he had first of all emerged. Though later he found himself capable of breaking out through any of them, or any area of water in the City, and eventually any area of anything, wood, stone, earth, that the City held. And he rose from all these elements with the same rapid and simultaneous ease. So that, appearing under water, as in the end he did so eloquently in front of Beatrixa, was only a facet of his scheme to ensnare her.

She had been primarily for his use as a weapon against Andrea. What could be more perfect—to ruin and destroy the enemy's daughter, as Meralda, daughter of the Scorpia House, had been ruined and destroyed through Andrea's heedless, thoughtless act—for what had Andrea had to gain, save the most petty of vengeances against the della Scorpias?

Silvio had *all* to gain. Such exercises fed him, as did the books, the art, the scenes of sun and shadow, the very stones of Venus, the very ground beneath the stones, the waters, the earth.

But, oh, Beatrixa.

Where the eels had leapt in the island lagoon, there was yet a slight disturbance.

Nothing Silvio could see caused it. But it went on and on.

I am causing it.

Silvio sprang forward, up into air, downward, through the opal mirror.

The garden was full of the evening scent of summer flowers, and under that, of the Triumph Canal. Beatrixa was used to both.

She stood among the firmly-shaped trees, watching two children of the house, a boy and girl, who were playing on the turf with some wooden toys.

"Whose are *they?*"

At the voice, everything in Beatrixa fell and smashed like a mirror. Her eyes dazzled over, cleared. She gave no outward sign of any of this, even her tawny skin, faintly flushed along the cheekbones with westering sun, camouflaged her change of color.

"My cousin's," she said.

"Aren't you," he said, "going to ask me what I want, and how I am here?"

"Not any longer. I've learned, you see, that you want things I could never imagine, and that you may come and go as you wish."

"Oh, Beatrixa, you could imagine one thing I might want."

She turned, and looked at him, at Silvio, where he stood against the trees. There was a statue there, too, a classical Apollo, brought from the Silvia Lagoon. Two fishing-boats had dragged it out years back, near the spot where there was said, by divers, to be a drowned Roman amphitheatre.

Both the Apollo and Silvio had risen out of the depths of that water. She knew it well, looking at them.

The two children began screaming suddenly, and to fight. They tore away along one of the paths, a flummoxed servant erupting from his doze to pursue them.

"There we are," said Silvio, lightly, "you and I, those babies. Our first quarrel at our first meeting. *You are my enemy*, you said to me. Get out, you said, or I'll call my father's men to hack you in bits."

"I remember what I said. But you went away, certainly."

"You're cold to me this evening.

"Well, it will turn cooler presently."

He laughed.

She stood there, listening to the music of it. How

beautiful his voice. Everything about him. This demon.

"I thought," he said, "you'd say to me, Silvio, why did you prevent my demanding of my father that awful question you had required me to ask him."

"Did you think that?" She shook her head. "No. I won't bandy words with you any more. Never." And turning from him, she began to go away along another path.

Instantly he was beside her. Strolling as if for innocuous chat, at her side.

"You are angry with me, madam."

She said nothing.

Silvio said, "Have you sought a priest, to exorcise you of my fiendish presence?"

"Well said. I will do it."

"Do. It will make no difference to me."

She stopped and turned again to him. They had entered the shadow of a topiary walk. Through tiny chinks in the dark hedges, the low sun glinted like watching eyes. It was in her eyes, too, so they gleamed with a quick, red shiver on their own blackness.

"Let me alone."

"Beatrixa—"

"If you are some devilish thing, which I think you must be, then I won't implore you for any mercy, since mercy must be like blasphemy to your kind. But this I will say. Hound me as you have done, and I'll find a way to be rid of you—yes, I promise you that. I swear it by God and by His kind angels, and by the Blood of the Christ. If it comes to it, even, I will *die* rather than be played with any more, as those children played with their toys. Do you hear? Do you believe? Kill me or be done. And be advised, *if* I am dead, I will come after you—yes, even to your master's stenchful bloody Hell-gate. The soul must have great power. And I will even damn mine, to come at you and tear you into *pieces*."

Silvio stepped back.

If, through her concentrated fury, she saw anything, it was how his wonderful face grew still and white, its own center seeming to fall away from it; the eyes wide, shocked, and old suddenly, older than the eyes of any man she had ever seen.

"My God, Beatrixa, my God, my heart's darling— what can I say to you to make this right?"

She had moved him unbearably, her rage and contempt, her controlled yet boiling passion, as human tears perhaps never could. He beheld all her pain and loss, her horror and wretchedness, and how she had fashioned them into a sword and cut him through. He had known he was hers, in any case, by now. And now he saw she perhaps was no longer his—

They stood frozen, changed to marble like the Apollo.

They stared into each other's eyes.

"In God's name, Beatrixa—if I were a man of your kind, I could take hold of you, I could kiss your lovely mouth and drink the poison you utter from it and die of it, if you wanted—but I can barely even touch you as I am, as you are—I'm like Christ in that one way, when He went about between two worlds, the countries of the spirit and the flesh—and said to them *Noli me tangere*— don't touch me—because he did not want to fill them with terror or break their hearts—but Beatrixa, I am not a Christ—not even the magician I must seem—no devil either—my only sorcery perhaps—is deception. What in the name of God can I do?"

He heard how she breathed, as if she had half perished in water.

"You can leave me alone."

"No, Beatrixa. No."

"*Yes*. I've told you what I will have. You are seductive, and I was lulled by it. You're some phantom of the Scorpion house, you make no bones of *that*. You have used me to persecute my own father. Oh, did you think you stopped me in time? Did you think I had not *seen* it—" she faltered. "I saw. In his face. As you told me I should. What he had done."

"I tried to prevent that."

"You tried too late. What do you care? Be glad, you damnable thing of Hell, to have unmasked him to me. What more lies do we need now? I am hurt. *Good*, you'll like that. Why pretend it is not so?"

"I've said to you before I want no fear or unhappiness for you."

"So you have *said*."

"I could never have harmed you. I wanted to come at *him*."

"*Him*? Andrea Barbaron—why? Oh yes, you indicate you are some ghostly friend of dead Meralda's—"

"Her son."

Again, the steel of her anger veered away.

"Is such a thing credible?"

"None of it," he said, "or all. I was in her womb when she died, unborn. She brought me forth on an island in some place I've thought of as Heaven, but it surely is not. No one else is there. Only she is, and I. I ventured out, as the son of a high family does. To learn and look about. And to achieve justice. But with you, there was no justice to be had. No. I'll spare your father, Beatrixa, for your sake."

The sun leveled like an arrow through a slot in the topiary. Beatrixa blazed with its red and carnal light.

"Spare him? Don't dare *anything* against him. I, too, have said. I will die and come after you."

"That would be worth killing him, then," Silvio murmured. "To have you with me."

"To rip your loose soul into fragments."

"Even for that. I'd let you, Beatrixa. If it were possible. Perhaps it is. But, my love, it's better that you live. You are so beautiful, alive. I never saw anything like you, alive, in this world or the other one."

She laughed once, hard, as if barking—or choking.

"Give it up. I told you, you needn't lie any more."

"I've never lied to you, as I have since seen."

The energy ran out of her as the sun drained away into the hedge.

She sank down on her knees and covered her face with her hands, and he heard her praying in the shadow as the darkness came.

Silvio knelt beside her. He spoke softly into her ear. And though she did not cease her prayer, she spoke more quietly (perhaps not knowing what she did) to hear him.

"Let me come to you one more time. Only one. There's something I want to bring you. Something of your world, not mine. Something that should be in your keeping, and no other's."

Still whispering the orison, Beatrixa became aware he had left her. It was as if the sun had gone down a second time.

Deep in the Laguna Silvia . . .

Foul rotted lights and mantles of obscurity.

Here and again, the leprous statues, pillars, ancient streets which the sea had devoured. Ships lying upside down. The skeletons of men. None of it concerned him. Or, only one thing.

There, below the rubble of civilizations and tragedies, lodged in the sticky mud: the Casket.

It was gold. He knew this, having once rubbed part of it clean.

He had read, Silvio, in the books, the libraries of Venus, all kinds of stories and legends. He had known about the box which held the Heart of the unrecognized saint, Beatifica, who once rode, they said, clothed only in her own hair, to the rescue of the City.

Why was it he had *found* the Casket, though? He could not recall. Could not even think, now, when it was that he had.

Stooping, he prized it free.

Disturbed, fish swam in the upswirl of murk and muck.

There at the bottom of the lagoon, among the sunken things, Silvio peered at the gold figures progressing around the Casket's sides. Each one was praying, he saw, hands upheld and heads bowed. As she had done, in the garden.

He hovered there in the water. He had never, in all his magical existence of joy and indulgences, known any pain. Now he did. The agony was like a sound heard deep in his mind, and like the sword that her words had thrust through him.

He had finally seen in her fury itself that she loved him, or why would she hate him in such a way? He had seen how she meant to destroy her love, and that she was stalwart enough to do it, and at what cost to herself. And by the glare of that, he saw clearly his own love for her.

Until today, love, too, had been a pastime and a joy, and easy. No more.

Now it was a love of the real world. It ate him up and had the taste—of death.

He had told her he would come back.

She could not want this.

Beatrixa became afraid to be alone. She was not often afraid, and it offended her.

But, pacing her chamber, every moment—she looked for him. It was the same as it had been when she was six, before she had sent him away. She had searched the palazzo—no, it was more like the time *after* she sent him from her. When she had resolutely *never* looked for him—and everywhere she had.

Twice they had come to this, then. The omen had been there from the start. *You are my enemy.*

Love your enemies, Beatrixa. Do good to those that hurt you.

She went to dine in the Little Sala. These dinners mainly involved only the higher women of Barbaron, and not even all of those. Andrea was seldom there, and tonight was no exception, which she was glad of. She had been avoiding her father, too.

There, she saw few of the males of the house. A scatter of the elder children, and younger cousins who giggled. An aunt, and two or three old ladies who all of Beatrixa's life had never been young. Then, Beatrixa's mother swept in, fanning herself with a flamingo-feather fan the Ducem had sent some years before.

"What a hot, oppressive night. We shall have a storm."

Everyone had risen, made various obeisances. A chorus of agreement.

"Ah, Triche. Come and sit here, by me."

To Beatrixa, her mother was a well-known stranger.

The young woman took her seat by the older, and their gowns rustled together, in a weird harmony, as if to say, see, you are both female—and besides, this one bore the other, so they must get on.

"You are browner than ever," said Beatrixa's mother.

She herself was old now, or thought of in that way, at forty-seven. Her pale complexion had withered like a dried petal, and her hair was streamered with white; she disdained hennas or wigs.

"Yes, madam."

"Oh, why you won't wear your sun-hat in the gardens . . . ? But then you're brown as a hazelnut, whatever we do. Like a native of the East, from Candisi, or the Africas."

Beatrixa, when a child, would have retorted something and perhaps earned a beating. Now she said nothing.

Her mother said, "But you have the finest eyes. I have always said so. And your hair is a splendor, when dressed."

Beatrixa glanced at her mother. The compliments upset her. She could hardly bear them. The battle with the other one had done this to her, stripped her of some essential upper skin.

Roasts of chicken had been brought in, with spiceries and rice, and round loaves of chopped meats. There were grapes and peaches, and a honeycomb.

Between the candlelight and the movement of servants, who stirred the hangings, there were flutterings all about, like half-glimpsed presences, ghosts—but none of them Silvio.

"Your father dines with the Strotsis tonight. There! When is he at home?" Beatrixa's mother lowered her voice. "He has a woman, on the Canal of Ancient Saints. It's best you know. We do not speak of it."

"No, mother."

This, her mother's life. Growing old in the house of Andrea, who kept one woman here, another there. Andrea who once, years ago—surely when little older than Beatrixa now—had delivered Meralda della Scorpia to torture and to murder. What had he felt? Indifference? *Pleasure?*

"What is it?"

"Nothing, Mother." Am I so transparent tonight? She can see through me?

"You're fidgety. It's the storm that is coming."

"Yes, madam. The storm."

Yes, the storm –

When she re-entered the bedchamber, it was in darkness. She carried her candle quickly to the others. The light soaked up. She thought, *Am I now always to be afraid of the dark?* Afraid of what the dark might hide in it—or that it was empty?

Then the light showed her something gleaming gold, there on the inlaid table by the window.

It was not hers. She had never before seen it.

Beatrixa recalled how he had said to her, ten years ago, that his own servants were invisible. Perhaps for a long while, visiting the City, he had not identified servants, even slaves, because he did not realize domestic and other tasks were performed by *people*, here.

Now Beatrixa, too, had an invisible slave.

For no one else could, or would have, come into this room tonight, without her orders, in her absence.

She walked slowly towards the Casket.

She knew what it must be.

They burned her . . . her heart would not burn . . . it was saved in a golden box . . . probably stolen . . . under Silvia, in the mud . . . I know where the Box of the Heart is.

In the candleglow it shone, cleaned of the dirt and debris of the lagoon. A small, attractive reliquary, with tiny saints praying all around it, who in the flicker of the light seemed to take little steps—

He had said he would come back, one time only. To bring her something. He had done so. He had left this for her.

Once, it had worked miracles, this box, or what lay inside it.

Beatrixa touched the golden lid with the tip of her finger. She withdrew her hand.

Then a leaden curiosity filled her, and she put both hands on the box and tried to raise its lid, thinking it would not open.

But it did.

Within the Casket, on a bed of damask that had faded and stained, lay the Relic itself.

Beatrixa stared down.

The Heart was black and shriveled and wizened. It had shrunk, and curled together as if for sleep, then changed to a black stone.

Even so Beatrixa, who had read widely, and had access to a great many books and treatises that young women did not often see, had studied among the works of such as Leonido Vinchi, and Plendar, called the Surgeon. She knew, from the descriptions, and the diagrams, too, that this was not a *human* heart. Had it *ever* been, in the box? It was the heart, or so she thought, of a dog of medium size.

She laughed.

She flung back her head, and felt the heavy, leafy shower of her own hair striking her, slapping the backs of her knees even through the silk of her gown.

So this was what had worked the miracles, and been stolen as a mighty treasure—and been perhaps discovered and so thrown away. Had *he* known, Silvio?

A dog's heart, not a saint's. Was *nothing* ever as it seemed? Nothing, in the world of men or in the worlds beyond life?

Beatrixa laughed. Then she wept.

Then, she was still.

What did anything matter, if the heart of a dog had worked miracles? What extremity was there in a father who was as base and terrible as other men, or a lover who was *dead*?

The storm that her mother had predicted broke on the house.

Lightning, and then, nearly at once, a blow of thunder that shook the palazzo to its roots.

All through the masonry, Beatrixa heard and *felt* the scurrying and short cries, the fright of mankind under the ever-aiming onslaught of all things—weather, time, Fate—

"Am I done with you then?" she asked the chamber. "You won't come any more to play your games and twist my inferior mortal existence? No? Can I be sure?"

She put her hand again on the box, on the rim of the box. And then, she touched the mummified little Heart.

How dry and hard it felt. How could it ever have beaten?

"Why didn't you burn?" she whispered to the Heart. "Oh, but of course, you weren't in any fire. This was done after. But then, *still*—how could you work your miracles—for I think you did. There are so many I've read of, the healings through Beatifica. Belief in her, that made the miracles happen, belief in her—and in you.

Faith. As we are told it will." She prayed to the Heart, which was still the Heart, her hand upon it, so it seemed to grow warm, and in it there seemed to wake the pulse which came from her own fingers' ends. "Give me back myself." Beatrixa raised her head. Her face was calm and her eyes shut fast. "You have. Now I know what I want. Then give *him* back to me. Bring him back—for I belong only to him and he to me. Nothing else. I don't know why it can be, or how. Bring Silvio back, my beloved."

So she stood praying.

She must have known he might be, anyway, in the room. Listening to her, seeing what she would do.

If he heard her, that, too, was as she wished.

She had always been brave.

But when she opened her eyes, the room was only filled with candlelight and the rushes of the storm.

She saw then her life, as it was. Its unimportant worthlessness. She saw how it would be. Her status (a Barbaron), some dynastic marriage, children born, at length her death.

Beatrixa looked firmly at all this, this *dust*.

She had always been brave.

He was gone from her for ever, as she had demanded. He was somewhere in his other world, not hearing her. Maybe he had only played with her love, too, her willingness a valued accessory, but only that, no more. And now he lost all interest in her.

Perhaps he would, after all, destroy her.

"Only be patient, Silvio," she said. "I am already dead. Though I walk about the world for another fifty years."

Against the lightning blast in the window, Silvio was standing.

Thinking she had only visualized this, she closed her eyes, opened her eyes, looked again. Now he knelt at her feet, and his head was bowed. He said, "Then, you are willing to love me."

"Yes," she said. "Who else have you left me to love?"

"I am ashamed."

"I too."

She kneeled down also, as she had when she had prayed in the garden.

She put out her hand.

"*Noli me tangere*," he said. "A sensible precaution."

"Are we sensible, then?"

They put their hands together. It was awful for them to touch. Each to the other, like a *nothingness*—an absolute of the forbidden and impossible. Yet they kept their hands together.

"Shall I die?" she said. "Should I be with you then?"

"I don't know, my love. I think not. There have been some I killed, whom I've never met after. I believed I sent them to Hell. But the island is void of any but ourselves, my mother and I, and what we invent for ourselves."

"We must make do then, with this."

She put her arms about him. He held her in turn. It was as if they held the storm, if a storm were without motion or energy. It was as if they held nothing at all, yet the nothing was *paramount*.

While on the table lay the golden Box, and the withered Heart that had once worked miracles.

And in the deserts of time, midnight beginning to sound from all the bells of Venus.

"I love you," she said again.

"And I love you. Oh, Beatrixa. I loved you before I was born, and that is why, I think, I was."

"Then it must be that I, too, was born—for this."

Each had read, yet neither remembered, what tomorrow would be. The Crab month had arrived at its last day which, in the near past, had been sloughed and thus for one year missed, by the edict of a pope. The thirtieth day, which had become the single Dies Manium. And, in popular talk, it had partly remained so, even now it was returned to the calendar. A day that had died, yet lived. The Ghost Day.

He could feel the texture of her hair. How extraordinary it was, under his hands, and brushing over them, too. Silken—yet also strong and harsh and so heavy, this hair, galvanically crackling with its vitality.

And her body. Her slim, firm structure, fitted tight and warm on its chiseled bones, which, too, he could make out, through the sheath of her flesh; the serpent of her spine. Her gown was silk. His fingers pressed, amazed, into the embroidery and the lacing of her bodice at its back—trying to guess the pattern of these things which, visually, he did not remember.

"Silvio . . ."

She clung to him, rubbing her face against his shoulder.

Beatrixa, too, seemed to experience his body now, as now he did hers.

But to him, she felt as only the illusory women had ever done—*real*. For even the gentle touches of Meralda —maternal—had never evoked this sense—not yet of desire—but of completion.

Then, drawing slightly apart, they looked at each other.

They did not ask, either of them yet, what had occurred.

Each noticed, confusedly, that the other had become more real also in their looks, and more perfect, for there had been degrees of perfection, and now the greatest of these was attained.

As he leaned towards her again, her face was like a lamp, and then he forgot everything about her, except that she was his.

They kissed long and hungrily, their mouths fusing, their bodies one pressed and devouring thing.

It should not have been possible, had not previously been. But now it was, and so everything had become heightened, an exquisite tumult of erotic appetite, live as fire, consuming as deep water.

When again they let go of each other, or almost let go (their hands, their clothes even, and their hair, still mingled and entwined) they were not, even in perfection, the same. Though outwardly they remained as they had always been, they were altered entirely, become other creatures. But they knew each other still. It seemed now that they always would.

It was Beatrixa, a pragmatist, who said, mutedly. "How has this happened?"

Silvio only laughed, and reached for her again.

And she did not resist, for a short while.

But then, "No, we must see, my love, what all this is around us—"

"Why? Who cares what it is? You are everything."

"And you. But nevertheless."

She pulled away from him, her body aching at the loss, the very edges of her hair aching, and her blood. But even so she did it, and turned her head, and saw.

From the sea, the land rose high. Below lay coves and headlands, rocks and islands standing out of the water. But it was an unfamiliar landscape, and saturated in the supernatural ending of a night, the lambent break of a dreamlike day.

In the distance, the pleated sea was sluiced in glowing cinnabar light, and the fold of every wave was silvered. Here, the sun was soon to rise. Nearer to the land, the sea was melted to the deepest green, first like a dragon's back, then like malachite; and from it lifted giant arches of rock casting long, violet shadows, and yet also glittering as if speckled by dark gold. The sky was brazen red, and new copper where it met the ocean. Then beyond it, the immanence of the sunrise, the sky, like the water, also grew ethereal, a mysterious translucent hyacinth that turned darker as it rose. And in its highest ceiling it was smalt blue, and a quarter moon lay on it like a boat of white, transparent horn, scattered around it trails of flashing crystal that were stars.

The ground underfoot had a dark, twilight turf, turquoise-green, every blade of grass silvered like the waves, from the stars or the moon or the coming of the sun. Trees were massed here and there, ink-black without full light, yet their depths lit with spangles like jade, or tan-red like the lowest part of the sky.

Silvio and Beatrixa could make out mountains across the water, gleaming and looking near, in the clarity of approaching dawn. Their high peaks burned moltenly like amber streaked with madder. Also, a city, or cities, were now visible, spread across the further shores and on some of the islands in the sea. Their buildings sparkled with golden points just as the rocks did. Their architecture, however, was not easily distinguished, save for several glimmering domes of powder-green verdigris, and others of volcanic brass.

He and she stood there, gazing about, for perhaps half an hour. They had not spoken again, nor had the sun risen any higher, though the conflagration on the water did not fade. Nor did the moon begin to descend.

Beatrixa turned. She saw their own shadows dyed in metallic umber on the turquoise ground, among the silvered grass and glassy flowers.

There was the scent of the sea, clean as in winter, although it was summer, here. And the fragrance of the enormous sky which contained everything, the aromas of the stars.

She said, quietly, in the stillness where the sea alone sounded like a distant breathing, "This is a mighty and a terrible place."

"No," he said. "How, terrible?"

"I don't mean there is any harm here. I mean, it inspires terror—by its beauty and its vastness. Its difference

"Don't fear it, Beatrixa. It's only another country of the lands beyond life. One I've never seen. And yet—it was as if I knew it. Look, doesn't everything seem known to you?"

"Yes. And I have never seen any land like this, or heard of one. Except—now and then in some painting by a great master-artisan, perhaps there. How do they know to paint it," she murmured, "if they are yet alive?"

Birds flew over them, alabaster white. One separated from the others, and came down on to the headland where they stood.

Beatrixa knelt at once among the flowers.

Silvio did not.

He said, "Are you real? What are you, then?"

"The reflection," answered the being on the headland, "of another source , which is quite real."

"No," Silvio protested, "you are—"

"Hush, my love," Beatrixa whispered. "It is an angel."

"Nor that," said the being. "You are in another place. Unlearn, and you may see."

It was tall, the reflection, or the angel, tall as two men one upon the other's shoulders. It had wings of white flame, which spread behind it and caught the ruby incandescence of the unrising sun. It seemed clothed in something that was pale and not wholly visible, and nor was any of it wholly there, for the sky showed through it, and a cloud of little stars. Yet it was solid as the earth they stood on. It had no face, yet it had eyes. These eyes were like the larger stars. They gave great light, so from the lovers on the grass, jet-black shadows now extended, three or four of them, while the flowers, even in this shadow, shone.

"Are we to be punished?" Beatrixa asked.

The being said, "For you, it will always be dawn. There can be for you, here, no night, and no true day. But dawn, you may have."

Silvio said, "Dawn is for ever, here."

But the creature rose straight up into the deep of the deep, raisin-blue sky, rose like a pillar of fire, leaving behind it a susurrus, as if a breeze had passed across the land; and the air sang for a moment, and it was like the music of the stars.

After a time, they were walking down from the headland, the high place.

Inland, huge woods and forests spread, sable, lighted as if by torches within, and far away were other mountains, tipped as if with palest gold-leaf. The sky was sea-green there, in what must be the west, and also starred over.

They kept to the margin of the coast, the ocean on their right hand.

They were lost. This did not disturb them. Both of them knew they had reached the Ghost Day of Paradise. They were on the outskirts of Heaven, and had been given an endless dawn.

But Beatrixa thought, although the thought seemed negligible, *The moon is infinitessimally moving. I think it is.* Really, she could not be sure.

And Silvio had taken her hand, and now and then they stopped again, to touch each other, their faces, their hair, the very sleeves and shoes, the garments that covered their bodies. For here, they could.

Then they stopped for another reason.

The slope ran over and away into a long valley, where the sea came in like liquid vitreous to a shallow spoon. And there was a palazzo there, or palazzi—a town of them. The buildings gave into and from each other, and all were open, with roofs which had no centre and pillared arcades and courts laid with floors mirroring the sky above, doorless, and huge arched windows without glazing.

People—if people they were—moved about there. There were horses too, in ornate trappings, as if for a festival or carnival, and the clothes of the people had also, even in the distance, that glamorous look.

Closer, there was something else.

"It is a graveyard," she said. "How can there be a yard of death in this world?"

"There can be anything," Silvio replied, "here." He knew more than she did of such areas.

But they stayed at the graveyard's edge for some time.

Like everything they had seen, this, too, was of great beauty. Beside it, Venus City's Isle of the Dead was a paltry slum.

For here, every grave had its upright and pristine marker, made of a mysterious opalescent substance that glowed inwardly like a coal. And these markers had been carved, or had evolved, each with a figure of the Zodiac, but everyone done uniquely.

The Ram stood guard in one spot, like silvery ice, with a rose-scarlet smouldering inside his horns. There was the Virgo, luminous and stellar as her star overhead. And there the Lion, flickering in his own golden radiance. Each of these monuments, and there were a great many, stretching away and away, was a masterpiece. One other thing there was, too.

"Do you see, Beatrixa—each grave's thrown open—like a bed."

Beatrixa looked. She held her breath, astonished that she still breathed at all. She thought concisely, *The astrological signs are the markers not of their birth, but their deathdays. Their return into this world—*

At that moment, a grave which was marked by the Archer trembled, tilted, and the lid of earth flew up and slapped down again beside it.

"Look, oh look," said Beatrixa.

"I see. It's a child."

The child lay in the grave. But soon it sat up, and next it stepped slowly out of the earth. It wore nothing, was naked, nearly formless, yet its face was full of anxiety. It was crying.

"Oh, the child," she said. "Shall I go to it? What shall I say?"

But Silvio held her back, and in that instant, the child's face altered. It shook its hair, which became burnished, and for a second it was male, and then he was clothed. And the child broke out in a shout of laughter. Opening wide his arms, he flew up into the sky as if to greet his friend.

"In God's name, it's myself—" Silvio said. "It is me—"

"No, my love. No, not you."

"But so I was. Look how he soars about. All fear gone. Everything before him. Ah, no then. Not myself. What did I have? He was a human thing once. And I never was."

"My love," she said, "my love."

They watched the child, as joyful, skillful, and wild, it darted over the twilight sky towards the town of palazzi below.

"Are we to go there?" Silvio said to Beatrixa.

"I think it's allowed us."

But they had put their arms about each other again. Not to kiss or caress, not for the reassurance of sensation and lust, but only to be sure of each other, and of themselves.

In their minds, the voice of the angel sounded still. *Dawn you may have.* But were the glittering wave-crests one notch brighter, the moon a little less high?

In dreams, things are sometimes suddenly changed. And here, too, it seemed, this might happen. When finally they had crossed the graveyard, they needed to go through a grove of silent trees, where a fountain fell down into a basin. And looking up, the beginning of the waterfall was nowhere but in the starry sky.

Silvio cupped some of the water in his hand. "If we drink it, we must remain here."

"Do you think so?" she said. She shook her head. "Don't drink. I don't think it will give us that. Perhaps it's forbidden."

"Oh, Beatrixa, you'll tell me next I mustn't eat the Apple of the Tree."

"Yes, I would tell you that too."

Silvio drank the water, a few drops lingering in his palm. "It tastes of water."

Beatrixa said, "If you have taken it, then I must."

Then he would have stopped *her*, not uneasy, only cautious for her, as she had been for him. But she caught a little and put the moisture in her mouth.

"No, it tastes of light."

"On my mother's island," he said, "the fountains taste of wine or flowers—whatever one wishes. But this one knows its own mind."

Then they ceased to speak and looked at each other.

"We, too," he said, "are invited to their festival. Whatever that is."

For their garments had altered. Without their feeling or knowing or, for a minute, seeing it.

Her gown was of a blood-red velvet figured over in blue with a design of hearts that were also fruit. And he was now clad in cloth-of-gold, the doublet slashed to reveal yellow silk. Both were crowned with flowers, the flowers of the world, roses, myrtle.

"The colors of our houses," she said.

Beyond the grove, in the direction of the palazzi, music began to sound. Earth's music, too, Venus music, violas, mandolas, the tabor, the reed—

"And the design on my gown," she said, "is for a bride."

"Yes," he said, "I think you are right."

She was troubled. He, carefree.

She said, "Is this truly to be? *Is* it a dream, then?"

The music was nearer, and Silvio came and caught her to him again, making her his, as she was, reminding her without words that marriage, to them, was a formality and a ritual only. They were already joined, not yet by bodily union, but by the iron couplings of the spirit.

Outside the grove, when they emerged from it, waited their bridal procession on the grassy road.

They stared, the lovers, at a hundred people or more, none of whom they knew, and who were yet familiar to them, as if from the memories of others . . .

The wedding-guests had dressed in splendor. Their faces were smiling and expectant—and Beatrixa saw that the expression of Silvio's face was quite like theirs.

What had he really known but such a world as this, a world of happiness and delights—what had she known and seen about her but the other world, the world of earth, of sorrow and disappointments.

Small surprise he stood there, this superlative man, childish in his pleasure and acceptance. Nor that Beatrixa was so still.

Musicians in crimson and yellow struck their pear-shaped lutes; to the tapping of drums, acrobats turned cartwheels and walked on golden stilts. The red and turquoise dawn lit every figure, every drapery, the silverwork and rainbow tassels of the horses, the mantles that seemed stitched with diamonds, the cascading hair, the masks of animals and birds with sequined eyes, the faces all unknown and yet known.

Some had led two horses forward, for the bride and groom. (There were no servants here, of course.) The hands which assisted Beatrixa to mount were courteous, helpful. Physically able to be experienced. Silvio was already mounted, used to horses as to everything from the illusory war-camps of his earliest living fantasies.

They rode slowly down towards the town of palazzi.

On the sea, at the very line of meeting between sky and water, there was now a single crack of sheer white-gold.

Over a bridge the couple went, one high-arched and lined by statues that held high torches of grass-green flame. Below, a river of obsidian flowed to the jade of the sea and to the outer sea, which was carnelian.

Walking alongside her horse, which was a white one, trapped in white patterned by golden towers, Beatrixa recognized the guardsman from the Castello Barbaron, he who had died two years ago.

"Good morning, Beatrixa," he said, smiling up at her. His face was fine, and full now, too, of happy thought and good-will.

"Greetings, sir. I am glad—to see you here."

"Best girl. I am content, for now."

Sharply she said, "For now? But this is for eternity."

But when she looked down, she found he had gone off a short way, and instead Jacmo walked by her. Jacmo, who had been killed by the della Scorpia sword, that night above the Blessed Maria Canal.

And Jacmo said to her, "Even forever changes, Beatrixa. How else? It is For Ever."

None of them called her *lady*; she did not expect them to. But they spoke to her as if they were now far older than she, even Jacmo. But then, then, so they must be, here.

Turning her head, she saw that Silvio looked away. What was it that he saw—or *who*?

Silvio saw his mother, Meralda, who was riding a little grey palfry to his wedding. Her gown was emerald green, and she, too, had been garlanded with flowers. *Her* face was happy beyond all others. Intuitively, not understanding why that should be—did his joy still fuel hers, even now that he had gone over to another? Silvio sought after their former unity, his and Meralda's. It seemed to him that it was no longer present. He had thought this had been the case since their last dialogue, when they had parted on her island. And even so, she was all gladness. Nor did she even look at him. No, she looked at the man who rode beside her, on the roan horse. He was dressed magnificently, as were all present. His hair was quite long, brown, and curling.

My father?

He is my father. In this place she has found him again, and he has found her.

Beatrixa thought, *He is angry. Why is Silvio angry?*

Was anger possible, in Heaven? Perhaps not to any but Silvio, or Beatrixa.

We have not earned our stay here. We have never truly died. He scarcely, for he has never lived more than a day or so, and that as an atom. (How did she know this now?) *And I never, in any form.*

They have given us this, she thought. *They—whoever they may be. Or God. Or what must stand for God, here, since even here, it is not quite God's country.* (How too did she know that?) *For that would be inexplicable to any but those who are worthy of it and reach it as their ultimate prize.*

The outskirts of Heaven, this. I've known always. We must visit them sometimes, in dreams—

Silvio had urged his horse mildly through the crowd, which graciously parted to allow it. He came up by Meralda, his mother, and the man who must be the soul of Lorenzo Vai.

"Well," said Silvio, "and are you here?"

They looked at him.

He saw through them, not in any actual way, not now, but to the inner core of them both. They, too, had become one thing. They, too, were lovers, coupled by spirit.

"She's been a long time from me," said Lorenzo Vai, or his soul, or what, here, his soul had masked itself to be. "I tried to find her often, long ago. She never could hear me, then. But you've set her at liberty, Silvio. Now she can choose where she'll go."

"I? Liberty?—I never *chained* her."

But they were already gone from him. No longer to be seen.

He, the arch-magus of two worlds, now had worked on him the true sorcery of that which *outstrips* sorcery. They were gone, quite gone. The man, his father, old as a sage inside his looks of that callow, gorgeous young gallant he had been, was no more. And she, his mother, whose blissful ignorance had aided and abetted Silvio's greed and need of her, now vanished altogether, with only the sweetest and most gentle of forgetting, vanishing gazes.

Bells rang, as they did in Venus. In a hall of open arcades above the sea, Beatrixa Barbaron and Silvio della Scorpia were married, not only in the sight but perhaps in the very shadow of God. Or not. Priests spoke to them, and boys chanted, witnesses presented themselves, incense fumed. Flowers were thrown, and colored confetti and jewels. Birds soared over them in the sky (if they were birds). The very stars seemed to dance in the midst of the open roof.

In another hall, they feasted under complex gilded carvings and arches of green boughs, where roses bloomed that were not of the usual shades, but auburn, saffron, apricot, and cherry-colored, or purple like the robes of an emperor, or blue as lapis lazuli.

The sun had still not risen. But there was a gap of light there, on the laval sea.

How long do we have, how long before the dawn is ended?

They were sung to their chamber, which was high in a tower, a walled terrace that looked into the sky which now, surely, was more blue, like the roses, than dark.

There were none of the nastier jokes of such occasions. But there were the recollected bawdy ones—which apparently were not reckoned improper, here on the edges of Paradise. The food of the feast had been that way, too. The roast doves and cakes, the fruits and wines—they could not be real, they were not necessary— only for pleasure, only to make happy.

These are the things then, Beatrixa thought, *which will outlast all else. Delight and love. The rest—even honor, even despair—all swept away.*

But what can last for us? she thought.

And she was sad, as she saw that he, too, her lover and husband, was sad. But their sadness did not belong here, as they did not.

She remembered the flying child, and how Silvio had said "It's myself." And he was so in error.

The guests ebbed from them. For them, what had all this been? Something kind they did, some dream or repayment for some other joy they themselves had received? A curtain fell across a doorway.

In the wide and open chamber, Silvio and Beatrixa stood together, alone.

"She has left me," he said. "I mean, my mother. Now there's only you."

And Silvio in turn recalled how Beatrixa had half-confessed, half-accused him, *Who else have you left me to love?*

"Am I enough for you?" she said.

"Always."

We have the dawn, she thought.

I must never lose her, he thought.

The dawn will end, even in a year. It will not be so long.

*I shall lose her. So much is unavoidable. How do I know?
But I know.*

There was a bed, like a bed of the City, heaped with costly covers and feather pillows.

To this they went, and, when they wished it, their clothes were gone from them. Naked as children, the man and the woman regarded each other. Speaking, they told each other each of the other's beauty. They moved together, and all things were dismissed, even Heaven and the world, but for themselves.

Across the flame-scaled sea, the sun began to rise. An inch at a time, a brilliancy that did not scorch or blind, but that filled the Heaven-country with immense and shining light.

Gradual as a dye dissolving in water, the turquoise dark grew thin, and the blue of the sky appeared, a blue more blue than blue. And in the day sky, too, there were stars, golden stars.

For the lovers, several comparative hours had passed. Silvio and Beatrixa had possessed them all. They had eaten up time, with each other's flesh.

Now they slept and did not see (yet in their sleep they saw, nevertheless) the waking sky, the sun that was like no sun.

In sleep, too, they spoke, for the last time in that place.

"It's over. Where will we go now?"

"Only God can know."

"We'll be parted."

"Yes, I believe so. We have had too much together."

"Punishment, then."

"No, not to punish us. I was wrong thinking that. There's no cruelty here, not even the flail of justice. We must work out our own amends, see to ourselves. Until we're fit, and whole. But you and I—it can't be, for us."

"Beatrixa, I would die in reality, any death at all, to keep you.

"I would die to keep you. But that's no use.

"Is that a nightingale singing so loudly?"

"A daylark, my love."

"This was worth more than the world."

"Silvio—it was worth more to me than Heaven."

BARTOLOME

YEARS AFTER, WHEN SHE EXPLAINED IT to me, which she did without compromise, and under such circumstances that I could hardly argue with her, most of me did not believe it. Not a word.

How could she know such extravagant things? Yes, she seemed skilled in witchcraft, if so I must call it. She understood the planets and the stars, herbs and salves. She understood the hearts of men and women. She was, besides, though not pious, spiritual. But she was a romantic, too, a teller of stories and a dreamer of dreams—and that was all well and good, especially in a woman who could be, as well, as practical and wise as Flavia—but in this, in this, how could I think such things had ever happened, and if she said she *knew* they had, not put it down to her wanderings at that lamentable hour.

Flavia vowed she had seen their history, those two, one of them dead or something stranger, and our history also, hers and mine, coming and going, like pictures in the fire.

"I told you almost from the first, that I had this power, Bartolo."

"Yes, my best love, so you did."

I have said, I would not, could not argue at that time. In her eyes I saw, though, the shade of doubt—not in what she had scried or had to recount, but in my acceptance of it.

On that night when she did tell me, there in the house by the weedy canal, to the south of the Diana Gardens, I listened to every utterance she made with tremendous care. Even some of it I wrote down, to keep it fresh for me, I said. Really to keep fresh her words, as I would have kept her voice if I could, inside a jar, as the sea keeps in a shell.

It was nearly two years ago, that night. Early in the season, in the Capricorn month, and cold. I remember the cold, like the cold in that dream I had of Meralda, down at the laguna's bottom. I remember that night as if it had been yesterday night, and tomorrow I shall remember as if it were tonight. To my final day on this earth, I will remember that night, the last I ever spent with my lovely one, my Flavia, south of the Diana Gardens.

Now, however, I must tell you that I believe it all, everything she said. That is, I believe it as much as one may do, here in the mortal state (for now and then, too, I doubt). I have come to it in little rushes, the way a child learns what is truly good for it.

I cannot give definite assurance of how or why. You may say, perhaps it is only I want to keep her with me still, and that is how I must do it, preserving the truth as she reckoned truth, along with her image in my mind.

It was then, that night, Flavia who told me how, all those years before, Beatrixa Barbaron was discovered by one of her maids, who had gone up to see, belatedly, to the candles in her chamber.

The door was unlocked, and going in, the maid found Beatrixa lying on the floor insensible.

For some while there had been a great storm crushing its way across the sky, and one thunderclap there had been which seemed to shake the palace to its cellars. The maid thought at once that her lady must have fainted from the shock of it, as one or two had done elsewhere in the house.

When she bent over her mistress, the maid saw Beatrixa's eyes were just opening.

"There, there, M'donna," said the maid, "the worst has passed on."

"Has it?" Beatrixa asked her. And then, as if from some way off, she added, "So much does pass."

The maid was concerned, and assisted her to rise.

Beatrixa was not her usual calm and ordered self. Indeed, the maid said later, she would never have believed Beatrixa, of all of them, would swoon at thunder. She seemed agitated and hurried, yet curiously listless too.

"How long has it been?" Beatrixa then inquired.

"M' donna?"

"I mean, how long have I been gone from the City?"

The maid, still thinking it was the thunderclap which had done all this, and eager to reassure her lady, said, "Oh, only a few minutes, madam."

"In God's name," said Beatrixa. She crossed herself. And then, startling the girl, she shook out her hand as if she had done something irrelevant, foolish even. She said, "It was only a sunrise, but I would suppose it lasted the length at least of a summer afternoon. But time would be different, there."

Something in all this attracted the maid's attention. She said, rather frightened, "*Where*, madam?" And then, since either she was no simpleton, or because she was ironically more credulous than most, "You have been to somewhere else while you lay senseless? Where, oh where?"

At this Beatrixa looked at her, and her dark face cleared.

"She said to me, 'Nowhere at all, don't be nervous. It was only my fancy.' But, oh, she said it to comfort me. I do think she had a glimpse of some other sphere. I'm afraid even to wonder about it."

Beatrixa, presently allowed the maid to see to her clothing, and prepared herself for sleep. When the girl was gone, Beatrixa lay down in the bed, alone. She thought she would always, hereafter, lie alone. For either she had sinned with demons, or she had been to a land above most others, and like the saints, who deserve to travel there, returning, undeserving, she was bereft. Besides, she had lost her love, her only love. When this happens, as I, too, know, snow falls on the heart.

But I will also speak of Silvio, and what Flavia said of where he found himself when he, too, woke, ghost, or whatever I must call him—I am unsure, though Flavia did name his condition, which was that of a character or personality existing without flesh or soul.

Silvio woke up and found himself lying, not on the island which had been his mother's, and which he himself had anticipated, but on the chill tesselations of a floor in a wide, high room. He knew at once he was in this world, our world, which was so drab after the island, let alone the panoply of that higher plane he had also seen.

Getting to his feet, he passed through at once, and before he thought about it, a heavy, ancient cabinet that stood against one wall. And this bitterly entertained him.

He saw he was yet, whatever else had been rent from him, a magician in the world of men.

The room, said Flavia, was a grand one, but bleak, dismal in the coming of an overcast earthly dawn. Cobwebs hung from beams above, but with these, certain blazons of the house. As the light flowed in like water through the thick-glazed windows, Silvio could be in no doubt of where he now was.

"When everything else is taken from us," Flavia said, "sometimes our only course is to seek close kindred, however alien to us they may be."

The banners hanging there were of the Scorpion, dulled gold and ochre, on a faded chestnut ground. The room was the great, old, neglected sala of the della Scorpia Palazzo, that lies behind Laguna Aquila.

Silvio himself was not best pleased to find himself there.

He walked about the sala, looking at objects in it indifferently. But he knew it was the memories his mother had implanted, in his noncorporeal body, these solely which had brought him here.

And where else might he go? Heaven (if Heaven it had been) had closed its gates to him. He thought he recollected even some voice in sleep which had turned him out, like Adamus from Eden. And the green island, he sensed had vanished, as emerald Meralda had, going away on her journey without him, her hand in that of Lorenzo Vai.

What then would Silvio do, here in this house of his ancestors where, presumably, in some inexorable way, he belonged?

If he were to live here, might he not still cross the City, and find out Beatrixa in her own venue at Barbaron?

No sooner did he think this, than a stroke of purest agony and sorrow thudded home against and within him. It was like a mortal wound, which he would never have felt. This was a spiritous one, and must be worse.

Silvio knew in that second that Beatrixa was gone from him forever. That what had joined them had been, by their very union—*broken*. To all the world, he might hereafter make himself known and seen, but to Beatrixa never again might he appear, let alone speak to her, or touch her. And in some terrible manner he thought, too, that she might be, of all things physical, *herself* invisible—to *him*. For they had joined elsewhere, they had been made one, but only for that given time. And the payment for it, which both instinctively had known, was eventual utter separation. Nor was this a *punishment*. It was mere logic.

He thought that he would go to the Castello by the Canal of the Triumph, would stride in through the walls and up to her bedchamber and find her, and see.

Then, his heart failed him. Silvio leaned against the wall and wept. He knew he did not dare this. Because, he foresaw also, it would be no earthly use.

He had lost Beatrixa, and she had lost him, perhaps—certainly—forever.

But he—he had lost everything save life—which anyway he had never had.

Exactly then, a door to the sala opened.

A woman entered.

She wore a black gown, and her pale yellow hair was confined in a stiff, gilded net. She walked straight across the floor, went to a chest by the wall, and pulled up the heavy lid.

Silvio watched all this. And then, to his slight, deadened surprise, the woman half glanced at him. She murmured, "Please, my wish isn't to disturb you. I only came—to look at this again."

She saw him clearly, as mortal things did when he did not mask himself from them. For an instant, he had a vicious urge to vanish before her eyes and alarm her. But then he saw, her face was marked with tears.

"My lady," he said, "what's your trouble? Can I help you?"

Why did he, of all creatures, say such a thing? Like calls to like, it seems. He had returned to the della Scorpia house, and in his own grief, he saw hers, and hated it for her, that dark companion.

"Sir, you're kind. But, no. Of course, you don't know me. I came back a stranger to this house."

"I, too," he said.

He had walked over to her to stand a few feet away. Curiosity had not left him, either. He gazed into the chest, and saw a penon-flag there, one which bore no resemblance to anything of the della Scorpias. It displayed a rust-red flaring disc he took for a representation of the sun, on a quartered ground of black and white.

"My husband's device," the woman said simply. "He died at Fensa, in Borja's army. The Duke Chesare was dulcet, and told me my husband had been one of his favorites among the Franchian captains. The Duke said he had always liked to hear my husband sing. Perhaps this was a falsehood, but I thought not, when he said it to me. Yves told me that Borja remembers everything, and every particular skill any of his men may have—in case one day it might be useful to him."

Silvio looked at her. From her words he deduced two things, that she was loving, yet pragmatic. She had, not peculiarly in this familial house, a little look of his mother, but without her beauty. Mostly, in those moments, this woman reminded Silvio of Beatrixa, unbearably of her, for it was more than he *could* bear.

"Oh, I beg you—don't shed tears for me. Who are you, that you have such a gentle heart?"

But Silvio drew back. He said, "Forgive me and excuse me, madam. I must intrude on you no longer."

And he turned for the door, to walk out of the room like a proper human man, and not add fear to her wretchedness.

But she called softly after him, "But tell me your name, sir, if you will."

"I have no name," he said, going out, "I am no one."

PART FIVE

The World

HAMLET:	Whose grave's this, sirrah?
GRAVEDIGGER:	Mine, sir . . .
HAMLET:	I think it be thine indeed, for thou *liest* in it.

WILLLIAM SHAKESPEARE
Hamlet

DIONYSSA

THE STUDY ON THE SECOND FLOOR had a window that faced that courtyard like a well.

Although the day was not sunny, it was hot; the window had been opened. The acacia, which had been slightly damaged, perhaps by the previous winter's blasts, had yet put on all its intricate foliage, and two pigeons were sitting there.

Como stood by his window, watching them. Marveling, as sometimes he did now, at animals, or the very young—at the careless, smug emptiness of their lives.

How quickly that could change, however, even for the young. How quickly and how horribly. Como was thinking now of his nephew, Dario, who lay screaming and part-mad in the priestly care to which he had been removed. It was the disease they called Franchian—the Siphilusic ailment, named from a poem, and passed during the sexual act, which destroyed first skin and muscle, then bone and brain, in unstoppable progression. How unlucky Dario had been. Como recalled ruefully his own excessive youthful dalliances—and here he stood, aging and uncomely—yet whole, alive. But, no more of that.

He looked back into the chamber then, and saw the woman had seated herself as she had been invited to, in the velvet chair. He thought, oddly, *She has more presence than I recalled.*

"So, Dionyssa, I imagine you're here on the same errand as your mother. Am I to infer you have already noted someone?"

She appeared composed and, if she was pale, that seemed natural to her; she had always been so. Besides, something had brought up a slight color in her cheeks.

"My lord," she said, "do you mean you think I wish, as my mother wishes it for me, to wed again?"

"Well. Would it be a crime?"

"No, my lord."

"Of course, in the eyes of the world, more time should elapse. Your first husband is dead . . . how long?"

"A year and approaching two months, my lord."

"You are exact."

"No, my lord," she said. "Did you wish me to be? I can tell you the precise amount in days, if you'd prefer."

Como reflected.

"Then it's taxing for you, Dionyssa, to be a widow this long a while. You yearn to be a wife instead."

She flinched. He saw it.

"Come," he said, "we agree, there's nothing sinful in that. You're young. And you must want children, too."

Then he saw her frown. It was a deep-cut and intent frown. She did not bend it on him, but on the row of books behind his table. Her finely made mouth tightened, not sulky but fastidious. Intrigued, he thought, *Willful too, in her way.*

"My lord, for a woman who wished for it, it would be the most natural thing on earth. I wish for anything but."

"I see."

"I say *anything*, my lord. I mean it. If my choice is marriage or to be sent away to some poverty-house of beggar nuns—which I think is quite usual in the case of a difficult woman such as myself—then I'll go. I'll go gladly. I will go," she said, and her eyes came up and fixed on his, defiant yet removed, "singing."

Como shook his head. He seated himself, too, and eased his stiff leg, which had become damnably stiffer with time, even on a summer's morning.

"Dissa—my dear girl—I won't force you to that. Nor to marry if you won't have it." Her face flooded with color. She seemed to take a breath that she had been without some while. "Oh, your donna-mother would like it, I know. To have everyone at their correct station, like a troop of soldiers. The men tailored and swaggering about at the Ducem's court, the women clutched in influential nuptuals, each pouring forth babies like a bee-queen." (He saw her eyebrows go up, and was not sorry. Como still liked women, he always would, and liked to tease and to amaze them even now. Even his relatives, and with a bad leg under the table, and his face giving way—God have pity!—like a wet dough—but God had had pity: whole, alive.) "No, no, my girl. If you don't want to wed, we will keep you here instead, to brighten our lives.

Then she lowered her eyes and sighed, and he saw her hands were shaking.

"I would have come to see you sooner, my lord. If I'd known. I've been so unhappy, thinking I would be *made* to marry.

"You went obediently to it the first time."

"Yes. I was afraid, but I was obedient."

"Was he cruel to you?"

She said, "No—he was—"

"He made you love him. Even though you had been afraid, and he was a Franchian."

"To love him very much."

"You *should* have come to me sooner. You should, Dissa."

"Yes. I would not have come today, but . . ." she paused, then said, "But my lord, I don't think, even with your approval, I can stay in the palazzo, if—if I refuse eventually to wed."

"The Lady Caterina will nag at you."

"My mother, yes."

"Dear God. I'll speak to her—"

"No—no. Let's have peace. She will only say one thing to you, and another to me."

"She, then, is *not* obedient."

Dionyssa smiled faintly. "Only to God and Jesu Christ."

"Well, it is a beginning, I suppose."

She stared at him, then broke out into a laugh. It was a pretty ripple of sound. She sang well, too. As her husband had done; even the Borja had remarked that.

Como said, "Where do you wish to go then, Dissa? Back to your lands in Franchia?"

"No. I would loath my life there, without Yves."

"What are we to do then?"

He saw she had something under her hands, something she had been crumpling up, and now smoothed. It was the old penon-flag that her husband's men had carried into war. She had been given it, along with the greater banner, on his death, and now brought it with her as a child brings its toy: one ally.

She said, though, firmly enough, "There is, if *I* may choose, the religious house at Santa Maria Sta' Bianca. I might live there, if you allow it. a secular life. I don't want to take the veil. But I should be more content in a . . . in a quieter home. There are gardens there, and pri-

vate land. I could go about as I wanted and be a her-
mitess when I wished. I could have my music and other
things I like."

"And in all comfort," he said.

"I think I can obtain funds from my Frankish
lands—it may take a short while, his cousins never wanted me to get the revenues—"

"That must be dealt with at once," said Como.
"Confound them, what are they, jackals? I'll see to it your
husband's legacy comes to you, Dissa. And meanwhile,
you shall have all you need from the della Scorpia cof-
fers. We'll gift Maria Sta' Bianca generously too, it does
no harm. Then you can go there as you wish. But now
and then, you must come here to visit me."

She rose to her feet and, going across to him, took
his hand and kissed it. "Signore-donno patrone."

"There, there. Now you're crying again.

"I'm happy."

"No, not yet. But it will come. Time runs away, and
the knives in our sides hurt less. We have rheumatics
instead, some of us."

But he thought presently, what a pleasure it had
been to assist her. In this at least, he had been able to
make some difference.

As she went back along the corridor, her husband's
war-blazon in her hand, Dionyssa de Mars was already
planning what should be packed up for her, and whom
she would have to help her in that—her escape.

Indeed, she *did* yearn to be gone, though she had
not insulted Como by saying it. To leave this dreary
house with its dusts and sickness, its slow decay,
enlivened only by feuds and jealousy, and a sense of
unquiet specters.

The sisterhood of Sta' Bianca was not itself unduly

rigorous, and though she would not now have to join it
Dionyssa was glad to be going there. She did not like the
idea that hardship was the only road to God. Why would
she? She had suffered, and thought the condition without value.

Now, however, everything was simplified, lightened.
And all that, how strangely, because of her words with
the young man in the sala this morning, which had given
her courage at last to seek out Lord Como herself.

Why had this happened? Who had he been, the
well-dressed della Scorpia noble, who had then left,
gray-faced and his eyes full of tears; so young and made
for pleasure he had seemed, and yet, and yet—

He had not tempted her, not even once (erotically,
strategically) to look at her life as an available woman. It
was not that. Maybe only like had called to like. And seeing his pain that her own, evidently, had stirred, she was
made angry. So she took her stand. It was a fact, which
she would never know, that not only had the de Mars blazon gone with her into Como's study, but a ghost. Even
while her meeting with him gave her new strength, Silvio
della Scorpia, unseen by either other occupant of the
room, had stood behind her chair. Silent . . . as the grave.

BEATRIXA

"YES, WHAT DO YOU WANT?"

How impatient he could be. How intolerant. What else?" And his voice would most probably change, when he heard her speak.

"My lord."

"Beatrixa—Triche—"

His voice had changed. Friendly now, and welcoming. He had gotten up, the papers and the cup of wine left on the table. In the candlelight, his reddened, sweating face, the malt-brown hair fell around it but left the dome of his head unoccupied. She had always thought his forehead broad and intelligent above the porker's face—and it was. Andrea *was* a clever and a knowledgeable man. And he smiled on her, showing that he loved her best, even if he did not properly admit it. And all that made it so much more terrible—what he, who could think and who could love, had once done, from some abstraction of petty revenge—worse, from mere petty expediency.

"Do I disturb you, sir?"

"No, Triche. I've been studying the reports of our traders in the East, and I've had more than enough. God send us soon some other continent to feed on. I'm glad to be diverted."

This will be more than diversion, Father.

Here she waited, the sword drawn in her hands.

"My lord," she said, "I have to tell you something of a very serious nature."

He will go mad. He will strike you. You're brave, what do you care—that's nothing to you—

It is perfectly true. I don't care. It is nothing. Not now. Not any more.

"What is it you've brought me? Is it for me?" Jovial again. Like Jove himself, god of thunders and lusts, another smasher of lives.

Oh, it is the sword, Father, that's what I've brought—

Beatrixa set the Casket down on his table, and drew away the cover she had put over it.

"Gold?"

"Yes, my lord."

"You're not often so formal, when we're alone, Triche. And yet, what an expensive present."

"There's a heart in it."

"Eh?"

"It's the relic of a saint. An unrecognized saint. Beatifica, Saint Fire."

"Bea-tifica. Wait. The witch who brought God's wrath down on the Jurneian infidel. Ah, yes. The Council of the Lamb waxed scared and had her burned. But this relic was stolen from La'Lacrima, was it not? How did you get it? Have you looked at it?"

"The lid won't open," she said. This was now also true.

Andrea tried. He was powerful, his hands could bend iron, as they said Chesare Borja could. But the lid stayed shut, as if fused to the metal of the box.

"Are you sure it's the reliquary?"

"Yes. It works miracles. It still does that."

"You haven't told me how you have it?"

"My lover." she said, "gave it me, before we parted. He fished it up from the Laguna Silvia, where it had been thrown."

"Your lover, eh. Who's that? Who's been making eyes at you? Better say, I know you're a sensible woman, but—"

"No, I've not been sensible, my lord."

Andrea stopped. His face became static. He was puzzled, like a bull, she thought, that suddenly sees the door of the pen is open, and yet something stands there, sword in hand.

"What do you mean, Triche?"

"I mean I have made a secret marriage, sir. And he and I have consumated it. We have lain together, I and my lover, and danced the dance which is performed on the belly or the back—"

"Don't speak in that way—"

"You'd have me not speak, but I tell you I have done more than *speak*. I have been, if you will then, well *wed*."

"You say to me—"

"I'm no longer a virgin, or even in the single state. In the market of marriages, I'll be useless to you from this day on."

He grunted. He turned, swung about the room, came back a short distance and halted.

His big fists were clenched. His face was swollen, bloodied from within. Yet not angry.

"You fool, if it's a fact—"

"I have said. Send a doctor to me. He'll soon tell you."

"Triche—Beatrixa—why, in the name—"

"*Why*? Why do you think?"

He opened his eyes. He said. "I don't know why. Tell me why."

"Because I have renounced my Barbaron honor, and yours, since our honor, *Father*, was despoiled long, long ago. Oh, come, sir. Have you never before heard a story of a young woman who lay down with her lover in spite of her House? I think you have. She ran away with him, it seems, but someone learned of it, and took them up in his grasp, and delivered them to the justice of the young lady's spurned betrothed, whose name was Ciara. *He* was a monster of the pit."

Andrea said, "Yes, I know the tale. He killed them both and flung the bodies in the lagoon—"

"You should know the tale, but you don't, it seems. I will tell you, Andrea Barbaron, I will tell you—"

She seemed to float in the air before him, shining with her hideous victory, her feet off the floor, come from some other world too dark, too full of light.

"Beatrixa—"

"My lover, you see, has told me what happened to Meralda della Scorpia. I can't remember when he told me. But what he knew, I do, too. And now so shall you. Ciara slew Lorenzo by cutting from him his male member, which was then cooked and given, in disguise as a dinner dish, to Meralda to eat. Then Ciara informed her of what he had done, and showed her Lorenzo's body, to prove the case. After this he sent her back to the della Scorpias, but on the lagoon, she threw herself in and drowned."

"Christ's love."

"What has *love* to do with *that*? I will say what is to do with it. Wickedness. Evil. *You*. That is what is to do with it."

Andrea clapped his hand across his mouth. He retched once, violently, turned from her and spat into the empty hearth. Then he walked to the table, refilled his cup and drained it. His back to her, he said, "I have never known."

"Now you do. If you believe me."

"I believe you. On both counts."

"Then, my lord, why don't you chastize me. You saw fit to give Meralda over to Hell-on-earth for her single transgression, which had nothing to do with your house. You think women who fall must be treated so. I am your daughter. You *own* me. What will you do to *me*?"

"Beatrixa—"

"Perhaps only run me through with a dagger. My lover is gone and I was never yet betrothed. This will limit your retribution."

"Be quiet," he said. His voice was quieter than the word. But it stayed her at last. "You have said enough."

She had.

She sank down in a chair and closed her eyes.

Silvio—she thought, *my love—my love—*

But there was no love in the world, not now.

This was the fee for Heaven. Death while alive. Loss until the Final Day. Beyond? She knew, oh she knew.

In the end, she became aware of him, the man who had been her father, moving about. Heavy, rustling movements of mantle and booted feet. The bull-pig, scuffing at the straw.

When she raised her lids, she was dully astonished to see the candles had almost burned down—they had mostly been fresh when she came in. Time here too, it seemed, did not always follow its own pattern.

Andrea had now sat down in a chair, some way across from her. He looked into the wall as he said, "I regret very much that you've come to hate me, Beatrixa."

"I, also," she murmured.

"What I did—was then."

"No," she said. But now she had no strength. She could never forgive, but to continue to insist aloud was not possible.

"Then," he said, "I accept I may not excuse myself to you. Although even to God I might."

"If you believe in God."

"I wonder if I do. Perhaps. I did, when young. In all of it. But then, God would condemn me too. More thoroughly than Ciara, even. I held the key, and put it there in the lock under his hand."

She could not talk to him any more.

He seemed to see this, and he said, "Know, at least, I learn now I was always stupid, in what I thought to be my task, my honor—my duty. For *that*, none of it—I can't apply that to you. I couldn't harm you, Beatrixa. If you had been Meralda, or she you, she would have been safe with me. And if any man had done for her what I did, then I would dismantle him with my bare hands. That told, I must send you away."

She said nothing.

He said, "You will be glad enough to go, of course. As things stand now. Far from me, and from my house. Far from honor, and the City and the lagoons, and all these dead."

After all she said, "Is there such a place, far from all these things? They aren't to be eluded." And then, "Oh, one place. But not there. Perhaps never again."

Then they sat in silence, and at a distance, he and she, while the candles burned right away, and the night once more filled the room.

Leone, her white dog, had avoided her since that night Silvio had come to her chamber and given her the question she must ask her father—the question now so irrevocably answered. At first she had thought the dog had been lost, and had sent searchers after him about the palazzo. She had looked, herself, too. But her mind had been on other things, and perhaps she did not search thoroughly enough. At length Beatrixa did find Leone herself. He was in the garden; hiding, she reasoned, under a hedge. When he saw her, he got up, shook himself apologetically, and ran away again.

She had known why.

And now she knew why he had come back.

While she rode to the outskirts of the City, first in the boat, under the hoop of the central cabin-house, next in the box-litter with its red and blue curtains down, lastly in the jolting carriage on the rutted road, Leone sat in her lap, or lay beside her on the cushion. Sometimes he would sit up, raise his white ears, and look about. He would look at *her*, inquiring, waiting.

"No, my little lion." Beatrixa said to him, "he isn't with me now. You're safe enough, Leone. Silvio will never return."

It was a tiresome, tiring journey, just as she recalled, to Veronavera. Three days it took, and half a morning, and then two horses of the escort cast shoes, and she was told she should not go on alone, and they did not reach the castle of the Barbarons until nightfall.

Torches had been lit along the approach, to welcome her. Indoors, all the candles, she believed, must have been got out of store.

The first thing that attracted her attention, or which made itself known to her, was the vastness of the mountains. An enormity not only of size, gargantuan, intangible, immanent. And later, going out on to the stone walk that led from her new room, the summer air was charged with their presence as if with invisible fires.

And Beatrixa thought, *I remember this. It was never here I felt it. It was—elsewhere.*

For it seemed the uplands and the mountains recalled her to the sharp nostalgia for heaven.

Leone ran back to her up the steps from the vine-walk below, because he heard her crying. Others who heard her kept their own council. Gossip had come ahead of her. She was disgraced, their lady, unmarriage-able and outcast. No wonder she wept. But she was still one they could be proud of, dignified and kind. She was yet theirs. And her own.

As the summer months went by, Beatrixa took on the management of the rocca-castle, assisted by Omberto, the Barbaron steward. Finding her apt and astute, Omberto quickly gave over the reins of authority. "She is like her father." he said. "She knows what she wants. Most unusual in a woman." "It seems she was woman enough somewhere else," said Omberto's son. "And too much of one." At which the steward said, "If we are to believe that. For my part, I doubt it. Look at her. Do you think her so light she'd flutter down at some man's whim? No, this is some other thing that sent her here." "What, then?" "God knows," said Omberto.

Beatrixa did not seem to pine for her home in the City, nor for her kin. And no one came to visit her. Letters came, it was true, from her mother, and two or three of her cousins, and later from her father. But Andrea Barbaron's first letter arrived in response to one of Beatrixa's own, in which she had asked him if she might, herself, have seen to certain repairs to the walls, and to several outbuildings.

Andrea's letter then was amiable and encouraging, but not effusive. He gave her good advice on workmen and on the repairs themselves, spoke of books that he had purchased for her and would be sending, along with other things for her ease, and generally of house affairs. He did not press for her affection, or any sign of contrition in her, or of her forgiveness. Beatrixa, reading the letter, beheld again, as if far off in fog, someone she recognized. She saw Andrea, too, had self-respect, and had kept his respect, such as it was, for her. She was relieved to find they could communicate without danger. She had been very afraid of what his first letter might reveal.

By late summer, all the running of the castle was smoothly in Beatrixa's hand. Everything seemed to have benefitted from her residence, and those who had actively professed their loyalty to her, whatever she might have done, now congratulated themselves. The rocca was far more of a house, as in ancient times, when a lord and lady were often domiciled there. It was not only in full repair but seemed sleeker, within and without, had grown more elegant and far more comfortable. The gardens flourished, pruned and trimmed and planted with successfully blooming experiments. The library swelled, and became impressive, with books arriving now almost monthly, not from Venus alone, but from the outer bounds of Italy, from Egypt even, and infidel lands. The servants went about, pleased that their virtues were now noticed and commended, and that any dead wood, as with the garden, had been removed. That now they had someone to go to for redress —Omberto had seldom been ready to make judgment in their quarrels. This, Lady Beatrixa did, however, and fairly. "Wise as Sheba," they said, "after she had lain with Solomon." By which maybe they meant sexual looseness could improve some women, providing it was gone about the right way.

They did not even look askance at Beatrixa when she went riding with just one groom, her hair mostly down, otherwise in the garb of a man, and astride the horse.

Let others mind their manners. Beatrixa Barbaron became a law to herself.

The hills were putting on their foxy autumn coloring. In the orchards and gardens the fruit burned on the boughs, and particular lanes ran with the purple of bled grapes. A time of plenty. Before winter began.

Beatrixa, on a black horse, galloped across the ridges of the hills, glimpsing now and then Veronavera (*vera*, for Truth) miles off below. That was to one side. Elsewhere the mountains rested in disembodiment, veiled in a blue fall mist.

It was about ten in the morning. In Venus, the Primo Pegno would be sounding, and dimly she heard it start up too from the churches and duomo of the town. Those bells, so slender and unmeaningful in the hollow air—

"Lady—M'donna, wait, if you will!"

Beatrixa reined in and the horse, vigorous and young, well trained and responsive to her, came swiftly to a standstill.

"What is it?"

The groom pointed off up the next hill.

"Other riders, M'donna. About ten or twelve of them. I don't know their colors. I saw them as I came over the last slope."

Beatrixa thought for a moment. Farms and vineyards lay near enough, the castle itself was only half an hour's ride off. But there was woodland between now.

Sometimes there *were* riders, of course. The noble families of Veronavera also enjoyed sport; they and others hunted the woods regularly for exercise, and meat. The hills were, they said, good pork country.

"Well, I expect they have their own business."

"Yes, lady, but they looked ruffianly, some of them, to me. And slovenly-dressed, all but one or two."

"We will turn down towards the town," said Beatrixa.

But at that moment the other riders rushed sweeping up from the dip in the hills, ran over the crest, and flew like arrows straight towards them.

If they were not smartly turned out, these men, and they did mostly look a rough lot, their horses were of the best.

"Ride back to the rocca," said Beatrixa to the groom. "I will stay."

"And leave you here—no, lady—"

"Do as I say. Get some of our own men and come back." He hesitated, and she said, "If you disobey me in this, you may cause the deaths of both of us. *Go.*"

And he turned and galloped off, his face undone with panic. Afraid himself, she had reckoned he would not be much help. If both of them were to flee, they would invite pursuit. She would remain and use her wits—or the knife at her belt. She did not say to herself, as she had not said to her groom, that, whatever this encounter was, she did not much care.

She was, as once before, in error.

She would have cared, had she known.

But the ruffianly band was already near enough that she could see their faces now, and hear the jingle of spurs and bridles. Two of the men had crossbows. A crew, indeed.

How curious though, that one, there, he had a familiar look. He was bearded, in the Spanish or Frankish fashion. And that one as well; she had seen *him* once, surely. Their leader, who rode, she noted, superlatively well, and with a sort of negligence only possible in perfection, now shouted in a clear, carrying peal. At once the charge halted. Then he, by himself, came trotting over.

His horse was worth a fortune, Beatrixa judged. And he was a handsome man, handsome to an extent that human things seldom are. Then she took in how his hair matched the autumn shades on the hills, and how despite his unprincely clothes, she knew him. How could she not? She had seen him quite close less than a year before.

"Good day, my lord Duke," said Beatrixa, as he drew up to her.

At this, he raised his brows.

"Can I go nowhere incognito? I did my very best."

"Certainly, your grace. My man thought you all a pack of bandits and I sent him to fetch assistance."

He said, idly, "Some would say he was correct, in any case."

She smiled. Since that must be a jest.

Chesare Borja looked at her long and stilly. And at his regard, which was unmistakable, Beatrixa felt the blood come up in her cheeks. But this was reflexive only. Though it perhaps pleased him.

"You must pardon me, madam, both for alarming you, and for staring at you. But I've not frequently seen a lady of good birth riding in such a manner. Of course, there was the Amazon, Caterina Svortsa, but I must confess, to count her as a woman, let alone an aristocrat, was usually beyond me."

"I find this way convenient, your grace. It's not generally immodest, as I seldom meet strangers, or if I do, I do not stop to address them."

"And I have improperly addressed *you*, I fear. And anyway I, too, and they, " he indicated the other men, who sat about now grinning or blank-faced, watching the interchange, "are in deep disguise. We're off hunting. Pork country this, I believe. We took you and your boy for two of our own party from the garrison, hence our precipitate advent. But tell me, how do you know me?"

"I was present, your grace, when you wed my City."

"Ah. Then that castle in the distance is yours. You're one of the Barbaron House, I think." He had known her colors. They said, he forgot very little, and that fragment not worth remembering.

"Yes, your grace."

"May I know your name?"

"Beatrixa," she said.

"The Lord Andrea's daughter."

Again, he looked very closely at her. Here she was, the sole legal female child (if he knew that—probably he did) of a high house in Venus, sluttishly galivanting on the hills in breeches, with the protection only of one groom.

She said, "My father has made me the rocca's Castellana."

"I see."

Yes, he doubtless did. Something, at any rate.

His horse sidled, and he gentled it charmingly. On his bare hand, clean and shapely, a ruby and a pearl. Otherwise he wore the garments of a servant, which fitted his spare and well-made body like the raiment of a king. He knew all that, too.

She thought, *What am I doing now? He is the most lethal and trustless man in Italy, in a quarter of the world.*

But she did not care. Cared about so few things. And besides, something—what?—not attraction, not anything like that—yet something, something—

He spoke now in a lower, more velvety tone. It was meant to touch her, and it did, like fingers flickering over her spine.

"I hope you'll forgive me, madam, but I must ask— where on God's earth did you come by such quantities of hair?"

"It grew, " she said, "upon me."

At that he laughed. Oh, his laugh. It was like Silvio's laughter, almost, almost. Beautiful laughter, given to enchant. False, in this one, cultivated. As it had been indigenous in the other.

"Well, you are to be congratulated," he said. "On your sorceress's locks, your horsemanship and your courage. Let me make amends for any worry I've put you to. Will you allow me to call on you at your Castello?"

One did not say no. Not to this one.

She did not, however, want to say no.

"We should be honored, your grace

"Oh, call me Chesare. Grace is for courts and churches. Who is at home, aside from you?"

"No one," she said. Guilelessly.

Guileless also, the arch-deceiver added, "Then perhaps, it won't be too inconvenient for you. It will just be myself, you understand. No need for ceremony. Anything will do for supper."

God's Heart, she thought, *he wanted to be fed, too.*

He rode a short way with her, off from his men, conversational, flirting now and then, to remind her what he was after, to show her he would be gallant providing she gave in.

She had heard some rumors here, how he came and went in Venus now, disguised, slipping in and out of the City and its satellite places, recognized sometimes, or not. He had his own wanderer, they said, for the canals. And his own favorite hostelry. She had heard also, that the Rivoalto bored him, and Nicolo the Ducem.

He had almost died, last year in Rome, and his father, the pope, Alessandro, who—if he had perished, would have dragged Chesare down with him, dead or alive. After that, you might do things differently. *Playing, playing . . .*

But he was yet no one to be trifled with.

What will happen? she thought. Oh, obviously. *If he finds himself in the same mind, he'll want a nice unceremonial bed, and to rig me in it. I suppose it will be a bed he wants?* (she had heard other rumors too of his vices, that he preferred rape, but also that he remained the priest he had been meant to be, and had no feeling at all for women.) *What does it matter? I am already welldighted.*

He could destroy my father, if I anger him.

Then she must care about that, at least, it seemed.

"You're very meditative, Beatrixa."

"Yes, your—yes, Chesare. I'm thinking what would be both simple and enjoyable for supper."

She told the house a nobleman was to dine with her. To no one did she say who he was. He had not said she might.

It had already been an interesting task, explaining to the rescue party she met, issuing from her castle, that the pack of bandits had turned out to be friendly, and well-born.

Not all of her people would know him. Some would, of course. Or might he arrive in an even more complex disguise, to catch all of them, and herself, out? (As Silvio had that time, as an old man?)

Why did she think so much of Silvio now? He had always been there in her brain, inside her, inextricable—she was accustomed to that. But now, she thought of him not as this intrinsic element within her. She thought of him as her lover, she thought of him as one who had lived but was dead . . .

She dressed in her most lavish gown, had her hair perfumed and arranged, and donned the cap of silver spangles she had worn to Borja's "marriage," when he had not noticed her. She put on rings, and a necklace of silver and gold. Not for allure, but to show herself his subject, and to flatter, as a subject must.

Even so, as the evening filled the countryside, and the mountains drew backward from the hills into the sky, she stood on her stone terrace, under the great towers of the rocca, and found she was excited. It was not fear. Nor arousal. She realized she, too, then, must like—to *play*.

She had never known this of herself. It had never *been*, she thought, till now, in her character.

Beatrixa did not know what had taken possession of her, only that she could do no differently than she did and would do, and would be *insane* to do differently. But—she did not mind it, it galvanized her. She had woken, if not to a morning, then to an evening of the world. Twilight then, she would live in that. Twilight, with some stars.

Only three men accompanied him. Everyone was finely dressed, and frivolous, one of them armed not with a crossbow, but a Spanish vighela, which from time to time he strummed. Even so, Beatrixa recognized the third of the men as Borja's most constant, and feared, body-guard, said to be consummate in the skills of murder, and the garrote.

He and she, though, dined alone in the small sala off the great Hall.

Omberto waited on them, and had chosen the serving girls himself. Although Beatrixa had omitted the nobleman's name, Omberto was not slow.

The dinner was comprised of roast kid, fish brought up from the Adza that morning and stuffed with eggs and capers, minestrone, braised tripe, peaches in wine and a gelatina with curdled cream—while plates lay about of olives, almonds, cheeses, and fruit from the castle orchards, to supply the air of artlessness.

He ate well, but not over-heartily. His manners were flawless. He complimented her on the dishes, and discussed with her the wine (which was naturally the best). He had also brought her two presents. The richness of these was less shocking than the evidence they gave of his knowledge of her. For he had brought a printed book, impossibly tiny, not the size of one of his own hands, made, he said, not in Venus, but Franchia. Its cover was gilded, and set with three polished smoky topazes. It was love-poetry, of course (Petrarch's), but quite seemly. This alone was probably priceless, and seemed to indicate he knew her a connoisseur well able to read Latin. The other gift, was, if anything, more disconcerting. A small, soft leather collar with gold-work and a pink tourmaline.

"It's for your little dog," he said, seeing her look of bewilderment.

"My dog—you have found out that I have a dog, your grace?"

"My grace has found out nothing. Chesare, who will

be pleased to hear you call him so, remembers your little dog from the Ducem's palace. It was such a good little dog. My sister especially noticed it. It never tried to chase the flamingo."

By now, everyone else, even Omberto, had withdrawn. Chesare's man had brought the gifts into the room, then left. Firelight ebbed and flowed. It was the first fire of the season, for the nights up here could be cold. Outside, the musician was playing the vighela, singing a lilting Spanish song, whose words gained appropriate mystery from not being understandable.

"I didn't think you would have seen me," she said.

"Really? I saw you very well. I don't miss much, Beatrixa. Particularly a woman of such power."

She glanced up at him. "*Power?*"

Borja smiled at her. *He has the face of a wolf*, she thought. But it did not increase her wariness. Oh no. She thought, *They are not alike, yet he is like him*. Like Silvio, she meant. This glittering quality, poised like a razor s edge between a maleness cultivated and sophisticated, and the unpredictable and ferocious, the lawless, the creature of the inner dark.

"Well," he said. He put his hand across the low table and took hers. She was prepared to find his touch electric. It was. "What shall we do now?"

He seemed to know her through, all there was to know. That was part of his trick, obviously. Yet even so . . .

What shall we do now? And Silvio had replied—

She said, "Why must we do anything?"

"Why indeed. Let me tell you what I would like. To go with you somewhere even more private than this. To remove your garments, but leave you your jewels and your silver cap, perhaps your stockings and your silk shoes. And then, I wonder."

She got to her feet and he rose quickly and came around the table. He took her by the waist, not at all bruisingly, and lifted her up high in the air. It was effortless. He stood there holding her up, her contact with the earth all lost to her, but for the grip of his hands around her waist. *Women must like this*, she thought. She thought she did. He let her down slowly, bringing her smoothly against him, and finally he put his hand behind her neck, fondling the mass of her hair, and bent his head and kissed her.

A rush of feeling, as if a sluice-gate broke, burst through her, dizzying, terrible, and glorious. She clung to him, and found to her horror she had taken fierce hold in turn of his hair, but before she could rectify this trespass, he laughed and said, "I thought so." And he pulled her with him now, up the side stair to the rooms above.

They ran, he and she, into her bedchamber. It was nothing like Paradise. The walls were dank stone and hung with faded tapestry, and the bed was an uncooked porridge of lumps and cavities. The door slammed shut. The sound of it went on ringing in her head as she tugged at his clothing in her need to seize him, in her need to strip him as he stripped her.

"Well, Beatrixa," he said as they landed on the riot of the bed, both of them half-undressed.

Her brain sat miles off and said, *Who is he, this one?* But she knew who he was. He was life. He was the world.

He pushed her legs apart. It was easy, she always rode astride.

"Yes," she said.

"Say no," he said.

"No, then." And she scored his flanks with her nails.

He said, "*Amor vincit omnia.*"

As he thrust into her, unexpectedly she felt the pain, a wasp-stinging tearing hurt, at which she cried out, and, not to be denied, let him force closer inside, wrapping his body with hers.

Into the night he rode her and she, him, absorbed in the tumult of it. He was silent, thrusting and burning in her, until obliteration came. It voided her, and took away everything, even her love.

She lay under him. Sweat, heat, their breathing. Where were they? Who were they?

He said quietly after a moment, "I was rough with you. I never knew you were yet a virgin. Perhaps you should have told me."

Oh, so that was the other wetness, not only sweat and lust, but blood. A virgin.

And he, and she, had thought she was no longer that.

"Yes," she said, meekly.

He removed from her and lay on his back. "An honor I'm very conscious of," he said, "to be first with you. You have been most generous, Beatrixa Barbaron."

She would say later, "He is always polite, chivalrous, with me. He treats me very well. I've nothing to complain of. Sometimes he even discusses politics with me, tells me something of his plan for Italy. Once he told me of a dream he had. He is very just. He's like that, with the places he conquers, so long as they are faithful and do as he wishes."

Amor vincit omnia—everything is conquered by love. She would write to Andrea too, warning him, in cunningly chosen words that gave away nothing and revealed all. It could be advantageous to him this, that his daughter won favor with such a man. Such things could always be turned to use.

She did not of course mention to her father that Borja had found her still a virgin, and perhaps prized her offering the more for that. Andrea believed, as Beatrixa herself had, that her virginity was gone. He would have credited a secret marriage much less. But a marriage there had been, and a nuptual. In Heaven. Where it had not counted, it seemed, or counted in some other scales than those of the world.

Chesare Borja visited Beatrixa, as the passage of his military affairs, and other endeavors, permitted three or four times before the spring. That first year he even arrived in the two weeks before Christ'Mass, leaving her only to go straight to Rome. His interest in her was beneficial also for the castle. Some astounding luxuries were accrued during those first months, and a couple more during the following year.

By the end of that first year, however, his fancy for her was on the wane. This, too, was handled diplomatically and nicely. It was only in bed that he was sometimes, as he said, rather rough. But even there, not always. He could be languid, too, and lascivious. Or careless. Only a battlefield ever gained his absolute attention, that or Italy.

Once the second spring was there, he had virtually ceased to call on her. Until there came to be one significant occasion. But it was before that he told her about the dream.

"I have never told any other," he said, "save for my sister, the Lady Lucretza d'Estro."

It was a sexual dream. (He apparently made no demur either about sharing it with Lucretza, or the fact he had done so, with Beatrixa.) He had married Venus to secure the City and the state. Then, on the Rivoalto, bored to distraction by the court of Ducem Nicolo, this dream.

"Venus herself walked into my room. Do I mean the City or the goddess? Something of both."

She had mounted him, he said, and used him. She was in her form bigger than most women, but provocative enough.

"The most intriguing thing," he said to Beatrixa, lying against her, his hand upon her breast. "was that her hair was blue."

"For the sea," said Beatrixa, "perhaps."

"Perhaps. But she marked me, I found it when I woke the following day. I sent for my physician, one takes no chances with those sort of things. He dosed me with some poison, liquid gold and arsenicum, I think it may have been. The marks went away."

Beatrixa had wondered if this were a lie, as so many things were lies—even, like her virginity, when told as truths. Did Borja perhaps have the disease which all Italy blamed on the Franchians, and all Franchia on the Italians? It was too late to be anxious now. Besides, he had no signs of it, nor she.

She had also heard, in a letter from one of her cousins, of a bizarre wonder corresponding to his dream, that had occurred in Venus. An island had surfaced, it seemed, in the Aquila Lagoon. A small mound of earth, cleaving the open water. Since it had appeared about nine or ten months after Borja's marriage with the City, popular wit named the isle *Filia Caesini*—Chesare's Daughter.

She thought he had probably heard the tale. Even seen the island, as now she never would.

Why a daughter, though? In the rumors, his

by-blows were always boys. Even his sister was supposed to have borne him a male child. And by the end
of that second spring, when really he very seldom came
to see her any more, Beatrixa, too, would have proof
that normally his seed formed men.

BARTOLOME

BELIEF IS NOT ALWAYS NECESSARY for a miracle, and disbe-
lieving seldom prevents disaster. I had no foreknowledge,
I knew *nothing*, until it was already too late.

It was winter, dark and icy cold. This was in the months
after I had turned thirty-nine years of age. I felt the cold
more, maybe, as an older man will. But otherwise it had
been a fine year. Pia and I were on reasonable terms, and
there had begun to be some talk in private at my guild-
house, which concerned my elevation to the Seven, that
is, the seven Under-Masters who serve only below the
Guild Master himself.

Other than all this, there was Flavia, whom I saw
now regularly once in every week, and in whose house I
stayed always on that night. I had told Pia, long before,
this recurrent absence was to do with secret business of
the guild, and she had accepted this from me without a
ripple. By now, for the procedure had now gone on
nearly three years, she was accustomed to it. Did I feel
guilty at lying to her so routinely, or that my lie had
included also the guild? No, I had no guilt. I too, was
accustomed by then. And Flavia—she was my life's

blood. It was my time with her that gave me life and reason for all the rest.

But Flavia had been gone at Verona the past three weeks, and the freezing weather had convinced me she would not yet be coming home. So when Pia said, "What, are you to be under my feet again tonight, husband?" I had said I was glad of the respite from my work.

We went early to bed. I seem to recall the Luna Vigile had sounded, but perhaps that came a little after.

Pia was asleep, but I lay thinking.

To this hour, I can recollect nothing of those thoughts but I know they were trivial, and of no significance.

Then came a pounding on the house door.

Both Pia and I sat up, she in a taking.

"Hush, Pia. Thieves don't knock. Someone wants to speak to me urgently, or he would never venture out so far." For the house, you will perhaps remember, lies by the sea-wall of Silvia, on a bare spit of land, with only a few blasted trees for company.

So I went down in my bedshirt, with a candle, and undid the door—Pia's cook and the boy, needless to say, had not stirred.

There at the door, bowed against the bitter night as if crippled by it, stood Flavia's younger servant, Anso.

For an instant, I made no sense of it. It meant nothing at all, and was only inexplicable. Then my guts turned to gall within me.

"What?"

"Oh God, Messer Bartolome—you must come with me now."

It was like the summons of death, not to be avoided, and everything at once surrendered to it—and so it was.

"Tell me why."

He told me. He was in tears.

Something made me turn, and there stood Pia in her mantle, shielding her own candle with her hand, although there was no wind.

I said, or someone who spoke for me, "Pia, I must go out. Something has happened. Don't be afraid. I am well, and will be back when I can, but it make take some time."

Then I ran upstairs again and got into my clothes, or I must have done, for later I found I was dressed, but I remember nothing of it. Nor of how I went with him and got in the waiting boat he had ready. We were rowed across the City, through all the never-ending twisting dark of night and water, and it seemed to take a century—and only that comes back to me, how long it took, but very little else, until we reached the house south of the Diana Gardens.

She had wanted, Anso said (as he stooped there at my door) to come back. She said she had more comforts for winter in the City, and only some dispute on the estate had compelled her away at that season. Also she had wanted, it seemed, to see me.

Even in such weather, she had spurned a carriage. To ride was quicker, she always said so, and indeed she was not in error. They had made fair time, and by that day's overcast, dreary afternoon, the City was in sight.

There are woods there, close to the thoroughfare. Abruptly four men came riding out of the trees and straight up on the road. They were a nasty-looking gang, and Flavia said instantly that she believed they were robbers.

Because of robbers, she always journeyed in her male disguise, and plainly dressed. As a rule, such cut-throat bands are more inclined to prey on the obviously wealthy, or on somewhat larger bodies of travelers, where there is more likelihood of booty.

But these fellows wanted dealings, it seemed. They partially blocked the road and said they feared a hard winter, and would the young gentleman spare them a few pence.

Flavia got hold of the bridle of her servant's horse, and rode straight up to the robbers, calling cheerily, "We've little enough, but you are welcome to it," and just as she was level with them she kicked in her heels and hit Anso's horse across its withers with her crop. Next moment, the two of them shot through the scattering bandits, and were pelting on down the road towards the gates of Venus.

"Their horses were nothing, poor ill-used, starved things, no better than sheep," said Anso. "She knew what she was at, too. They had a bad eye, those men. It was more than money they wanted." It seemed they had liked the look of two young men, both seeming not much more than boys, for though to be a woman on the road is chancy, to be a youth is sometimes no better.

Of course, Flavia could ride as well as any man, and both their mounts were good ones. Behind them the gang did their best to pursue, but made a sow's ear of it by all accounts.

Anso was even laughing, with excitement at their narrow escape, and the breakneck speed of their flight. And the arch of the Porta Vene, as I have said, was in sight and getting closer by the second.

"We were safe by then, Messer Bartolome. That was it—we were *safe*."

There was traffic ahead there, he said, some carts approaching the gate though it was almost evening, before the City should close herself to the land. And then a kind of explosive yet soundless severance came, as if a piece of the light had snapped and toppled out of view.

Anso looked over his shoulder. He was brave, Anso. Despite the robbers, when he saw, he jerked his horse around immediately and galloped back.

It was a stretch of ice, less in width than a ribbon, he said. Her horse had hit this ice with its left front and back hoofs, skidded, and gone down. As it fell, unable to help itself, it threw Flavia on the ground, then rolled across her.

He said the first thing she said to him, as she lay there and he came up, was, "Is the horse well, Anso?"

"Yes, lady," he said. For he saw it had now regained its feet, shaking itself over and slewing its eyes, but unhurt. Then he drew his knife and faced along the road. But the cutthroats had already vanished back into the wood. He realized presently that some of the men farther down near the gate (carters they were) had seen the incident, and were now running up, and this was why the robbers had made off. At the time he only saw that he could now concern himself with Flavia.

He kneeled down and asked her what he should do.

Her eyes were shut. Her face, he said, had no blood in it, and he thought no wonder, it was out on the road—but then he saw it was not blood, only wine from a skin that had been on the saddle. And then he hoped.

But she said, "I must get home. When they come, tell them to lift me. It won't matter how."

"But they must take great care," he said.

"No need," she said. Then a small thin trickle, like the wine, ran from her mouth, and he knew, as she did.

The carters assisted them, and after that, others. They got her into a boat, and so through the City to her house, where she was carried in. She told Anso to bring all the herbs and powders from her chests, and she would instruct him in what to mix and how, and he did this, and when he had the tincture ready, he and the other servant helped her to drink it. Then she seemed better, and she said, "You must go and fetch Bartolo, please. As quickly as you can. I am so sorry for his wife, but it can't be avoided."

Then, by my door, Anso wept again. There had been, he said, so many delays, and it was night by then, and he had been in a fight with a wanderlier who would not take him, thinking him drunk or mad. But here he was at last before me, and I must come at once. Pray God it was not already too late for her to bid me farewell.

When I went into her room and saw her on the bed, which I had so often shared with her, I, like Anso, thought she had been mistaken. She was propped up on the pillows, her brown, dark hair combed out, and though she was pale, her eyes were clear and intelligent, as I had always seen them. (Like stars, I had said, like stars.) But then, something about her—I think it was her utter stasis, as if she were already from her body, only there still, in the eyes and mouth, to see me and speak to me—well, then I knew her looks lied, and she and Anso had not.

I have seen and attended the dying and the dead many times. What else, it is my trade.

But this was not like that.

"Sweetheart," I said, "here I am. What can I do for you?"

"You can listen, Bartolo," she said. "I have a lot to say, and you must hear it through. I should have spoken before, but there was never the proper hour for it, and now it's late, my darling, but I have just enough time. If you will be patient and attend."

So I sat down in the chair, and I listened, and she told me all she had perceived, through her curious and pure magic. She told me the life of Meralda, which I had known already, and of Meralda's son, Silvio, who had never lived in this world until he was a man, and of Andrea Barbaron, and of Beatrixa, and of Dionyssa de Mars—of them all.

I did not once contest what she said, although, as I told you, I did not think she could know so much. Not that I judged her a liar. She believed in all she said. After, as I have told you too, I also came to believe it. Or, if you will, for six days I do so, and on the seventh, I rest from believing. For even God had to rest, it seems, from the unconscionable wonders He Himself had wrought. And we tiny atoms are sooner tired than a god.

I remember her voice. I can hear it now, if I will only listen. I do not mean that she comes back to me like those ghosts and personalities and souls she told me of— or if she does, the physical mote in my spiritual eye blinds me to her. No, it is only love, I mean. It is only memory.

But in the end, she had told it through, every single particle of their lives, and ours, all so strangely inter- twined. And then she told me *why* the tangle was.

Forgive me now, that I will not yet give you in turn that last note of the song. But as I only came to credit it fully through another circumstance, which happened at a later date—which happened four days ago, to be exact, and which is the reason I have sat down to write all this—allow me also to set that before you in its turn, before I render up the final answer.

You may not, even then, believe *me*. You may say *I* am the liar, the romancer, or the madman. Or you may say death is the lie, the greatest madness and falsehood in all this world. Even if, perhaps, on the seventh day, you rest from thinking that, and holiday once more in doubt.

I hope it is death which is the great lie. But Flavia at least I know did think so. Whatever else she was that night, she was not afraid, and though sorry to leave me, without any lasting sorrow, thinking we would meet again. And God knows how well I, too, long for that.

When she finished speaking, then I saw the light run out of her. She seemed to grow small and old, yet she smiled at me.

"Come here and kiss me," she said.

I kissed her, lightly, as one does with the very old, or the frail.

"Be friendly to Pia, Bartolo," she said. She sighed, "Be kind to yourself. I'm tired now. It must be time, I think." When she said this, it was as if my heart tore open, as if the walls fell down. But then she smiled once more at me. "Until again," she said, and then, looking past me, her face suddenly became not old but very young. "Why," she said, in a different voice, a girl's, "'Chesco, is it you?" (Franchesco was her dead husband's name.) "Oh, then, of course I will. And Mumma, too—" at which her face lit up, full of a happiness even I had never beheld. Like a simpleton, I turned my head—though it was irresistible—to find who she spoke to. There was no one there that I could see. When I looked back, she had gone.

I thought it must have been the next day before I saw that I was at home in my own house, and that Pia stood there looking at me, and that she had been crying.

When we were young, she and I, she was jealous

over small and petty things—if I noted a pretty woman on the lagoon, or in some other house, if I spoke even of a legendary classical beauty, such as Helena of Troy, or Dido. Then Pia would flare up at me, "Oh, you show me *my* place, Bartolo. You show me *my* worth to you."

Now Pia said, "Bartolome—Oh Bartolome—it's so terrible a thing."

"You know," I said. I was vague, callous perhaps. I thought she had found out, as she must, and was now to unleash her howls and spite.

"Know?" said Pia, "I've known these four years and more. Oh, I was raw at you, then. But you didn't abandon me, or despise me. She made you easier, if anything, your Flavia Tressi. I've learned not to mind. But this blow you've taken is a heavy one. I will do whatever you want, whatever I can."

I gaped at her as if I had never looked on her before. Perhaps I had not, properly.

Then she went off and came back with a bowl of thick, hot soup, the dish she herself would always make, rightly not trusting our cook.

"Eat a little of this now. It's three whole days since you've taken anything but water. Look, here is some Roman wine. Micaeli who lifts the stones brought the barrel. The Guild Master sent it. And here is the spoon."

She treated me like a child. I was one. I have said, I think, she was always at her best with children.

SILVIO

During the morning and the afternoon, Dionyssa was generally occupied. At Sta' Bianca, there was plenty to do. And though naturally, no resident lady not herself a nun or lay-sister (there were five such residents here) need do anything, those that did were welcomed.

In Dionyssa's case, the welcome was quite hearty. She excelled in certain areas, they found, as with the gardens and the herbarium. (The other resident lady who sometimes liked to help, was less proficient, and now and then needed tactful, time-consuming redirection.) But Dionyssa was a gift to the nun-house

It lay beyond Venus, on the Veneran plain, quite near to the town of Mariamba, where once a saint had lived, they said. Strangely, for nuns, they seemed unsure which saint.

On clear days, the mountains far off along the plain, drifted closer. And in winter, their tops were white as the moon.

The grounds of Santa Maria Sta' Bianca held endless variety. A herb garden and a physic garden, a coppice wood (where local farmers were permitted to graise their pigs, in return for a regular fee of choice pork), also several ponds with fish. For recreation there was a cedar walk, a cypress avenue, and a curious topiaria, cut to the shapes of the Last

Supper, with Christ and eleven Disciples carefully rendered, but with Judas left out. "There *was* a Judas," the Mother of the house had told Dionyssa, when first describing the grounds, "But that bush died. A minor miracle. We did not dare put him in again."

Dionyssa had surveyed the spot. She had thought, *Is there no forgiveness then? Even from the One who said we must forgive?*

But then she had crossed herself and asked His pardon. It was not God who did not forgive, but the thoughts of mankind, even of the generous nuns, who hated the Betrayer Judas, and would not suffer him even in a bush.

By day, Dionyssa was often at work in the gardens, summer and winter. She would put on the dress of a lay-sister, tie up her hair in a scarf, and work beside them. She was usually at the ten o'clock morning service, too, and once a week at the evening one. She was not overly religious, but she liked to attend—most of the five other permanent guests did not bother, save when they must. It seemed a courtesy, to Dionyssa, since she lived now in this country, to observe some of its customs.

Also, it passed the time.

Other than the gardens and the herbarium, where she had brought a little knowledge and soon gained more, Dionyssa would take an hour or so to play her viola-lute, and the lap-harp. There was reading too, and in the library of Sta' Bianca many books, not all of them concerned with piety. Other books came to her as well, by the kindness of Como della Scorpia. Some of these were in the Frankish tongue, as she had requested. Aside from all this, Dionyssa had acquired a black dog. He was from a litter of pups born to the Mother-minora's own canine companion. "The disgrace," had said the Mother-minora, laughing, "everyone of them black or brindle,

and she such a perfect grey. Whose are they? Some imp's
I shouldn't wonder."

The dog, whom Dionyssa accordingly named
Beaumal, was mostly about her through the day.

But, after the day, would come the night.

"What, do you want to go out again?" The dog
stared up at Dionyssa, whining. "You are more like a cat.
Or a wolf. Are you a wolf, Beaumal, that always you want
to run away when it's bedtime? Go then. I will see you
tomorrow." And letting the dog from the door, Dionyssa
closed it once more, and was alone with darkness.

Such an affectionate and loyal dog. Why did he run
off always at night when she went to bed? It happened
now and then during the days, too, but then she supposed he found some other activity—he was friends with
everyone—and she was often busy.

At night, she missed him. He would have warmed the
bed. She might have spoken to him as she lay awake, or
when she woke, off and on, both of which she did so often.

But it is Yves I miss.

Would the pain never leave her? No, it seemed not.
She did not weep now, but had hardly ever done so. The
hurt was too deep for tears.

She could only hope she would grow more used to
it, her loss. That she would feel it less keenly if not less
frequently. But it had been years now. Perhaps nothing
could change.

At least, Beaumal came back with morning.

"Good evening, my love," he said.

Dionyssa lay smiling in her sleep. There had been a
time when she would not have understood even that
small phrase, spoken as it was, in Franchian.

Ma chère amie . . .

She opened her eyes and saw Yves de Mars sitting there on the bed.

He was, in the dark, clearly to be seen, although there was no moon, and few stars.

I am dreaming. Let me not wake up, not for a while.

"Yves?"

"Yes. Here I am. I see you haven't noticed I was gone at all."

It was what he had been used to say to her, returning from war. His eyes laughing and his face doleful, and behind it all, the shadow which, after a day or so, would fade. Until the next return. Until there *was* no return, and the shadow had him.

"You're well," she said. "I'm so glad—to see you like this."

Jolting her, he said, "Ah, you mean because I'm dead. Let me tell you, *mignon*, it is an ideal state. Nothing wrong with it."

Dionyssa sat up in the bed.

She said, slowly, slowly, "You are a little older, Yves."

"I wish to keep pace with you, though naturally you look as young as the day we met. Even so, years have passed."

"But—do the dead change?"

"Of course, sweetness, if they want. It's only mortal stuff that's subject to earthly laws. I prefer this, unless you would like a younger husband."

"Are you a vision? Have you come to me in a dream? Is this you?"

"What do you think? Do you think me a vision or a dream? Are you afraid? Don't be afraid."

"I'm not afraid. How could I be fearful of you?" She looked him up and down, at his dark eyes, his hair, his

His eyes, sunk in pouches of discolored skin, looked round suspiciously. As if he guessed the library-haunt was there once more.

Then nevertheless he seated himself and, taking up a pen, began to write on a sheet of fine Arabian paper.

Silvio moved forward and stood behind Andrea, where his unseen shadow might fall across the sheet. He read, *Beatrixa—*

That was all. That was all the old man, this old Andrea Barbaron, had written.

And then he put down the pen and pushed back the chair and stood and turned and confronted Silvio, standing not ten inches from him.

Andrea's eyes wandered over Silvio's features.

"What do you want of me? Haven't you done enough?"

"Yes," Silvio replied. He had felt Andrea's breath on his face. "As much as I meant to. And considerably more."

"What are you?" said Andrea.

Silvio thought, *He can't see me, or hear me, yet he knows I am here. He too has gained another awareness than he had.*

"Your daughter's lover." Silvio said.

But now Andrea said, "What? *What?* Are you there? *What* are you?"

"Some things, then, you don't like to hear, so you won't. I took her from you, old man. But she was taken also from me.

"I will have a priest to this room," Andrea said. "See if that works."

"It will work," answered Silvio.

He passed by Andrea, not impertinently going through him, and took up the paper on which Beatrixa's name had been written. Perhaps it was a letter. Even though it entailed only one word.

Andrea watched the paper skimming off across the room.

Then slowly he grinned. He did not, then, look so old any more.

"Take it, if you want," he said. "Do as you like."

And then he turned and went out, leaving behind him the burning candles, which Silvio himself presently extinguished.

So he took her written name away with him, and one other thing, too. It was the Casket of the Heart, which had lain till then in a cabinet in Andrea's apartments. Silvio knew this, once he set his mind to it. He seemed always able to know everything, in this fashion—everything that was of the physical world, or had been. (Only one thing he could never learn—the light beyond the light.)

Silvio undid the cabinet by psychic pressures on its locks, and lifted out the Casket, and sprang out through the window with it. The closed window, that was.

Perhaps Andrea had been sleeping in his bed while all this went on. Silvio had given up any interest in Andrea now. He did not even go to see.

The Casket then, Silvio bore to the lagoon. Not Silvia, but Aquila. He drew it with him down deep into the black, icy winter water, the cold of which would have killed a live man in seven minutes. He sank to the floor of mud, and there he walked, Silvio walked on the sandy mud which was the sea-bed there, the earth-bed under the ocean.

Glacial fish issued sluggishly from the glooms and quivered back to them. Others lay asleep in apertures of stone, looking like sleek daggers.

He skirted drowned boats, wanderers, fishing-craft, one vessel with an illustrated sail done in gemmy dyes, which now the water had bleached to—ghosts.

Silvio noted the skeletons of men here and there. There were always these. He glanced at them, but had no need to investigate them, despite the fact it was bones that he sought.

She had gone in just by the church of Maria Maka Selena. But currents swilled about the lagoons, and seasons and more than three decades had also done this.

Silvio found the remains of his mother at last, simply because they were hers, and his *mother* was what she had been, if only for a day or so. He found her death then, in the lagoon. (And his own death curled inside her, no longer there in any form that might be recognized. There, for all that.) As in the world, bones were all she had finally left him.

He thought he was far off from the City now, but he was not yet against the irregular shallows of the sandbars, out where the open sea began.

Silvio gave the Casket of the Heart of Beatifica to his mother's bones, positioning the box where he himself had lain, at the pelvis. He murmured to the bones what he did, that he put into their keeping the relic of a saint. He did not know either that it was the heart of a dog. He had never looked. And anyway, however well-read and clever, he might not have known the difference.

With his hands, as a mortal man would on the land, Silvio built a mound above the burial spot. He made for her, and for the Heart, a bed of earth.

But then, because he was not, and never had been a mortal man, Silvio gouged great torrents of the mud out of the laguna's floor, and hauled them by will alone towards this place. He piled it up, earth upon earth, pebbles, shale, shell, shawling sand, marine detritus, pieces of the rocks. He piled it high, and higher, rising with it. The active fish fled away. A silver shark, which came to observe, swerved off into the calmer water.

Up and up. Until in the end, the mound broke out of the surface of the lagoon. Even then, Silvio made it a little higher, and a little more wide.

When he was done, the winter moon was all that was there to watch him, and one black streamer of gulls blown by their wings across the sky.

This now, his mother's island.

He named the grave, standing on its summit under the moon. "Meralda, Filia della Scorpia."

In the air, supernaturally, the name remained. But like so much, grew altered.

For it was the island the City came to call Filia Caesini —Chesare's Daughter.

And at its core, that pair of secret things, sleeping on for ever.

That night, too, Silvio returned to the Palazzo della Scorpia.

To start with, he only strolled about. He picked at the flaking murals and rattled the rings of curtains. Then he went to the sala and looked into the chest, the one where the battle banners had lain. The penon-flag he had been shown was no longer inside. And he remembered that the woman, too, had meant to go away.

Beatrixa, had he known—surely he might have done—was at Veronavera. Between himself and her, however, was an angel with a flaming sword.

Silvio turned his mind, his *senses*, through the winding corridors of night and time, and saw instead Dionyssa de Mars lying in her bed at Sta' Bianca, on her yellow hair.

Now there began a new thing.

It had nothing to do with love or revenge, and very little to do with death or Heaven. It was born of the world, and the world's vast desire for survival, justice, and happiness.

Like all those dread ghost-beings of ancient stories, precisely so Silvio must have traveled across the dark, and manifested, unseen, there in Dionyssa's room in the house of nuns.

And also like one of those dire spirits, just in that way, he must have leaned over Dionyssa, gazing as if feeding on her. But the food he absorbed was her sorrow and her yearning. And everything she knew of one man.

This was to be a schooling of many nights. Of some years, in fact, actual years, spent on the earth.

Accompanying her as she worked by day, sitting beside her as she read and sang. Lying by her as she slept and dreamed. Listening, and learning it all. All of her, and all of her love.

Even that other language of the Franks was to be learned in such a mode, by one such as Silvio, who might learn anything, anything but one thing—which none, it seemed, could learn, who had not first come from it, the light beyond the light.

Learning, Silvio gave up himself. He became another self. A form and a personality that was not Silvio della Scorpia. But that was Yves de Mars.

He did it for Dionyssa. Not because he was infatuated with her, but because he was alone, and so was she. And because, in marriages such as this too, sometimes love will come.

That he would be lying to her, he did not even see. He could make her happy, prove to her that death was nothing, provide justice in a world of wreck and dislocation.

Not every deceit is to be condemned. Not every truth is good.

And anyway, he had not usurped the soul of Yves—that was gone. Only Yves' personality, which Dionyssa's mind had kept so well.

The dog was afraid of him, though. Animals, when they saw him—which often they did—always were.

As Silvio became more unlike himself, more like his reborn self—Yves—the dog called Beaumal (Fair Badness) grew less certain that it distrusted and feared him.

It still ran off, nevertheless.

Somehow, he was concerned at this. Probably because it disturbed Dionyssa, and his whole aim—Yves' once, now his, therefore Yves' once more—was to protect and cherish this woman.

That eventual night, when he made love to Dionyssa, he lulled her after to sleep with caresses, and left her in peace.

He had determined everything must be gradual, now. As for the love-making, it was as fundamental, as marvelous, for him, as anything he had experienced with Beatrixa. While for Dionyssa too, he had unmistakably seen the anticipated quiet violence of her pleasure. That he could touch her physically, and she, him, he did not trouble with. (That was still his knack, not to waste thought on such slight problems.) But of course, he had learned touch also, and (with Beatrixa) the ability to transcend his own unmatter, to meet, where he would, flesh with—flesh. As if he were as *real* as his partner. One more needful, benificent lie.

It would take more time. Many years, even, perhaps, to win Dionyssa to himself-as-Yves, and so make her truly "glad."

Tomorrow, and for several tomorrows, she would

think it still a dream. Then she would think her reason, maybe, was at fault, and he would need strategies, which he was already preparing, to ensure her belief in his—in Yves'—presence, and that her brain was sound. Then they would learn to communicate, clandestinely, even in daylight when others were there. In the end, they would be content. They would be happy.

He did not, as Yves might have, think either of the future hour when her death would rob him again. Or of what would become of him then—for her, he knew she would be safe, since death was an insurmountable wall only to Silvio's kind.

He did not once, not once, wish ill to God or anyone, because he might never get free of this world, or the second magician's world of divine illusions. For sure, he *never* thought that, by what he did and would do, he too had begun for himself a process of chameleonism, body to body, persona to persona, which was the lot of souls. Or that he, not a soul, but only the memory of one who might have lived, behaved now as a soul did.

It did not occur to him to ask of what material a soul was composed, which made it so entirely not like himself. Or if the difference were truly unnegotiable for all eternity. . . .

In the gardens of Santa Maria Sta' Bianca, Yves de Mars (who had been Silvio della Scorpia) met, as if by another eccentric appointment, Beaumal. Who was indeed part wolf, and would soon enough show it by his grown size, if nothing else.

Yves spoke to Beaumal in Franchian, giving the dog's name its proper accent.

Beaumal lifted his nose and stared with his innocent, feral, *human* eyes.

Then, for a short time, he allowed Yves to walk

beside him, before suddenly running off again into the fascinating wood that smelled of pigs.

There would be a night, not so far away, when Yves would be throwing sticks for Beaumal. Also smoothing his head, or rolling with him fiercely on the ground, impervious, of course, to bites or scratching claws.

And there would come a morning, too, when Dionyssa would wake up to find her husband sitting by her, with Beaumal stretched at his feet, his black and by then very wolfish head settled easily on his boot. It would be that morning too, naturally, when all doubt would leave her for ever.

VALENTE

FOUR DAYS AGO, I saw my son.

Let me gather my wits and sentences together, and tell you how that came about.

One wet autumnal morning, the Guild Master sent for me. Seeing I was by now one of the Settera, the Seven under-Masters who serve him and the guild most closely, to be called was no great surprise.

"Bartolome," he said, when I came in. "be seated, if you will. This is not all guild business, though partly. Some of it is your private business too. I am sorry to grieve you, but it may chafe either way, most, I thought, if I did not speak to you at all."

Then I *was* surprised. I wondered what was coming, and then if Pia's elderly father, the stonemason, had died, and news of it come here first.

But the Master said, putting all other thought to flight, "This concerns Flavia Tressi."

Stupidly I said to him, he, the Master of the Grave Guild, "But she's dead."

"Yes, Bartolome, I know that she died. It will be two years since, won't it, in the Capricorn month."

"Yes."

We won't speak of the past, perhaps. But something has been brought to me, and I am to choose an upper guildsman to see to it. When you've heard what it is, you may want to be that man. Or if you do not, that's well enough. But it seemed to me you should be the one to decide."

Now I did not know what to say, and sat there. We, he and I, had never spoken her name between us, until now. I knew that he had been aware she was my mistress, these things do get known, here and there, within a guild. I knew too he must have prevented the stonemason from also hearing about it. The guilds also know how to keep their secrets. The Master had seemed to guess too, something of what she had meant to me, for I remembered, after I lost her, when he sent the barrel of Roman wine, there was a verse in Latin with it:

Nobis miseris
vinum donum
dei dederunt,
cum lacrimis.

Curis levandis
quas per ipsos
deos patimur
cum lacrimis,

Usque adeo
vinum curae
exsiccentur
cum lacrimis.

'To man the gods gave wine, to ease those cares they must let us suffer, till wine and tears are done.'

I have never known the source; at the time I did not notice who had written it. But the words, as you see, remained.

The Master now said this, "I have been sent a letter from the Palazzo Barbaron. The Lord there, Andrea. wants two things from us. Firstly he tell me plainly enough, he wishes to give back to the della Scorpias that burial land they have always claimed for themselves on the Isle. He says he has no idea whether it be theirs or Barbaron's. But he asserts they may have the ground without argument, and hereafter Barbaron will respect and uphold their rights to it. That is the first matter. The second is the one which concerns the Tressi family. Here I'm not certain what you know, Bartolome. Perhaps the lady herself told you that she had always been accounted a child of Andrea Barbaron's youth, though born inside the wedlock of another."

I got my voice and said that I did know this.

"Now it seems Andrea wishes to place in stone on her tomb, alongside the Tressi insignias, that of Barbaron. The Tower, and its motto: Joy in life, fearlessness in death."

I said, "That would be true of her, at least."

The Master knew I had not seen to her burial. Others had done that. It had never shamed me I could not do it. She would have understood. And if she was elsewhere, as she had reckoned to be, I knew also she did not mind.

Neither had I ever visited her grave. It was not on the Isle of the Dead, but at Veronavera, by the Tressi vault there, close to her husband Franchesco's ashes, that she had so honorably seen re-housed.

For a while we sat in silence, the Master and I. I drank some of the wine he had put by for me.

"Well," he said, "it's a strange circumstance. I would have thought Andrea Barbaron himself near death, to be so urgent for these affairs, but it seems he's hale.

A man over sixty, I believe. Perhaps he realizes it must still come."

"It does come," I said. I rose and thanked him for his care of me. "I will see to it, sir. Both matters, if you wish. My earliest experience of the Isle was the della Scorpias, ranting over their burial-ground, while one of their number went into the earth. As for Flavia— I think she'd smile. And the old lady at Tressi, her sister-in-law—does she live? Then she must be in her eighties. She'll be as proud as if it were Tressi's own armorial."

When I went to call on Como della Scorpia, I thought the palazzo looked dreary and wan in the rain. The years had not been friendly with it, they never had.

I was shown into his study, but he was not quite alone there. A group of the family's old people were present, and among them the stiff and black-wigged Caterina—the very woman I recalled from when I was thirteen, at my first earth burial.

The message had already been delivered, it seemed. They had gathered like birds of prey to seize up the dead thing and swallow it down.

Only Como, sagging and ugly, had any look of normalcy in his face. He was very courteous to me, as he had been at our other meeting, all those years before, when he told me I must be a bastard of his house, I looked so like his kin, and that because of this, if ever I had need of it, he would be my patron.

"Well, Messer da Loura, is it true, this Barbaron change of heart?"

I told him it was.

"It is a stroke of great good fortune, and says much

for Andrea Barbaron, that he will do it, and unprompted. For generations his family have been our enemies over this, and we theirs.

"They fear us still," rasped Caterina, in her cracked and loveless voice.

"No, madam," he said, glancing at her. "Let's be intelligent. They have no requirement to fear us any more. Particularly now that they enjoy the friendship of the Borjas. This is Barbaron's kindness."

"Then I spit on it," she flared. She was like a dusty crow on a fence, fussily cawing and flapping, an omen of discord and shadows.

But Como said, "You may do as you please, Caterina, providing you do it privately and alone. For my part, and I am the lord here, I welcome the generosity of Lord Barbaron. I shall write to him this very day. I think it only sensible we meet, we two old men, who were at daggers drawn in youth. There's no longer anything to fight about."

When the documents I had brought had been accepted and put in the clerk's hands, Como took me aside. He thanked me for coming personally, and asked how I did. Some days later I heard, he did meet Andrea, and the City marvels now that this feud is going out like damp fire, after a hundred years or more of sparks and flame. Barbaron and della Scorpia exchanged gifts, and it seems there may be a marriage soon between the houses, one of Andrea's sons, of whom he has several, some youngish, and a granddaughter of Como's.

To me Como also very graciously sent a gift. It was a set of goblets, twenty of them, of the precious Venus glass which is called Empyrean. They are like blue air with golden stars caught in them, the colors of Heaven. Pia is always very taken with them, washing and drying them herself, having them every day on display, but, "No, Bartolo, how can you even *think* of drinking from them."

Going to Veronavera, especially in rainy blowing weather, was no holiday for me. I could not help but recall how she and I had gone that first time to her house in the hills. We had been back there only twice together, and counted ourselves lucky to have had the occasions, when I had been sent to the town on other guild matters.

It was not possible to see the house or the vineyard from the road. I was thankful for that. The most horrible part of my journey had been at its start, of course, just beyond the Porta Vene, where the woods approach the roadway... but I had sometimes traveled some of the route before, since her death. The horror never lessened, but I was used to the horror.

There was a storm beating over Veronavera when I reached the hills. Everything else, near or far, was lost in cloud and lashing rain.

Gaining the town, I went immediately to the Tressi house, where the old lady, Franchesco's sister, received me as though we had met only yesterday. I was thankful to find her looking so fit and spry, and much as I remembered her. But I thought too how curious it is, how we the living age, while those that die in youth, or when they are yet young, stay always as they were, immortal in the mind.

Flavia had told me so very much before she died, and I had come to believe it—and still I doubted, of course I did. Even then.

And I knew when I had to go and regard the tomb in which she lay, my Flavia, then I would doubt it more than ever. For if ever she came back to me after death, it was in such a subtle way I could neither see nor feel it. While the tomb was made of stone.

The weather changed during my hour with Franchesco Tressi's sister.

When I came out on the street, the sun shone, and Veronavera's wet, red walls were glowing like ripe fruit.

As I stepped from the door, I had half noticed a little. calvalcade passing across the street's end, where it gave on another, only some two or three houses off from the Tressis'.

There were outriders, and a woman in a somber rich gown, all riding excellent horses. And a mule was there, with, I thought, a servant on it.

Then there began to be a commotion. I looked to discover what went on, and saw the servant struggling with something very agile and slippery, which turned out to be a child. Next moment the child was down from the mule, landed in a puddle and paid no attention to it, then came racing up the street where I stood.

He was a very wonderful-looking child, I saw swiftly, a boy about five or six, with gold hair, and a face mothers often believe their sons to have, although generally they are wrong.

Then, I realized this golden child was running straight at me.

Only when he reached me, did he stop.

He stared up smiling at me, and his eyes were alight with excitement and pleasure. Before I could speak, he spoke to me. "Dadda," was what he said.

Poor lad, I thought, *He's mistaken me for another. In a minute he will begin to cry.*

But the child did not cry. He went on gazing up at me, alive with joyous finding. And had he been my son, no father could wish for a sweeter greeting, so content was he to see me, and so obviously satisfied, in every particular, with me and what I was. And I in my Master guildsman's grey clothes, with the badges of office and the crossed circle of death—the very image certain fools use to distress their children with, so on the canals and in the alleys of Venus, sometimes they turn screaming from such men as I.

After an interval I collected myself. I bent down and said, "Well, I'm honored to meet you. Will you let me pick you up now and take you back to the lady over there?" For I knew they were all halted there, although peculiarly none of them had come over.

"Mumma," said the boy, and then, very proud too of this, "My mother, Lady Veyatripsa Barbron."

I was unable to move a second, reaching out, but then my arms went on, and I had him, and lifted him up.

He made no objection, assisted me even, and sat there in my grasp, beaming on at me, and then back at them, delighted with all of us.

He was warm and light yet strong, and he had that wondrous smell of new things that young animals and healthy children have.

I walked down the path, and reached the cluster of horses, where I looked straight up and met the eyes of Beatrixa Barbaron.

For it was she. Her dress was indigo-colored, and her face very pale. Her complexion and eyes were like Flavia's. I had forgotten that would be so, but they were both Andrea's daughters.

"M'donna, this young gentleman tells me he belongs to you."

"Yes," she said. She sat there, sidesaddle on the horse, rigid, and her hands showing the bones whitely as she gripped the reins. Where *he* had looked at me in approval, Beatrixa seemed the stricken one, the one who was afraid. Then she mastered herself. "He is my son," she said. "I am Beatrixa Barbaron."

"He told me that you were," I said.

I found I too had begun to shake. The child sensed it at once, and stared at me again, now concerned. So I smiled and shook my head at him, and I, too, mastered myself.

She said, "You will perhaps let me have your name, 'ser."

"Bartolome da Loura. Settera Master of the Grave Guild."

She nodded. "Yes. I noted your guild. You must excuse us, my son and I, for interrupting your business."

"It's seen to for now, madam."

Her servant was beside me. He was reaching finally for the child, to put him back on the mule where they had both been seated. I found I did not want to let go of the child. But naturally, I gave him over instantly. *Then*, he began to cry.

The servant murmured, and coaxed him, but it was no use. Nor did he weep as children normally do, loudly, effusively. They were low, rough sobs, as if he could not help them. And all the while, he was looking back toward me, this child.

"Give him up here," said Beatrixa. The servant carried him over to her, and handed him up. The boy now went willingly enough but, seated in her lap, clasped in her arm, still he looked and looked at me. He said nothing. We should all, the rest of us, I believed, be most relieved at this. Beatrixa's son was attributed, and by the father himself, to Chesare Borja. It would hardly be fortuitous, if he called me *Dadda* now.

"Perhaps," said Beatrixa. Her eyes were on the boy. "Perhaps, Valente, you might ask Messer da Loura if he will visit you this evening. Providing that he is free to do so."

My head was spinning slightly. The sun was flashing from every point of the world. I did not know quite what to say, I, an aging man in his forty-first year. But then she was in her twenties now, a woman evidently accustomed to wise judgment and self-command, and she was not quite steady. We were in the presence, she and I, and he too, the golden child, of some other thing, which was a mystery and a terror. We knew already what it was, yet did not know. Or *would* not.

The boy—she had called him Valente—spoke, his eyes dry and shining again.

"Come to see us, Messer da Loura, come this evening. We live in the castle. Do you know the one?"

"Yes, sir," I said.

The child frowned. It was only then, for that moment, I saw Borja in him, too. "Not *sir*," he said.

"If not, what shall I call you?"

Beatrixa said, softly, "His friends call him by his name, 'ser Loura. And so may you, if you desire, seeing that, obviously, you are his friend."

So I swept him a bow, and promised him I would attend them, and employed his given name, since she had allowed it, *Valente*.

She had named him, even, for Chesare, and Chesare had permitted this. In Franchia, it was Borja's title, for his lands there, Duc Valent-en-Oise. Italy, when it called him that, made this out as Valentino. Valent—Valentino—Valente—one might suppose it apparent enough how the boy's name derived.

I had heard long before about Beatrixa's child, and that the father, having seen him, had legally recognized him. For the mother, they said, Borja no longer had a sexual appetite, but they stayed on good terms. As well, for he kept a regular consciousness of the son. One way and another, Borja had not sired many children, and some of these, as with his wife in Franchia, were possibly dubious. You could not miss the fact that the boy's unusual combination of extreme beauty and, for want of better words, the air of lawlessness about him—less in his demeanor than his eyes, and more ethereal than animal—might have been at once evocative to Borja of *himself*. In that way, Valente resembled his presumed father greatly.

Nor did anyone doubt he was Borja's offspring. Beatrixa was infinitely sensible. She, of all people, would not have played Chesare false, which would have been the act of a madwoman.

And there was the other proof, the proof that none but she and Borja himself could possess (but which Flavia had scried and told me of, when she told me all the rest): Beatrixa's virginity. Borja was the first with her, and knew it. Otherwise, the time of conception must correctly coincide.

I thought, as I rode up to the rocca late that afternoon, over the drenched hills, what did the boy call this true father then, if he addressed *me* as *Dadda*?

"Oh. " said Beatrixa presently, in response to something else, "he will call Chesare nothing but 'my lord.' Valente is vainglorious of Chesare, also. Boastful even. And his grace the Duke has himself no difficulty, that his son addresses him like his adoring servant."

"It would be hard for anyone," I said, "not to fall under the spell of your son."

"His spell," she said. She looked at me intently. After our earlier meeting, she had sharpened her glances it seemed, with a wetstone. "Are we to speak of spells?"

But I am ahead of myself, and I must not jumble up my text so.

Let me arrive firstly at her door.

The dusk was beginning when I reached the castle, and stars were breaking through the opened roof of the sky. I was completely unsure what was to happen now, and had come there in the most odd condition, between dread and a kind of exhilaration. I felt young again.

Let me say at this juncture, for perhaps I mislead you, neither my hunger nor my love had been stirred up by Beatrixa. (I would have been a fool, and worse, an old fool, I thought, if it had—to allow myself such feelings for a high-born lady half my age.) But no, the very thing which drew me to her—her look of Flavia—made me not able to consider her, even frivolously, in such a light.

I had seen Beatrixa long ago, you may recall, at the Ducem's feast for Borja. I was very taken with her, then. And so I pondered now if, just as the shade of Flavia was summoned for me by Beatrixa, my liking for Beatrixa at sixteen had been a premonition of my love-to-come for a woman my own age.

However. I was politely conducted through a court-yard of the rocca, up some stone stairs reasonably ancient two hundred years before, and across the great hall, where the history of the Barbarons—banners, tro-phies, swords—hung like bats from the beams.

She received me in a sala off this hall. It was the room where she had first dined with Borja—Flavia had described it, and now I saw it for myself, and Flavia had been accurate. But then, perhaps Flavia had even physically been here, once, when little, and long ago. As she was Andrea's daughter, it was not impossible.

Beatrixa stood up when I came in. She wore a far more homely gown, but her magnificent hair, which had been dressed and bound up for the Veronavera streets, was loose around her. In this way I saw, as I had not earlier, a little strand of grey was in it. Yet she was not more than twenty-three or -four.

She invited me to sit down. I did so. So did she. And by her chair, an old white dog glanced up at me, dismissed me, and went once more to sleep.

She said, "You are my son's guest, 'ser Loura. But before he comes in, let's talk a minute."

"Of course, madam. Whatever you think best."

"We go down frequently to the town," she said, as if inconsequently, "Valente and I. He has always wanted to. And when there, he has always looked about him carefully." She waited.

I said, "A town can be an intriguing place to a child."

"More," she said, "as if he looked for something. Someone."

There started up in me again that vibration which was not fear or exuberance—and yet which was a relation to both.

She seemed to see how it was with me. And I, too, could see she was the same as I.

So I said, "Madam, let's be plain. What is this thing you wish to say to me?"

"Oh do I have something to say?"

For all her authority and her sense, I saw she was a woman.

"M'donna—"

"Oh," she said, "dispense with that. Use my name. I am Beatrixa. My son has trouble in speaking it still—as I did until I was more than six. He insists he use it though. So I am Veyatrida or Beatrilsa or some such. I think he only calls me Mumma when he wants to startle me. He has his own rules for names, and titles. Oh, he will call Chesare nothing but 'my lord'—"

And then we had the conversation I have already reported, which ended in her saying to me so sharply, "Are we to speak of spells?"

"Why should we?" I said.

"Messer da Loura—Bartolome, if you'll allow—we are *caught* in a spell, you and I. And he, my son. And you, I think, know it perfectly well. And I wish us to be frank and thus decide how we stand, before I can let Valente see you. Is my meaning clear?"

"Yes. But not what I can say to you."

"You can tell me," she said, "why you are the exact twin of my lover and my son's true father. He was most often, for me, a very young man, not twenty. But once he was old, and many ages between. When momentarily he was forty years, then he looked as you do."

"What?"

Despite everything Flavia had said—or because of it, of denying it, being bemused by it—I stared and stumbled.

Beatrixa said, "I don't mean either, my lord the Borja, as you well know. I mean the man who was the son of Meralda della Scorpia and Lorenzo Vai."

"Silvio," I said.

I heard her breathe very deeply inward, and out again. "*Yes.* Oh now, Bartolome, there's no going back for you. For you can only know his *name* if you know everything."

"I do know—I've been told, by one I trusted—I do know everything."

"Why?" she said. She gazed at me simply now. Her eyes were limpid, her fine hands folded on her knee.

She waited in patience for me to tell her. And you also have waited, and for longer perhaps than she. I ask your pardon that I made you wait, as I asked hers. I will render now the last thread of this tale, as my beloved one did, like her not knowing if you have believed any of it, let alone if you can believe this.

We are between deaths.

That is, between the waters of the outer life, which surround this one. And, while living in the world, between the last life we have lived—and died—here formerly, and the next death, which must come.

This, Flavia told me. How a soul moves from body to body, at bodily death returning into the light, leaving the light to return again on to the earth—till all is accomplished. Whatever that All is thought to be, for that she never explained. Perhaps she did not yet comprehend.

It was *I* who was to have been born the son of Meralda and Lorenzo Vai. My soul it was which haunted the atom of life then growing in her womb. My soul which therefore accompanied her, stricken, into the depths of the Aquila Lagoon, and saw her perish there, and her own soul, paying no heed to mine, go far away.

Silvio was what I should have been, what I had intended to be, in this, my life. A nobleman of Venus, or an illegitimate urchin scrambling in the war-camps or studios of Lorenzo's luck. Whatever else, and by whatever other name, a della Scorpia in partial blood.

But that I could not become, for Meralda had drowned herself, and with her what I would have been. Instead, the character I was so busy moulding for myself about the fleck of flesh in her womb, *that* became the ghost—of what had never lived. *My* ghost, if I—that other intended I—had survived.

As for myself, there was my life gone before I had had it. Yet I would not go back out of the world. For I had a cause there, a committment. It was more than the will to live again in body. It was a bond I had made before birth, with another unborn soul—Flavia's.

If I meant to be a bastard child of della Scorpia, she was to be (and this she achieved, and was) a bastard of the enemy House of Barbaron.

And so, our scheme: at thirteen it would have happened, through the seeming vagaries of random chance, she and I would meet. Our earthly union would then have formed. How we were to have accomplished its fulfilment I cannot imagine, and nor did she. But we had, it seemed, vowed. To love, and so to wed, and so to begin the repair of the Barbaron-Scorpia feud, which had existed all those decades, and was set to go on for centuries, the murderous emnity over the Isle graveyard and the right to a bed of earth.

With Meralda's death, this plan was lost to us. And yet it seems my soul would not utterly give up its attempt to gain the world and the City. And so it searched for another embryonic life, one either unwanted by, or else awarded to it (to me) by the generosity of some other soul. This life—the best I could hope for at such quick notice—lodged in the womb of my drunkard mother, the progeny of my drunkard father. A sentence to likely death for any child, if it were not tenacious, and, once born, also of likely death—if not rescued. But I took my place there, it was all I had to take. And tenacious I was, and in due season, rescued I was too.

And so I am here, Bartolome da Loura di An'Santa, Settera Master of the Gravediggers Guild and citizen of Venus.

We met, Flavia and I, if not as we had planned. Love, it transpires, persists both sides of the grave. Love is everywhere, and I have known it well. It is the most holy thing and the most fearful, on the earth, but what we have of it here is but the phantom, as all things are, of the love to which we return.

And yet, I am here still. I am here, and she is gone. Oh, Flavia.

Flavia said my will was so strong, even in another body, it kept for me the appearance I should have had as Meralda's son, resembling her father, Justore, but with *her* beauty—which in myself I can never find. This likeness was imprinted on the human form I took, perforce—which should have had no look of that at all. I wonder my drunken sire did not doubt me after all. Perhaps he did, and it made his beatings more brutal. Silvio, too, assumed this same look, Silvio who should have been one with me and I with him, two parts of one whole man. Silvio, who had removed now, so Flavia said, to another life in this world. But it would seem *he* had an uncanny glamour I, and no other man, ever has had, lacking as he did the anchor either of soul or flesh. This quality he has, somehow, extended to his son.

For Valente is Silvio's. Though he did not break Beatrixa's chastity more than light breaks crystal, it *was* taken, and his essence filled her up. She carried this second ghost invisibly within her, almost, she said, aware of it, until the seed of a living man—and of all men, Chesare Borja—quickened her.

Yes, Valente is Silvio's son. Flavia knew, Beatrixa knows, and so do I. Silvio's son—and therefore mine. I, who never in any liaison of my life have got a woman with child, as if I, too, must wait until some other might complete physical creation for me.

I see Silvio in Valente, as I never saw Silvio. Yet, he and I are linked, while I linger in this world, and in this body. Flavia demonstrated that what I might learn, Silvio might, if he willed, discover. For example, as with Euniche's betrayal of Meralda, of which I was told, and which Silvio therefore knew, and so acted out his vengeance from it. He was drawn to me in other oblique ways, but only ever once directly. That was when he rose to this earth by my house on the Silvia Lagoon, scaring the cat and annoying Strabica. He named himself for that lagoon, too. He could not get closer to my own name.

But it was when he met Beatrixa Barbaron that the last magic—Flavia's and mine—worked itself out. For they, like we, were tugged together by a cord of steel. They took our places, never seeing what they did. They played our love-scene, which we had meant to play. And so, by the strangest ways, they worked the ending of the feud.

Beatrixa informed me that night in her sala, that she herself was responsible for this. She had suggested to her father by letter (they never otherwise communicate) that he might give up the burial-land to the della Scorpia family. "He sometimes values my advice," she said. "He has no religious feelings on ash burials, not now. And it's better they have the ground than no one."

Did she know, in saying this, that she showed me, too, how she had now finished her part, that part which was not truly hers, but what *we* had vowed, our aim, Flavia's and mine.

But I do not anyway remember our spiritual plan. I do not remember how it was. Only Flavia, and her voice, telling me all she did, as she lay dying.

For a great time, then, it seemed Beatrixa and I did not speak. Then we exchanged some ordinary talk. We spoke of the harvest, I recollect, and a smoky-dotted foal, bred from the leopard-spotted horse that Ducem Nicolo gave to Borja, which foal was her son's other pride and joy.

The old, white dog got up while we were at this, chatting with each other as if we had been familiar all our lives, as we had. The dog padded to me, and sniffed me, then lay down against my legs.

"He was afraid of Silvio," she said. "My Leone is choice in his fellowship. But he has no quarrel with Valente."

Soon after, the child came to the door, from the stair that led to the floors above. How he knew to arrive then, I cannot determine.

He was as I recalled, but for one thing. His mother had schooled him somewhat, and he no longer called me Dadda, but Bartolo. His face though was still keen with affection and expectancy. And now I might admit to myself why I loved him.

Since I have been back in the City, I have looked very long at myself in Pia's mirror. I can see the resemblance. It would be gross to deny it, now, it is striking enough. He might well be mine, or the della Scorpias', at any rate, and I a della Scorpia too. But he has also that element of Chesare. Thank God, for all their sakes.

And Chesare it seems, thinks him all his own.

"He said to me, Bartolo, 'My sister had hair just that color when she was a child. My younger brother, Guffri, has it still.'"

Pia has come to the door now, telling me I have labored too long over the affairs of the guild, and I must shift for bed.

She and I get on very well at last. We have rubbed each other smooth enough we can lie side by side and not grow sore. She is caring and tender in her own way. I can never tell her about the boy, or that sometimes I shall go to see him. It is worse than a mistress, perhaps, to have this hidden, secret child that she may never suckle or rear or exclaim of, "My son."

Outside, the sea wind is lifting, a great gull on the water, clapping its black wings. We shelter here within this small, warm, vulnerable place, and it seems all there is to us, and only night and harsh weather are beyond. But over the ocean of night lies the morning, beyond that morning, night again, and again the dawn. I do not see what else there is to say.

L481be

Lee, Tanith.

A bed of earth (the
  gravedigger's tale)

DEMCO